"Come forth, dogs!" the barbarian challenged. "Is this the cream of Kothian soldiery? Step through, I say!"

But his taunts were vainglorious, and the soldiers knew it. In mere moments a second crossbow was raised, screened this time by the armored shoulders of two guardsmen. No command or warning was given.

Conan looked death in the eye, realizing that it could be smaller than a hummingbird. Through sheer, blind reflex he raised his sword at the moment of twanging release.

There was a jolt to his hand, and the sword-blade snapped in two before his face, miraculously deflecting the crossbow bolt. While its broken end clattered on the floor, men swarmed through the doorway. The foremost of them tripped Conan with a spear as he tried to run, and others surrounded him and laid into him with feet, fists, and weapon-butts.

CONAN
THE RENEGADE

Look for all these Conan books

LEONARD CARPENTER

CONAN
THE RENEGADE

A TOM DOHERTY ASSOCIATES BOOK

CONAN THE RENEGADE

Copyright © 1986 by Conan Properties, Inc.

First printing: April 1986

A TOR Book

Published by Tom Doherty Associates
49 West 24 Street
New York, N.Y. 10010

Cover art by Kirk Reinert

ISBN: 0-812-54250-9
CAN. ED.: 0-812-54251-7

Printed in the United States

0 9 8 7 6 5 4 3 2 1

To Cheryl

Contents

Haloga

HYPERBOREA

Tundras

Deserts

BRYTHUNIA

Steppes

KEZANKIAN MTS.

TURAN

HYRKANIA

CORINTHIA

ZAMORA

Sultanapur

KARPASH MTS.

Shadizar

Arenjun

VILAYET
SEA

KHITAI →

T H

KHAURAN

Isle of
Iron Statues

IKHORAJA

Deserts

Akit

Aghrapur

Samara

Zamboula

Khawarizm

Zaporoska R.

Kuthchemes

Zapur

Preion

Aghmnrath

KESHAN

Kassali

PUNT

Keshia

Ilbars R.

VENDHYA →

KINGDOMS

ZEMBABWEI

IRANISTAN

Trial by Steel

"Who goest?" The sentry's voice rang harshly on the rider's ear and caused the black war-stallion to break its pace. With a scuffing and stamping of heavy hooves, the horseman reined the great animal around and faced his questioner.

"I am Conan, late of Cimmeria." The speaker was a formidable-looking man near his prime, with a square-cut mane that rivaled in color the midnight hue of his mount. His face and arms were tanned deeply and evenly, as by the glare of northern snowfields. "I am a fellow mercenary."

His choice of steed was justified by his size and the weight of his weaponry—for he was both tall and broad, and his mail shirt was contoured to accommodate the heavy muscles beneath. From his saddle depended a sword, ax, buckler, helm, and spear, along with rolled fur robes dangling over slack saddlebags. He spoke in Kothian with a barbaric accent. "Whither the way to Hundolph's camp?"

The sentry, a fork-bearded Corinthian, looked Conan up and down while making no haste to reply. He lounged on a horse-saddle he had laid over a strut of the makeshift barricade flanking the dirt road. Though his posture was lax and unmilitary, his hand rested with an expert fondness on the recurved bow in his lap. A quiver of arrows bristled by his side. "If you be Hundolph's man, where is your tabard?"

"I am not of his troop." Conan's horse whickered restlessly. "At least not yet."

"I see." The sentry watched him lazily. "Another hungry buzzard circling to the killing-ground." The man shrugged. "Pass, then. Hundolph's is straight back to the fifth terrace, and left." He shifted in his rude seat. "But if you want a good posting, try Brago's pavilion, just ahead there. His men always gain more battle-spoils."

The Cimmerian inclined his head noncommittally as he wheeled his steed around. "I know Hundolph of old." He spurred the horse smartly up the road.

The camp of the Free Companions was set amid terraced vineyards under the walls of Tantusium, a provincial city of western Koth. Conan, fresh from barren lands, was surprised at the extent of the place spreading before him on the rocky slope in an immense straggle of tents. From scores of fires, plumes of gray smoke trailed away into the hazy blue Kothian sky that faded almost to white near the horizon of hilly, stone-walled fields and pastures.

The encampment was carelessly laid out. Its nearer borders conformed to the lowest of the terrace-scarps and to a shallow ravine that cut slopewise across them. But Conan could see that the camp gained little defensive benefit from its perimeters, which consisted of mere heaps of stone and rubbish atop the low embankments.

Even the city itself seemed to rely more on its natural crest position for safety than on any works of man. Tantusium was visible above the tents and sprouting vinestocks as a white rampart overtopped by the town's jagged rooflines of slate and tile. The wall appeared at this distance to be of rough plastered masonry. It had no great height or steepness, and probably had but a narrow guard-walk at its top. The only real stronghold in view was a well-built rampart of cut gray stone, which merged with the city wall at the steeper end of the ridge. It was higher than the other wall and notched with toothlike crenellations. Likely, it was the ancient citadel or palace precinct.

Conan continued his tactical appreciation of the scene as his stallion wound its way up the cobbled road. He passed the gaudily fringed pavilion beneath the dragon banner that must be Brago's. The tents grew thick on either hand, and the vineyard terraces between the low, sloping fieldstone embankments turned into a close-packed canvas slum. A few trampled, ravaged areas were roped off for horses, but otherwise there was little open space. Most of the tents' occupants seemed to be loitering in the road.

The mercenaries made themselves laxly and slovenly at home in the camp, and the only order was rowdy disorder. The produce of the vineyard was in evidence on all sides, sloshing from hand to hand in earthen jars and beakers. From smoke-seeping tents sounded oaths and the rattle of dice in wooden cups, as well as the occasional squeals and coarse laughs of female camp followers. Men in wildly varied modes of dress and undress talked, disputed, and strove together in trials of strength among the rocks and straggly grass.

Conan had to edge his horse around a pair of freckle-skinned Gundermen, naked but for kilts and sandals, who were battering each other skillfully with fur-padded poles. They grunted and dodged, oblivious to the ring of enthusiastic onlookers who cheered them on. Farther along, a group of Shemitish youths in sheepskin coats were hurling javelins up a straight reach of road into a tattered straw-bale; grudgingly they stepped aside to let Conan by, resuming their sport as soon as his horse's tail was past the target.

Those who preferred not to roister sat before their tents talking, polishing their armor, or honing weap-

ons. A few tossed rude remarks as Conan rode past;
an odder few merely sat and stared into vacant space.
These Conan watched most carefully of all, knowing
the quirkish, dangerous temperament of some of the
men who rode to mercenary service. He scanned the
throng for familiar faces, half in hope and half in
wariness.

Vultures stooping to a fresh kill, Conan thought.
Aye, indeed, the sentry had been right in his picture
of this gathering. Conan himself, on his recent sojourn among cousins and old comrades in Cimmeria,
had felt sorely overleisured. The wild cliffs and hills
of his boyhood now seemed strangely confining. Rumors of rebellion and strife in Koth, carried northward by merchants and spent travelers, had come as
might a musky, far-off perfume to his nostrils.

And so, with the passes open and with a hard-won
purse of silver weighing at his belt, he had armed and
provisioned himself and headed southward.

But not, he told himself, for a mere living, like
most of these fugitives and starved-out farmers—with
the chance of easy wealth just tempting enough to
offset the far greater chance of a bloody death. And
not in search of vainglory and praise, nor of the less
wholesome rewards that lure darker souls to free-
bootery.

No, Conan knew vaguely that he was capable of
more. There were strengths in him that he longed to
try out, skills he could wield. Whether they could
prevail in this harsh world would have to be seen.

His mulling thoughts were interrupted by a rasping
voice at his knee. "Conan, old sneak-thief! Do you
come to join us, then? Our prospects are bright
indeed!"

"Well—Bilhoat, is it?" Conan turned in the saddle to smile on the thin, wizened man who stood
looking up at him. "You've taken up honest work
since Arenjun, eh? As I have."

The elder man creased his leathery face in a laugh. "Aye, and there are others here from the Maul—Pavlo, and Thranos! We should all get together and carouse again."

"We shall, and soon, by Bel's swollen purse! Are the lot of you in Hundolph's band?"

"Nay, Conan." Bilhoat shook his head. "We ride with Villeza. A pity—the Zingaran is a foul-tempered knave. I wish I were with Hundolph. But I have too much pay overdue from the black-hearted rascal to abandon him now."

"What campaign is this anyway? We press the cause of an upstart rebel princeling of Koth, I am told."

"Aye, Prince Ivor. A firebrand—a young fellow, and the darling of the locals." Bilhoat reached up to rub the nose of Conan's stallion. "Full of new ideas, and dead set against his uncle, King Strabonus."

"Yes, I know the king for a murderous rogue." Conan scowled. "This Ivor is a reformer, then? He can have my good arm in any fight against bloody Strabonus! And these Free Companions"—he gestured at the drunken mercenaries cavorting around them—"they rally to him just to advance the cause of good kingship?"

Bilhoat laughed and stroked the animal's black mane. "Indeed, no. Some of the dog-brothers already grow restless, saying that the action is too sparse, and the booty sparser." He winked at Conan. "But I'm no glory-hound, and to my mind the prospects are good. Word is that any of us who want can stay on to receive land or regular rank once the rebellion succeeds. It could be a tasty deal." He slapped the horse's neck.

"Tasty or tart, I need a posting." Conan lifted his reins. "I'm for Hundolph's. 'Tis good to see you again, Bilhoat." He spurred his mount away, calling back over his shoulder, "Seek me out when you can."

Keeping count of the terraces, Conan threaded his way up the road. He turned off it at the fifth, between two rows of tents, to see before him a square-based, pyramid-topped pavilion where hung the banner of a gold ax on a black field—a device he recognized from Hundolph's shield of old.

But the three ruffians who loitered in front of the canopied entry to the tent were unknown to Conan and inscrutable even to his seasoned eye. Hard-looking men all, half-naked in the afternoon sun, and each with a weapon ready to hand.

Sullen-eyed, they watched Conan dismount and tether his horse to a shoulder-high grapestock, which early summer had transformed into a dazzling spray of green fronds. He took his swordbelt from his saddle and draped it over his shoulder. Then he turned and walked to them, his buskined feet learning once again the feel of solid earth.

"Hundolph's tent, I see. Is he inside?" Conan pitched his voice loud enough to be heard regardless of the men's presence. There was a long silence before the stoutest of the three, a swag-bellied, gap-toothed worthy, stepped forward to address him.

"No. He is away. I am Stengar, commanding in his place." He tossed a severe look at his companions, then faced Conan again. "You are . . . what? A Northron of some kind." He looked Conan up and down. "Hyperborean, I would guess."

"Cimmerian," Conan corrected him, scowling.

"Oh, a hill-barbar. Well, what would you have of our captain? State your business."

"I hear that Hundolph is laying on men."

"He may be." Stengar frowned and took his time speaking. "What of it?"

Conan's eyes narrowed. "What might you suppose, man? I was thinking of hiring on."

Stengar glanced again at his companions, then back to Conan. "You think yourself good enough, then?"

Conan looked the three up and down. "I thought that Hundolph would hire good men." He shrugged. "I could be wrong though."

As this remark sank in, Stengar's scowl deepened. He thrust his paunch forward and raised his voice, putting an irritating edge into it. "Tell me, outlander, why did you choose this troop? Why ride all the way up here instead of joining that rabble camped down below?"

Conan eyed the man warily, deciding to say as little as possible. "Hundolph's troop has a good reputation."

Stengar smiled with mock encouragement. "True, outlander. A good reputation. Or, to put it another way, we of Hundolph's are the best." He smirked back at his fellows. "Now, can you tell me, outlander, from all your experience of remote, uncivilized corners of the world, just why that would be?" The stout man's overexaggerated oratory was causing other mercenaries to emerge from nearby tents and watch the scene with interest.

"You tell me." Conan stayed motionless.

"Very well, outlander, I will tell you. We are the best—and a posting with Hundolph's troop is so highly prized, even by a footloose ruffian like yourself—because, out of all those who seek to join our band, we accept only one half." He folded his arms across his chest and gazed around his audience with a self-satisfied air, as if he had explained something.

Conan balked, smelling a trap. He shifted his swordbelt forward under his arm so that the hilt was within easy reach. "One half," he said.

"Right, northerner. One half—the survivors!" Stengar threw up an arm and beckoned theatrically to someone outside his listener's vision. "Come forth, Lallo—here is your match!"

Conan wheeled to the sound of thudding footsteps and a low, inarticulate yell. A hulking youth was running toward him carrying a heavy two-handed sword. The weapon was raised high to cleave him in two.

So swift was the attack that Conan had to throw up his own sword before it was quite clear of the sheath. The two blades met aloft with an ear-stabbing clang, at which the onlookers raised a lusty cheer. While Conan's swordbelt was still rolling and skidding in the dust, the youth unleashed two more wild slashes at his victim's midsection. Then at last Conan was able to fend him back with his point.

"And so, comrades," Stengar called from the sidelines, "which one is to be our new recruit? The staunch woodcutter, Lallo, a child of these very Kothian hills? Or the northern barbarian? My choice is Lallo. I'll take any wagers to the contrary." An eager murmur of voices followed his speech as bets were laid.

Meanwhile Conan dodged and parried. The lad was quick, as his onslaught had proven. His height and reach rivaled the Cimmerian's own, and his headlong recklessness was such as to bring him into danger time and again from Conan's blade.

"You, lad—Lallo! Leave off this foolishness," Conan called in Kothian between strokes. "There's no need for us to butcher each other just for these jackals' sport!"

But Lallo gave no sign of comprehension; his eyes followed his foe mechanically while his mouth hung slack. He aimed a wide, curving stroke at his enemy's head. Conan sidestepped, sparing the youth the backslash that would have laid open his arm.

"Oho, the barbarian wants to quit!" cried a watcher. "Gutless, he is! Double my money on Lallo!"

"Mine too," another chimed in. "Everyone knows these hill-barbars are clumsy fighters!"

Clearly Lallo did not see that he was being coddled. He swung his great slab of sword like a timber ax, stalking his quarry deliberately, as if the Cimmerian were merely some strangely elusive kind of forest tree. Conan beat the lad's blade aside and tried to box his head with a mighty fist—but the blow missed, leaving the Cimmerian dangerously overextended. Only by a straining twist of his torso did he get back behind his sword and save himself from Lallo's return stroke. He kicked a foot out then to trip the youth—and had the hairs close-shaven from one side of his leg for the trouble.

Whether the boy had a full portion of wits or not was impossible to tell. But he was swift, too swift to be allowed to live, as Conan came to see. Repeatedly he was forced to exert himself to keep from hurting the lad.

Finally he ducked under one of the woodcutter's broad slashes and spun, catlike, so that for an instant he was behind his opponent. Lallo's head turned, but his sword was hopelessly out of action. Conan arched his whole powerful body into the stroke that would end by splitting his adversary's drooling, wide-eyed face.

But then a heavy hand shoved Conan aside. The force of his death-stroke was expended in empty air, though Lallo sprawled to earth in ducking it.

The barbarian snarled. He balled his fist to smite the intruder, but at the last moment he recognized the man's gray-stubbled face and barrel chest. "Hundolph!"

"Well! Conan, the Cimmerian!" The gray stubble bristled in a grin. "And in a fight, as usual. Hold your blows, man, we'll talk." The mercenary chief turned to the others with a gravel-throated shout. "You, boy—stay back! Zeno, Stengar, disarm that brat. I know not what sort of prank this is, but I want no more of it.'' Hundolph shot an angry look around the circle of men, many of whom seemed suddenly to remember that they had urgent business elsewhere. ''Well? Who is responsible for this?''

Most of them avoided their commander's gaze, but Stengar spoke up from his place beside Lallo. ''It was just a disagreement between these two recruits, sir. I had no authority to interfere.''

''That is plausible, Stengar''—Hundolph nodded— ''to a blind, puling infant! But I know Conan, and I know that he could have had this boy's head in a moment had he wanted it.'' He swept an arm around the assembly. ''I fine every man of you five coppers. Meanwhile, induct that young fool so that I may thrash some sense into him. Conan, come to my tent—my groom will see to your mount.''

2

Hundolph's Left Hand

"Still slogging the mercenary road, eh, Conan?" Hundolph, reclining on an embroidered mat in the corner of the tent, tilted a jeweled goblet to his lips. The mercenary captain had dressed down to a plain cotton jerkin and trousers. The air under the sunlit canopy was close and warm, but an afternoon breeze stirred the tent's lower edge and let in fresh drafts.

The old warrior squinted at the Cimmerian. "I had thought that by now some plump noblewoman would have seen in you a good Chief of Household Guards, and your place in the world would be set."

Conan grunted, sitting cross-legged in the middle of the pavilion. "A shrewd guess, Hundolph. More than one has tried." He swilled from his own jewel-bossed cup. "But it was never my way to be a pampered lap-dog, no matter how well-padded the lap."

Both men laughed, and Hundolph said, "I had my share of offers, too, at your age—and I rode like a tempest to escape them." He smiled wistfully. "Would that I had accepted one, or mayhap two."

Conan laughed, rubbing his back against the tent-post to scratch an itch. "And yet you seem to have prospered since our freelance days in Corinthia. You lead a large mercenary band, with good repute among

11

sword-slingers.'' He raised his goblet to the elder man. "I salute you."

The mercenary chief shrugged as well as he could, with the weight of his barrellike upper body propped on one elbow. "A good reputation, perhaps, which serves to attract to me a larger rabble of such rogues as you have seen. Not many like you." He shook his head of black hair shot through with gray. "This is not enough for me, Conan. I still seek a permanent place. And I begin to doubt that these rebellions and provincial squabbles will gain me one. Would that I could settle down—if not here, then among the grain-fields of my native Brythunia—once I can raise enough of a stake to retire on."

"Do you expect to find much profit here?" Conan leaned forward, elbows propped on his massy knees. "I know little of the situation—Ivor's rebellion against the king of Koth." He knit his brow. "A risky venture, but workable, perhaps, in this forsaken corner of the kingdom."

"Oh, yes. Prince Ivor has a strong play against his uncle." Hundolph grinned wolfishly. "Strabonus's reach is overextended, and there is deep unrest in Koth. Tight-fisted as he is, the king fields costly forces to keep the peace elsewhere. Hence the high taxes that rankle the local farmers and herders."

Conan stroked his chin. "Might he not send a legion or two here to crush Ivor's revolt as an example to the others?"

"I think not." Hundolph pulled himself up to a sitting position. "Other mutinous districts lie much closer to the capital. Strabonus can ill afford to have a legion cut off from Khorshemish. He dares not send enough troops against us to win decisively."

"Might he make a peace offer, then, and end our employment?"

"Not at risk of lending heart to the other rebels." Hundolph twirled the dregs in his goblet. "No, Conan, it looks to be a long, leisurely campaign, with our dogs nibbling a bit here, and harrying there, but no pitched battles.'' He glanced at his guest from under bushy brows. ''To be followed, likely, by an uneasy peace.'' He smiled. ''Prince Ivor may need our services permanently to guard his newmade kingdom.''

''No chance of settling it quickly, then, with a decisive stroke. That would be my way, and then move on to the next war—'' Conan was interrupted by a growing clamor of voices, hooves, and creaking drayage somewhere outside the tent.

''Sounds like a new arrival. Mayhap the pay caravan.'' Hundolph set down his cup and stretched, then climbed to his feet with a drawn-out, grunting exhalation.

Conan rose silently alongside him. ''Caravan? Where is our pay to come from, then?''

''From Turan, the Sunrise Empire—from your former employer, the Emperor Yildiz, to be exact.'' Hundolph unhooked his sword, his casque, and a light mail shirt from a corner-pole of the tent, donning each in turn. ''That is another reason why Strabonus can never settle with Ivor—he has struck a deal with Turan, to make himself a thorn in Koth's side.''

Conan grunted. ''The Turanian Empire was ever hungry for allies and client states—and ever eager to split off chunks of neighboring lands.'' He followed Hundolph to the tent's entrance. ''But can we trust old Yildiz to pay off, even as rich as he is?''

Hundolph paused just inside the entry. ''Where Ivor gets the gold is his problem, not ours. He himself is no pauper, and he cannot well default on payment with three thousand Free Companions camped outside his city gate.'' The chieftain stepped out to meet the troops who clustered around him. ''Well? What is the news?''

''A pack train from the Eastern High Road, sir. Heavily guarded.'' The speaker was the one called

Zeno, compact of build, with features framed by curly red hair. He had armed himself with a broadsword sheathed at his kirtle-waist, and he looked ready to escort his captain.

"As I thought." Hundolph nodded to him. "I must go to the citadel. By the way, Zeno, in your capacity as my lieutenant, I shall be needing you to remain here." He looked the man up and down and laid a hand on his shoulder. "I have required a keen sword at my side, and a keener ear, when I go among the nobles and the other mercenary captains. But that station can now be filled by Conan. After today's mischief"—he glanced at Stengar, who slouched at one side with his face averted—"it is clear that I need a firm hand in camp. Understood?"

"Aye, sir." Zeno gave a grudging nod, flashing a look of hatred at Conan.

"Good." Hundolph turned. "We go on horseback. Conan, keep to my unarmed side, and slightly to my rear."

A soldier approached, bringing up their saddled mounts, with Hundolph's black-and-yellow tabards spread behind the saddles. As Conan swung up onto his steed and started down the dusty lane between the tents, he saw Stengar, the false lieutenant, muttering darkly to Zeno.

Soon his attention was drawn ahead, where baggage mules and horsemen were passing along the main road through the vineyard. The panting beasts were laden with shapeless, rug-covered bundles and deep baskets. Their long ears sagged in fatigue as they were driven briskly by wool-jacketed Turanian pack drivers astride lathered horses. The way was lined with mercenaries who made their customary jeers and shouts at the new diversion. Yet something about the scene seemed to be provoking even greater vehemence than usual among the troopers.

It was some moments before Conan could identify

the cause. Then he realized that it was the armed guards, who spurred their agile Hyrkanian steeds alongside the pack train. Four of them were in sight near the rear of the procession, and so muffled were they in armor, furs, and travel-stained robes that it was hard to tell at first. But finally their contours and the lightness of their movements were unmistakable.

"Women!" the raucous cry came to Conan's ears. "The emperor of Turan sends sword-bitches to guard our pay!"

The hoots and yells of the watchers expressed simultaneous outrage and delight. "Forget my pay! I'll take the paymistress!" A red-faced youth among the many who straggled after the caravan came running up. In an eyeblink he had vaulted heavily onto the hindquarters of the rearmost guard's horse. He tried to grab its rider for purchase—but a leather-sleeved elbow jabbed out, catching him in the midriff. Then the arm recoiled and struck him again across the jowls, sending him thudding into the dust. At this the watchers hooted in derision.

Hundolph and Conan fell in with the caravan behind a rattling, black-canopied wagon drawn by two donkeys. It was a tall, angular vehicle with two large brass-bound, spoked wheels. The rims were pounded out of shape by long travel, so that the wain lurched from side to side even on the rare flat portions of road.

Its driver was screened from view by the faded black cloth that was stretched across hoops over the bed. As Conan tried to catch a glimpse of him on a curve of a switchback, his attention was diverted. Another rowdy trooper farther up the line was trying to seize the reins out of the hands of a female guard. Her steed, well-schooled to its rider's will, sidled against the man and bowled him over. He was left rolling in a pile of horse-flop, howling and clutching a mashed foot. Conan and Hundolph guided their steeds to either side of him.

Then a horsewoman came trotting from the head of the caravan. She shouted orders in Shemitish in a forced, grating voice. "Form up, there! Tighten the line! Arm yourselves." Her breastplate of green-tarnished bronze was female-shaped, with twin snarling cat's-heads sculpted over the breasts. The open faceplate of her helm allowed Conan a glimpse of austere good looks under short-cropped blond hair; an instant later she wheeled and galloped back up the column. She carried an unsheathed cutlass propped against her shoulder. At her command the guard-women drew their swords and carried them likewise.

"That one is Drusandra," Hundolph said. "I saw her fight at Phlydea. Merely a lone, desperate wench she was then—now a captain in her own right!" He shook his head. "Strange times indeed."

The sight of raw steel seemed to have a restraining effect on the freebooters, and the caravan flowed more smoothly toward the gate of Tantusium. The men continued their catcalling, but there were no more physical assaults.

Then the main city gate loomed before the riders. It looked imposing, with its stout round towers flanking the tall, metal-studded wooden valves. But Conan saw that there were no defensive works overhanging the gate itself; it stood open to the sky. The only outwork was a stone bulwark, made to block the motion of a battering ram and to force road traffic to either side, under the towers.

"Prince Ivor plays a risky game," Conan observed. "His city is none too tough a hazelnut to crunch."

"Hence his reliance on the Free Companions." Hundolph saluted a phalanx of city guards who stood on a low ledge inside the gate, and their officer responded with a nod. "All the better for us, I say."

Beyond the portal was a small plaza flanked by inns and shops and further encroached by merchants' stalls and taverners' benches. A few of the mule-packers turned their animals aside here to unload trade goods under the eyes of merchants and tax officers. But most proceeded out of sight into a narrow avenue of the town. Those mercenaries who had filtered in from camp with the caravan milled about the open space or turned their attention to the refreshment-sellers.

Hundolph and Conan followed the donkey-wain into the winding, climbing street, which was barely wide enough for two horsemen abreast. The way was roughly cobbled and, in the steepest places, surfaced in broad steps. In the intersecting streets and alleys cityfolk crowded to watch the procession—a light-skinned, round-faced people with brown or blond hair. They were well-clothed, most of the men wearing the aprons of different trades, the women brightly clad in embroidered dresses and shifts.

"Thus the prince's men restrict our movements," Hundolph said as they passed a second cordon of guards in a road-fork. The gray-cloaked men were turning away all but mounted travelers. "They allow our troops just enough of the town to squander their money in, and bar them from the rest."

The lane twisted and divided often enough to be confusing even to Conan's wilderness-trained senses. He rode between unbroken rows of crack-plastered buildings, from whose scanty doors and windows peered inquisitive faces. The height of the overhanging tenements restricted vision on all sides except for an occasional glimpse of battlements against a sky of deepening blue.

Only when he passed through a cullised archway of square-hewn stones, to emerge into a broad, stone-paved courtyard, did Conan realize that he had entered the citadel.

3

A Sending of Sorcery

The caravan had halted in the spacious courtyard under the sun-gilded façade of the palace. This was a gray stone pile, porched and battlemented at its third story, and receding there to a central dome and roofed towers. The palace was joined to the citadel walls on either side by stone wings two stories high.

Through its great doors, open and flanked by guardsmen, streamed courtiers and footmen to meet the new arrivals. The yard was filling with cityfolk who had followed the caravan through the streets, and its walls echoed with shouts, the clatter of hooves, and the braying of animals.

Conan followed Hundolph to a hitching rail along one side of the yard, where pages were setting buckets of water in front of tethered horses and mules. Dismounting, the two found themselves beside another pair of armed men.

The elder was a scar-faced, deeply tanned man with a long blond moustache. His dirty-looking yellow hair was plaited back in a pigtail at the base of his neck. He shouldered past his companion, a stout, scowling youth badly in need of his first shave.

"Conan, let me introduce you to my ablest brother-in-arms—and my staunchest competitor." Hundolph addressed the blond man. "Brago, this is Conan—a new recruit, but an old friend. Doubtless he knows your fame, and your troop's.''

"Aye, the leveler of Scilda.'' The Cimmerian looked in the warrior's face, not acting overly impressed. "A much-praised victory.''

Brago smiled, showing large yellow-stained teeth. " 'Twas a town rich in booty, and stupidly arrogant to oppose us.'' He clasped each man's extended forearm in turn—hands to wrists, in the legionary style—but did not bother to introduce his second. "Should you want to be part of such exploits, join my troop!'' He winked at Hundolph. "You, too, old man, if your ax-banner ever grows too heavy.''

"Keep wishing it, Brago.'' Hundolph turned his gaze away to scan the courtyard. "Most of the captains seem to be here. Yonder is Villeza''—he indicated a stocky Zingaran standing by the central well—"and there comes Aki Wadsai.'' The latter was a black, slightly built, turbaned rider borne across the flagstones on a clean-limbed desert steed.

Brago watched with him and nodded, frowning. "Doubtless they are as eager to lay their hands on some gold as I am.'' He smoothed the wings of his moustache with thumb and forefinger. "Plunder is scanty in this backwoods province, and Ivor's promised bounty has yet to be seen.''

"It is well that we all witness the unloading, lest our employer try to hold something back.'' Hundolph started toward the palace doors, with Conan taking station at his left elbow. Brago and his man followed.

Near the palace's low veranda, where guards kept a space clear of city gawkers, mules were being eased out from under their pack-saddles and led off to the stables. Drivers and quartermasters moved among the stacked baskets and bags, as did a gray-cloaked man, whose guard of four lightly armored housecarls showed him to be of noble rank.

He was short but robust, with a solid neck and a

stately, clean-shaven countenance that turned with dignity to survey the scene. His age was not much more than Conan's, amounting to three decades at most. His bare head was crowned with unruly brown hair. Under his cloak he wore a vest of fine link mail over a loose linen shirt, velvet pantaloons, and riding boots. No weapon was visible on his person.

"There is Prince Ivor," Hundolph said, halting a few paces away. "We have to stand and await his summons."

The prince was examining one of the pack-baskets. He unlaced its cover and drew from it a long bundle of oiled cloth. One of his guards unwound the wrapping, to leave him holding a sword by its sheath.

When the sheath was removed, Conan saw that it had a single-edged blade, lightly curved and pointed. It was simply made, and unembellished, with a brass ring-hilt wound in sharkskin. A light weapon, requiring no great skill to use. Yet efficient, perfect for arming untrained men, Conan thought. The basket held a score or more such bundles—and there were dozens of baskets.

The prince fitted his hand to the sword and slashed it experimentally in front of him. Then he thoughtfully scanned the crowd in the courtyard.

In a moment his head canted forward decisively. He strode away from those around him, moving a dozen steps across the flags. Coming to the well, he sprang up agilely onto its broad stone curb. Bracing his left hand against the wooden winch, he stood half again as tall as anyone in view.

"People of Tantusium!" he shouted. His voice rang boldly over the hubbub, which diminished at his cry. "My people! Listen!"

A thousand heads turned to face him, while his guards hurried up to take positions around the well.

"My friends and countrymen!" He waved the sword

on high. "Fellow victims of the tyranny of vile Strabonus! List ye to me."

He had them by the ears, Conan saw. The square was quiet except for the low scuffing and talking of the saddle-beasts.

"Long we have suffered together, my friends, and we have embarked, together, on a daring enterprise. We have bloodied the grasping hand of royal power." He raised his free hand clawlike over his head, then flattened his palm and swept it aside and down. "We have sealed our borders and called together many valiant allies." His glance took in the mercenary captains standing at one side.

"Not rashly did we take these steps, to secure our freedom and our nationhood. We had the wisdom and the patience of the earth—like farmers laying out a new field to nourish and enrich us. We knew that this plot would be a rocky one, steep and dangerous to plow." He shrugged impatiently, as if throwing off a yoke. "Yet, compared to the thousand iniquities of Strabonus—the exorbitant taxes, cruelly enforced; the offenses of his troops against our manhood and womanhood; his persecution of my father; and his constant, hateful sullying of our homeland's autonomy and honor—compared to these, the farmfield of revolt seemed an easy one to till indeed, as smooth as lush river-land to our plow's keen edge. And when our future has been in doubt, and the demands placed on us by our national struggle have been burdensome, we have walked on resolutely, our eyes fixed unswervingly on the dream of independence.

"But now, my friends, our desires are closer to our grasp than ever before. We have received today not just material aid toward our goal, but a prophecy, a virtual guarantee of our success!

"For the ruler of the most powerful kingdom in the world, Emperor Yildiz of Turan, our neighbor to the east, has lent us his aid and support in our trouble. He has foreseen the inevitability of our triumph amid the rising tide of rebellion against Kothian cruelty. Months ago he told our emissaries that he would aid us. He sent guarantees and written recognition of our young nation, affixed with his exalted seal.

"Long we wondered and anticipated what form his aid would take. Would he send us gold? Would it be troops to help press our campaign of liberation? Or sage advisors steeped in military affairs? For the wealth of Turan is great; greater yet its powers of generalship and statecraft.

"Well, my friends, today we know what aid has been sent. Not troops or advisors—rather something more durable than frail human flesh. And not gold! No, something more precious than gold. What, then, is our boon?"

No voice broke the pause that ensued.

Ivor brandished his sword in the air, slashing it back and forth before him. "Steel! Yildiz has sent us steel!" The prince's triumphant cry bounced off the courtyard walls. "For in his farsightedness, our ally knows that only with razor-sharp steel can the farmfield of civil war be tilled and fertilized! Only with steel"—he swung the sword against the beam of the winch at his side, hacking away a great splinter of pale wood from its edge—"can we reap a rich red harvest of the malefactors who stand between us and our national honor!

"Yildiz calls on you, and I call on you, to arm! Take up arms and fight for what you cherish! Let every able man be prepared to defend our beloved homeland should the king's bloody-handed assassins try once more to fasten the slave-collar on our necks. And better, let us carry the fight into their own camps, and into the very strong-rooms of Strabonus!

"To this end, I am forming a militia . . ."

Conan looked around the audience and saw that they were rapt. Farm squires, farm wives, and folk of the town—traders, artisans, apprentices, and stable-hands—all watched Ivor and followed his theatric gestures. When he raged with special intensity, a light gleamed in their eyes that was more than a reflection of the sunset deepening in the sky behind the prince.

Among the mercenary chiefs, the response to Ivor's words was less enthusiastic. Conan saw Hundolph frowning and heard Villeza, the Zingaran, cursing under his breath; Brago and the black desert-rider Aki Wadsai stood nearby with fixed skeptical expressions. Conan also saw a handful of officers and nobles in Tantusian mail standing on the veranda eyeing the mercenaries from moment to moment and noting their reactions.

"And so I say to you, countrymen: Do not fear an assault by Strabonus!" Ivor's voice was level but building to another climax. "Rather, welcome such a foolhardy act. For if a tyrant should ever march into our beloved land, the whole province shall rise as one! His hosts will scatter and die before our righteous blades! The very hills shall yawn to devour him as the ancient stories tell!

"Such, my people, is the strength of our determination. Such is the justice of our cause. And victory—victory will be ours!"

At the finality of Ivor's words and his frozen heroic posture, his hair disarranged, his sword-arm raised, the crowd burst into frenzied cheers. Hats were thrown high and the people swirled excitedly around the well.

The prince leaped down and went among the throng. His guards moved in to bracket him closely, but he continually reached past them and allowed admirers to touch and kiss his hands.

"There is no doubt that he has the people on his side," Hundolph observed at length to his companions.

"Indeed. It makes me wonder what he needs mercenaries for," Brago said.

Aki Wadsai appeared noiselessly at his shoulder and spoke in a low voice, accented like the desert wind. "What of this . . . this militia he speaks of?"

Villeza grunted, his Zingaran accent sounding deep and guttural. "I like it little if we are expected to fight beside raw recruits and stableboys. And all the less if his militia is to be turned against us someday."

Just then the prince moved clear of the crowd and came toward them, his guards falling back to his flanks. There was cordiality in his smile and in the way he extended both hands to grasp those of the captains, two at a time. "My fellow warriors! A halcyon day! I am elated at the way Emperor Yildiz has strengthened our cause."

"Wonderful, my prince." Brago cleared his throat and smiled tightly. "But there is the matter of our pay, which was to be subsidized by Turan. . . ."

"What? Oh, yes." Ivor raised one hand to brush hair from his eyes. "I fear that your payment will be delayed further. The gold is to be sent in a special shipment, for greater security. There is no telling when it will arrive."

"Sire," Hundolph put in, "if you could give us at least a portion of our first share, from your own coffers . . ." He folded his battle-scarred arms across his breastplate. "Our expenses are high here. And the morale of our men is always a consideration."

The prince gazed blankly at Hundolph. "That would be inconvenient just now. But it will pose no problem—" He waved one hand dismissively. "I shall order the city merchants to extend you credit. As for morale, that will flourish well. I expect us to be in action soon." He smiled around the group confidingly. "Very soon.

"But my main purpose now is to introduce your new comrades in arms." Ivor stepped back slightly and to one side so as to broaden the group. "Captains, this is Drusandra, whose able captaincy you saw today. She will be joining your encampment."

Striding up to them was the warrioress—uncloaked, but still arrayed in tarnished breastplate, thighplates, and greaves. Her plumed helmet was under one arm, revealing her short blond hair. Her face was smooth-featured and attractive, but with a hard look about the mouth. She was taller than she had looked in the saddle; as she strode forward, her height overtopped not only the prince's but also Villeza's.

"Hundolph, Brago, other worthies. No need for introductions—each of you has a peculiar fame which, like a fragrance, precedes you." She nodded around the group with a tight smile. "I command a score and three of dog-sisters. Here is my lieutenant, Ariel."

She indicated a black-haired, leather-armored woman at her side, who looked fit and alert, though shorter and slimmer than her captain. Her features were pocked slightly by marks of an old illness that gave her beauty a feral, hungry air.

The other mercenaries nodded and muttered, taking in the appearance of the two, but Villeza spoke out curtly. "You will have to quarter your women far from the rest of us. I may not be able to control my men."

Drusandra wheeled to gaze down on him. "Have no fear, Villeza. If you cannot control them, I will." She smiled more broadly. "My dog-sisters are used to unruly men. They enjoy making examples of the first who try anything."

Villeza reddened and looked to the other captains, but the prince interrupted. "I want the strictest discipline maintained by every captain." He flashed a stern look around the group. "Our plans call for close cooperation by all the elements of our force. Of which, by the way, there is still one whom you must meet." Ivor nodded to one of his bodyguards, who turned aside and beckoned, calling out, "Warlock—come over here."

In the twilit gloom, apart from the bustle of unloading and the festivity that was commencing around a bonfire in the center of the courtyard, stood the black-canopied donkey-wain that Conan and Hundolph had followed through the town. From its shadow a dark, thin figure now detached itself and moved toward the group.

"The Emperor Yildiz's generosity is boundless, it would seem. He has sent even more than I told of in my speech." Ivor extended an arm. "This is Agohoth, a wizard of the Sunrise Court."

The person who drew near was notable, first, for his extreme height, and then for his youth and frailty—a pale, gawky boy with a large beak of a nose and black ringlets of hair clinging to his scalp. He was clad in a disheveled black smock and pantaloons belted by a travel-soiled yellow sash, with pointed slippers of the eastern style. A black silk cape hung unevenly from his bony shoulders. His appearance drew a snort of amusement from Villeza and one or two others, while the rest of the captains looked on skeptically.

Agohoth halted and stooped forward to squint at the company, exposing a considerable length of front tooth. "Greetings, warriors. And you, prince. I am sent . . . these many leagues from the court of Aghrapur—" He halted. His awkwardness seemed more a result of bashfulness than of any language difficulty. His Kothian was good, though strangely accented. Finally he turned to Ivor and addressed him only. "My mission . . . the emperor and my masters have bidden me, ah . . . to ensure your victory by my skills."

His words were greeted by an amusement, and a guffaw broke from Villeza's lips. "Prince Ivor, this is too much! Instead of gold, Yildiz sends tin swords and armored women to vex us—and now a tongue-tied temple scribe!'' His eyes rolled back in outrage. ''A stuttering acolyte to delay us further and befog our plans with star-readings and omens. We had enough of that foolishness in Zingara! What good is it, I ask you!''

Ivor's eyes narrowed as he gazed on the Zingaran, but his composure did not falter. ''Well. That is a question indeed.'' He shifted his gaze to the gangling youth. ''Agohoth, what good are you? Can you give us a demonstration of your powers—something discreet, please?''

The sorcerer looked nervous. ''Oh, there are many things—my prince. I have certain . . . talents.'' He groped in his sash and produced a small scroll wound on two wooden spools no more than a span in length. He unrolled it and held it before his eyes with one hand, while the other drew from the neck of his smock an amulet that glinted oddly in the rays of the distant bonfire.

''Bring a torch,'' Ivor bade one of his guards.

Agohoth spoke absently. ''No need.'' He was holding the parchment before his face and peering at it through the scintillant gem, as though reading, impossibly, in the fire-tinted darkness.

The circle of faces watched him, except for one that drew furtively away. It was Aki Wadsai. Conan thought that the desert chieftain eyed the wizard with a knowing look, a look of fear. The easterner moved to the fringe of the group and stood as if ready to depart swiftly.

Meanwhile Agohoth had put away the scroll. He was muttering indistinctly and making tentative passes in the air before him with one hand; the other was at his brow, which was knit with a look of incertitude.

Then something passed about the circle. Nothing material it was, yet it could be sensed, and it provoked uneasy movements among the men and a gasp of surprise from Drusandra. Conan felt it as something soft and cool, brushing sinuously against the skin of his throat. His nostrils flared at the stink of sorcery.

There was the sound of a violent slap, and Villeza grunted. His hand flew to his face for a moment—then it dropped to the hilt of his dagger. He glared at those around him, but the prince's hand shot out to lock on his wrist, holding the hand down and the weapon firmly in its sheath.

"Make no retaliation, I order you!" Ivor said.

Already, quickly as it came, the visitation had departed. The guard was returning with a flaring torch, and by its light Conan glimpsed the angry red print of a hand on Villeza's cheek. A glimmer of panic was also present in the mercenary's eye. He shook his head in baffled consternation, then walked away from the group, massaging his face.

Agohoth was looking embarrassed and diffident. The prince went to him and reached up to clap a hand on his shoulder. "Welcome to our cause, wizard." He looked earnestly around the captains. "Rest well tonight, all of you. Tomorrow, our council of war."

4

The Jagged Dawn

The stockade's spiked edge loomed high against the sunrise. The eastern sky was a pale splendor that seemed to be formed of torn red pennants trailing under the plump pearlescent bellies of clouds. Against the dawn's glow the timbers of the wall were etched darkly, with sentries' heads and shoulders silhouetted at two places on its length. From behind it sounded an occasional voice or faint stirring—otherwise, silence.

Conan inclined his head against the brushy stump before him, relaxing his strained neck muscles. His body ached from a long vigilance during the coldest part of the night. Moving carefully to avoid alerting the fort's Kothian defenders, he flexed his cramped limbs. The labor of lying in wait was a hard one, harder even than that of creeping into position slowly and silently by night.

To either side of him, more mercenaries lay hugging the damp ground. They sheltered behind stumps of the cleared forest and the small bushes that the Kothians had carelessly allowed to grow up near the fort. Conan wondered how effective the sparse cover would be in the morning light.

Now a whisper came to his ear. "If that gate doesn't open soon, they will see us! We may have to storm the wall yet."

"Curse this for a suicide mission!" a huskier whisper replied. "They let the crazy barbarian try it only because they want him killed. . . ."

"Hsst! Quiet!" Conan twisted his neck and glared at the men, though they were visible to him only as dim, prone blurs in the mottled darkness. He waited, straining his wilderness-tuned ears for any hint that the exchange had been overheard from the fort. But there was no sound, and the sentries' heads remained in sight, unmoving.

Settling back to irritable watchfulness, Conan wondered if the men's mutterings were true. In the cold, fireless bivouac of the previous evening, Hundolph's plan of scrambling over the timber walls from horseback had sounded unreliable and potentially costly in men. As an alternative he suggested this ploy of stealth, learned in his youthful days of warring against the land-grabbing Gundermen.

Oddly the first one in the war-council to support his proposal had been Zeno, his rival, urging that Conan himself lead the advance party. Hundolph had consented with few words, but with an appraising glance at Conan, and Drusandra had given her leave as the second captain. Later Conan had seen Zeno whispering once again with Stengar, his other enemy, who was now lying somewhere along the wall to his right.

Conan's brooding was interrupted by new, faint sounds. He heard movement behind the wall: the muffled clop of a hoof. Then a spoken command, and the grating creak of timbers. Conan raised himself to his elbows. He watched a thin wedge of sky appear at the setback in the wall where he knew the gate to be.

"Dog-brothers!" His shout cracked the morning stillness. "Up, rogues, and forward!" He was already on his feet and running, ax in hand.

He heard the clink of a harness ahead, where a

mounted courier had just exited the compound. When the man saw dark shapes rising from the earth about him, he gave a yell and spurred his horse forward. Conan glimpsed blades flashing palely in the gloom. He heard a brute scream of agony and a thud as the horse went down, hamstrung. Conan ran on without stopping, drawing ahead of his companions.

Above him on the palisade an impact sounded, and a groan. The nearer sentry writhed and toppled, transfixed by a spear.

Then Conan was at the gate. The open half of the double door was scraping forward, nearly closed; he set his shoulder against it to shove it wide again. But there was firm resistance from behind. He crouched low and pressed harder, his buskin-soles grinding against the hard-packed earth of the road. The gate began to give back, creaking.

A flutter of voices came from the other side of the timbers, along with the whisper of a sword unsheathed. The pressure on the gate weakened, and a human figure darkened the narrow opening between the doors.

Conan hurled himself up from his crouch, ax in hand. The weapon lashed down, clanking on the visor of the man's helm. Instantaneously it drove back upward into the victim's face, striking flesh and bone with a dull sound. The gatekeeper crumpled backward.

Meanwhile the wooden portal slammed into Conan's side. Again he put his shoulder to it. This time it gave way more easily.

Then it swung suddenly wide, leaving him staggering. Two more sword-wielding guards were upon him.

"Crom blast you both!" the barbarian roared. With a wrenching heave of his shoulder he hurled his ax at one attacker, striking him in the chest and knocking him over. His sword whistled swiftly out of its sheath to meet the other's blade, and the air commenced to ring with clashes of steel.

Conan drove his opponent back and back, onto the crumpled body of the first attacker. When the Kothian stumbled, the Cimmerian's sword was ready. It hacked through his faltering guard and cut deeply into the side of his neck. The man went down with a gurgling cry.

Conan turned back to meet the other sentry. The soldier was picking up his weapon painfully, as though nursing broken ribs. A two-handed sword-blow to the back of his helm laid him flat again.

Something whizzed through the air past Conan's head—a thrown mace. Then a yard-long arrow thunked into the gate and stood out from it, vibrating against the bare skin of his arm. He looked up to see a mob of soldiers, half-dressed in Imperial Kothian uniforms, charging toward him from the tents and barracks at the center of the compound.

Conan wheeled. His thought found its way unbidden to his lips: "Where are my men!"

A dozen paces behind him in the dawning light, a gaggle of mercenaries stood silently over the butchered remains of the courier and his horse, watching him. Some of them looked indecisive; others had been leaning on their weapons with no apparent intention of approaching the gate. At Conan's stare, a few raised their weapons uncertainly and cheered. Then others followed suit, infected by the enthusiasm. "The gate is ours! Secure the gate," they began to shout, running forward. Stengar, at their backs, belatedly drew his sword and gave tongue to the cries.

The mercenaries rushed to form a defensive cordon inside the entrance. As they charged past, Conan felt their hands thumping his shoulders in congratulation.

"You men! Open the doors wider! Drag these carcasses aside!" He barked out orders and got prompt obedience. At his signal a long-bearded warrior raised a goat-horn to his lips and blew a shrieking double blast.

While he marshaled the men against the first onslaught of the Kothians, Conan could hear hoofbeats. The main mercenary force was finally approaching from the forest rim a hundred paces distant. He heard Hundolph's hoarse cry, "Take the garrison!" counterpointed by Drusandra's shriller tone: "Stay clear of the village, by the prince's order!"

In moments riders were pouring into the compound. The waxing light showed that the place was nothing more than a circular stockade with tents, corrals, and a few log barracks. It was nearly theirs already. Conan retrieved his ax and dashed forward with his fellows to engage the foe.

Combat swirled in the center of the camp. The Kothians had tried to make a line at the edge of the tents, but there were too few spearmen to hold off the attacking cavalry. Mercenaries leaned low from the saddle to hack down half-armored men, then spurred between the tents or directly through them. Once there, they waded their mounts amid ropes and billowing canvas to turn and ride down more Kothians from behind.

Meanwhile footmen of both sides charged up and down the tent-lanes. They met in brief and furious sword-battles, whose outcomes were determined more by weight of luck and numbers than by any fighting skill.

Conan joined the assault on the barracks—sturdy buildings of mud-packed logs standing between the tents and the stockade wall. At first the defenders kept the space around the structures clear by deadly arrow-fire from the doors and window-slits. The mercenaries were balked by the sight of a half-dozen of their skewered companions writhing or lying inert in the dust before the stronghold. Their armor and bucklers were inadequate to keep the shrewdly aimed quarrels and shafts from piercing a knee or an eye.

Hundolph and Conan ordered the men to hack down the nearest tents. These they raised before them as rough canopies, supported by spear-ends and posts. The improvised siege-shelters baffled the archers' aim and sapped most of the force of their projectiles. With pairs of mercenaries advancing side by side and holding the curtains up in front of them, the officers were able to lead assault parties forward.

When the attackers drew close against the wall of the main barrack, they blocked up the narrow loopholes with canvas. The door of thick planks had been shut and barred in their faces, so Conan and two others set to work on it with axes. Hundolph ordered a half-dozen men to stand ready with spears, waiting to contain a desperate rush by the trapped Kothians.

Finally the door buckled outward on its lower hinge of frayed leather. But no men at arms issued forth.

"Surrender in there!" roared Hundolph.

There was no reply. Conan seized the wreckage of the door and dragged it aside. Hundolph was first through the entrance, with Conan shouldering it at his back.

He had to squint to make his vision pierce the cramped darkness; then he saw that most of the defenders were climbing out through a hole they had broken in the roof at the back. Two of them turned to meet the intruders—a tall, scowling man in the cloak of a Kothian major-at-arms and his simian-looking corporal. Both men raised their swords and struck toward the doorway to clear the room.

"Back, hireling scum!" the major snarled. His sword scraped against Hundolph's, grazing his bronze breastplate, and the chieftain responded with a deft counterthrust.

Then the corporal engaged Conan. There was no room for the other mercenaries to press in behind.

Conan was glad of his ax. His height was handicap enough in the barrack, forcing him to crouch low, and a sword would have stuck in the rafters. His shorter opponent made wide slashes that seemed easy to block—until one of them turned into a crafty lunge that nearly gutted him. Red wrath flamed in his breast. He grabbed up a stool with his free hand and hurled it in the squat man's face. Charging in fast behind it, he clubbed his foeman with his ax on the side of the head. The fellow went down.

Conan turned to see the major-at-arms driven backward against a long table by Hundolph's strokes.

"Filthy mercenary!" The Kothian put everything he had into a vicious, sidelong slash at neck level—which Hundolph effortlessly ducked. He danced forward and drove his sword up under the officer's chest-armor, deeply, to the heart. Then, methodically, he shook the groaning, thrashing body off his sword and left it motionless on the floor.

Conan went to the end of the table and grabbed the last of the fugitives by his ankle. He dragged him down from the hole in the roof and thumped him on the back of the neck with his sword-hilt. The man fell limp to the tabletop.

Then the room was still. Faces looked in at the doorway and turned away with salutes and fierce grins.

Hundolph and Conan faced each other—and both of them burst into laughter. They tossed down their weapons and sagged against the log walls, trembling with mighty drollery. Then they blundered together and clapped each other on the back.

"Just like Corinthia," Hundolph gasped. "Do you remember the Vildar keep?"

"Yes, yes, and the duchess's four eunuchs!" Conan rumbled, gusting out laughter. "What a fight!" He shook off some of his mirth. "You've forgotten none of your swordmanship, I see."

"Indeed. But it was your skill that took the outpost. You must have learned some new tricks."

Conan glanced at the doorway, which was momentarily clear of mercenaries. Then he turned to Hundolph with a dour look. "Did you know your ruffians wanted me killed out there, before the gate?"

The older man met Conan's gaze innocently. "Perhaps." He shrugged. "I thought you could handle it."

Conan frowned, dubious, then nodded. "I suppose I could." Both men broke into laughter again.

Finally Hundolph slapped his knee and rose. "We had best find out who won the battle." He stepped through the door and barked at the soldiers outside. "Go in and get those captives! Make sure you disarm them. Search the place for loot and documents."

5

The Reckoning

On leaving the barrack Conan saw that dusk had paled to somber, overcast day. The sun was lost behind a canopy of rain-swollen clouds. He found the atmosphere darkly invigorating, reminiscent of his northerly home. It was a perfect morning for battle—a steel morning.

The would-be escapees from the hut had all been cut down or caught by Hundolph's men, as attested by dead bodies and a desultory group of prisoners and wounded at the back. A fire was burning down one of the log barracks, and Zeno's men were still routing a few die-hard Kothians out of the tents—but it appeared that the garrison was well-nigh subdued.

Good so far, Conan reflected. If the other two detachments of Ivor's mercenaries had gained their objectives half as handily, then King Strabonus's imperial teeth would be pulled, at least for the moment, in this neighborhood. The rebels would be safe from immediate retaliation, and Prince Ivor would be well pleased.

As he walked through the compound his attention was caught by an open doorway at a point where buildings stood near the outer wall—a postern gate. Cautiously he approached it and peered through.

On that side of the fort the land sloped away toward a village of thatched cottages that straggled down to a muddy stream. Beyond were farm-fields and forested hills, looking greenish-black under the lowering sky.

It was impossible to tell how many others might have passed this way during the battle, but now Conan heard sounds of conflict. Curses and a woman's screams issued from among the nearer dwellings.

He hesitated only a moment, bethinking himself of the standing order to stay out of the village—all the more reason for him, as an officer, to investigate. He jogged across the fort's defensive slope and down the rutted lane that led between the huts. As he ran, cool, tentative drops struck his bare forehead; the sky was striving to keep its promise of rain.

Rounding a plank fence that curved away from one of the cottages, he saw the source of the shouting. Two men in motley mercenary garb were struggling with a village girl. She was slight and barefoot, dressed in a woven skirt and a torn shift. As Conan drew near, the shorter and stouter of the two assailants wrenched a shapeless bundle out of her hands. He threw it to the ground—a screaming infant, half out of its swaddling-cloth. It lay in the grass and bawled.

The other mercenary, a hulking lout, was pinning the woman's arms from behind while she kicked and struggled vainly. His moon-face wore a strangely complacent expression; Conan recognized the doltish Lallo.

The stout man's back was turned, but Conan could guess his identity. "Ho, Stengar, what's the matter? Is the baby too small for you?"

The swag-bellied one turned and stared. Then he raised his eyebrows in mock surprise. "Well! Here's Lieutenant Conan, the hero of the day!" He saluted with a flat hand leveled against his chest. "What say you, Sir Barbarian? Did you come to partake of the spoils of battle?" He reached out one hand and ran it expressively down the girl's writhing body. "If so, run along and find your own wench."

"You were ordered to stay away from the town, Stengar." Conan halted three paces from the man, adjusting the scabbard of his broadsword with his off hand.

"Oh, was I?" Stengar marveled a moment. Then he sneered, showing his decayed teeth. "Well, I countermand the order. My rank is equal to yours."

Conan jerked his head to one side impatiently. "Yet you don't have Hundolph's authority for it— nor the prince's leave to molest his people. We both know that." He hefted his ax meaningfully. "Just as we both know whose mace it was that nearly brained me this morning at the gate." He nodded to indicate the spiked weapon dangling at the man's straining belt.

Stengar looked blankly at him. Then, with surprising quickness for one so stout, he reached both hands across his belly and drew sword and mace simultaneously from his belt. "A fight, then!" He stood at ready, holding the short four-bladed club in lieu of a shield. "As you wish, barbarian."

Conan had armed himself similarly, switching the ax to his off hand. Now he whirled his broadsword over his head once, twice, then gave a yell, "Hiiaa!" and drove at his adversary.

Stengar dodged and backstepped, clearly dismayed by the fury of the assault. Conan's sword, though wielded in one hand, was longer and heavier than his, and Stengar was forced to give ground with every stroke. When his mace took the force of the Cimmerian's blows, he drew back his arm as if stung. His own sword accomplished little against the net of steel that was woven blindingly around him.

Then the point of Conan's blade clashed across the front of Stengar's breastplate, and the stout man winced in pain. "Lallo!" he cried. "Give aid!"

The big woodcutter had been left some distance from the fight. He was still pinioning the girl's arms and pensively watching, his mouth hanging open. Now he shoved her aside. She scurried to her infant whose squalls had subsided to whimpers. Meanwhile, Lallo began lumbering toward Conan.

But as the youth groped at his belt for a weapon, something else intruded on the scene—a level geometric line, seemingly sketched in empty air. It intersected with Lallo's chest and stopped.

It was a spear. Its impact was followed by a long, grating moan from the youth's distended mouth. The brightly painted shaft wavered in space before him until its end slowly sagged to the ground. He leaned on it awhile, his face working in pain. Then he slumped sideways to the dirt and lay still.

"Crom." Staying in his fighting crouch and sidling so as to keep facing Stengar, Conan glanced back to see Drusandra's yellow-polished armor and leonine head. She was flexing and rubbing her arm, which had apparently been strained by the spear-cast. At her side stood dark Ariel, with sword drawn.

"So die all tormentors of women," Drusandra announced. "Do you need help with the other?"

Conan's glance away from Stengar was short, but it almost measured his life. As his eyes flicked back to his opponent, only a savage, primal instinct made him fling his ax up before him to clash against Stengar's flying mace, a mere handsbreadth from his face. The cruelly pronged weapon fell and rolled in the rain-dampened dust.

Stengar's back was already turned to Conan, his desperate feet hurling him away from his now-rampaging nemesis. The Cimmerian gave a bellow and charged in pursuit. "That makes three tries, Stengar, all that Mitra grants a man in this life!" As he overtook the running mercenary, his sword flashed in a barely visible arc, down across his victim's shoulder. It clove flesh and armor alike, ending deeply embedded in his spine. Stengar slumped heavily to the ground, pulling the swordblade down with him.

The blade was stuck in bone and plate mail, and Conan had to set his foot against the body to withdraw it. It came free with a metallic squeal.

"An excellent stroke, northman." Drusandra's husky voice was appreciative as she approached him from behind. "Most impressive. It proves that a brawny arm can be almost as useful in fighting as skilled swordswomanship." She stood at ease a few steps away, while Conan finished wiping his gory blade on the fallen's man's pant leg.

Ariel was silently helping the village girl back into the hut with her child. Under the warrior's leather-mailed arm, the woman crooned over the babe and held it to one of her plump breasts.

"Kindly spoken, Captain." Conan shifted his gaze to the shining one who stood over him, arms akimbo. "But I hope that you won't make a frequent habit of killing my men, or Hundolph's."

Drusandra raised her pale eyebrows under her blond mane. "That depends, Lieutenant. Do your men include many such scum as these?"

"It matters not." Conan scowled at her. "If killing is their lot, I'm the one to do it."

"I can see that." The captainess raised her spear to her shoulder and made ready to leave. "But I must say, you give me scant thanks for saving your life!"

"Saving my life?" Conan looked up at her in genuine surprise. "You almost got me killed!"

Drusandra tossed her head but gave no answer as she walked back toward the fort. Ariel turned around once with a wary look, and they were gone.

Conan eyed the two corpses dubiously for a moment, then muttered a curse to himself. A vile mess, he thought, and possibly an incriminating one, but there was nothing to be done. At least he had a witness in the matter—and an accomplice.

6

Silver Rain

Conan turned away from his fallen foes and walked a
short distance down the street of the hamlet, looking
for further signs of pillage. He saw none. The cottages of plastered stone were shut up tight, and the
open plaza at the center of the town was vacant, its
communal firepit untended and cold. The musty smell
of new rain was in the air, and a light spatter of
droplets was falling. The only other sound was the
barking of dogs from behind barred doors; the only
glimpses of humanity were of frightened eyes peering
between shutters.

But as Conan passed the scene of the recent car-
nage again at a distance, he saw a ragged farm youth
crouching over Stengar. The boy was gingerly trying
to drag the fallen warrior's sword from under his
grisly corpse. He was barefoot and straggle-haired,
clad in patched trousers and a shapeless, soiled smock.

Conan started to call out to him, but checked
himself. Let the brash lad keep the weapon, he thought;
perhaps he'll be a great war-chief someday.

The boy looked up—at the noise of his passing,
Conan thought first. But no, the lad was staring
around himself at the rain striking the earth. And
indeed, it had intensified. Great, cold drops were
hitting, but not wetly.

Conan scanned the ground nearby and realized that

it was hail—large pellets at that, bean-sized. They began to clink on his mail and strike his scalp with stinging force.

Freakish weather indeed! He hastened his steps toward the shelter of the stockade. A real crop-stripping storm this could be, judging from the blackness of the sky overhead.

The hail continued to increase in intensity. Soon Conan was trotting, while slivers of ice showered about him and rebounded from the earth and the battered-down weeds.

Then a shrill cry sounded from behind him. Conan paused and turned, to see the village boy clutching at his shoulder, where a dark stain was spreading. The youth took his hand away and stared in horror at its redness. Then he let go of Stengar's sword and sprang up to run; but as Conan watched, the boy staggered as if smitten fiercely from above, and dropped to his knees.

Great stones were falling over the village, silver blurs dashing visibly to earth. Conan looked to the ground and saw that the hailstones had become daggerlike both in size and shape, sharp-edged and cruelly curving. Some shattered when they struck, adding to the silver litter on the ground; others embedded themselves in the earth with a thudding that Conan could feel through the soles of his buskins.

The village boy was beaten down to earth now, with red stains starting from many places on his motionless body. Conan had given up any thought of trying to help the lad; he himself was running through the open, his ax held aloft to shield his head. Frequent backward glances told him that the hail over the village was far deadlier than the rock-hard shards that were striking his armor. Black tendrils of cloud were gathering and writhing in the sky behind him, and he saw the falling knives splitting fence-planks in the town and driving straight into the thatched roofs of the huts. Muffled screams sounded from within the dwellings.

As he ran, the hail striking him grew less vicious. A few small, cold daggers had driven into his bare forearms; he cursed as he plucked them out and threw them aside. Deep in his gut an awareness was forming—the sick, writhing clench of sorcery.

He went on in a blinding haze of panic and anger. Then he realized that there was no more hail striking, nothing but a gentle rain. He was on level ground near the stockade. Faces lined the parapet above him, and a crowd of mercenaries stood just outside the postern. They met his eye with guilty fascination, then resumed staring past him to the village, where the ice storm continued audibly and violently.

Drawn up before the stockade to one side stood Agohoth's black wagon and two quiescent donkeys. Nearby, at the top of the slope, was the sorcerer. He stooped absorbedly over a contrivance from which a weird light was playing up into the sky.

With dawning awareness, and with a rage inside him as icy as the storm, Conan turned his steps toward the wizard. The objects the Turanian was bending over were really two, he saw—a wooden scroll-rack carven with gryphon's feet and wings, from which a yellow parchment sagged, and a stranger device.

This was a stand something like the first, but it was made to support a large circular plate at a variable angle. The shieldlike disc seemed formed of crystal or silver metal; it was difficult to tell, because its surface was iridescing so strangely. But it was set at a slant, and it seemed to be gathering light from the sky and reflecting it in a beam toward the gravid gray clouds rolling toward the village. The play of the light-shaft was limned by the glint of the raindrops passing through it. Conan noticed that the drops that struck the disc sizzled about, as on a hot skillet, but fell to the ground as ice.

Agohoth's role in the process was unclear. The gawky youth stood behind the contrivance, peering at the scroll-stand and muttering distractedly in an alien tongue. Occasionally he leaned forward and fumbled at the knobs at either side of the disc, as if to tighten them; otherwise, his hands hovered ineffectually in the air.

Conan halted before Agohoth and clanked his ax against his chest mail to get the wizard's attention. The youth glanced up with a slight air of irritation, and Conan spoke through clenched teeth. "Making hail, are you?"

"Yes," Agohoth said, looking back to his work. He seemed scarcely to notice the burly, blood-splashed barbarian who hulked beside him. He continued to fidget with the device and mutter vaguely, "Astonishing results . . . never seen conditions so good . . ."

Conan interrupted him. "You're destroying the town."

Agohoth flicked one hand dismissively. "No matter. The town is mine . . . for testing."

Conan's blood-streaked arm swung high. "Well, test this!" He hurled his ax downward at the silver disc.

It struck with a dissonant clank that seemed to reverberate in other dimensions than that of mere sound. The wood frame was riven by the force of the throw, and the plate was seen to shatter in a flash that chilled the skin of all the watchers' faces—although, when the dazzlement was past, there was no remnant to be seen of the strange, silver metal. Conan's ax was there on the ground, to be sure, but its tempered steel substance was fractured into a dozen or more angular, scattered shards.

"My threnalium!" Agohoth looked from the wreckage to Conan, his lip curled up from his soiled front teeth in an expression of shock and outrage. "How dast thou . . . !" he mouthed.

"Do you really want to know what I dare?" Conan said, his hand wrapping about his sword-hilt.

"You dare too greatly," Hundolph's voice rasped in his ear. The captain interposed his bulky shoulder in front of the barbarian. "Spare him, wizard, please." His rough old voice had taken on as earnest and respectful a tone as it could manage. "He is one of my best men. He was unhinged . . . mazed by sheer awe of your spells!"

Agohoth glared suspiciously at Conan as Hundolph turned and pressed the barbarian back by main force. Then the adolescent mage shook his head disgustedly and turned back to his scroll-rack, commencing to furl up the parchment.

Hundolph hooked his arm into Conan's and pulled him into the parting crowd of mercenaries. They passed through the postern gate and stopped under the overhang of the parapet, out of the rain, and out of sight and hearing of the wizard. Only then did Hundolph turn to upbraid his officer.

"You must learn deference for authority, or you will never last in the mercenary trade." He thumped an angry knuckle on Conan's breastplate, and his gusting voice vented some of its deeper registers. "It was a vile spectacle, I know, but you have to control yourself. Otherwise you will stand in opposition not only to Agohoth, but to the prince!"

Conan shook his head sullenly. "That sorcery served no purpose of ours. The wizard was flouting good sense. Ivor is calling on the people to support him!" He folded his arms. "He would not want his followers cut to pieces, and his future militiamen riddled!"

Hundolph shrugged. "Who can say? The villagers were provisioning the fort and consorting with royalists. Perhaps he wanted to make an example of them." He swept one arm aside impatiently. "Such decisions

are made from afar. They are not yours to question—
nor mine, for that matter. Just watch yourself in the
future. Now let's have an end of it!''

Zeno was standing to one side, watching the
dressing-down with interest. A gleam of satisfaction
was also apparent on his rain-beaded face fringed by
its short, damp curls. After a moment's respectful
wait, he strode forward and saluted Hundolph. ''Sir,
we have one hundred twenty-four prisoners. The rest
of the Imperials are dead or flown. Our own casualties are twenty-two wounded, eight slain.''

''You can add two to that last number,'' Conan
interjected. ''I ran into Stengar and Lallo. They were
in the village, against orders. I . . . left them there.''

Zeno flashed a suspicious stare at Conan. Hundolph,
eyeing the two of them, spoke up quickly. ''Doubtless both were killed by Agohoth's rain. Zeno, send
six men to retrieve the bodies, and warn them to
beware of retaliation by the villagers, if any still
live.''

Zeno hesitated as long as he dared, then departed.
Conan said, ''About Lallo and Stengar . . .''

''Quiet.'' Hundolph spoke over his words. ''I can
imagine. And I would rather not know. Their deaths
will justify your actions against Agohoth in the others' eyes. As for you, Conan''—the captain regarded
him sternly—''our victory today is still due to your
initiative. Therefore I shall announce that I am making your field promotion to lieutenant permanent.''
He shook his head gravely. ''But you have not made
it easy for me. Henceforth, steer clear of the wizard.''

''My thanks, old friend.'' Conan nodded and laid
a hand on Hundolph's shoulder. ''But as to Agohoth—
mark my words, we would all be better off if I had
slain that sorcerous whelp.''

7

The Entertainment

The vaulted council-chamber of the palace of Tantusium, though normally an overlarge and gloomy place, was festively arrayed this day, and richly peopled by nobles and officers. They reclined on cushioned divans and stood in glittering, fur-draped cliques, gossiping of state affairs. Some promenaded into the palace entry hall and out through the arched main doors onto the veranda.

The largest and most resplendent group stood about the steps at the raised end of the chamber. They clustered around Prince Ivor, who stood, lace-shirted and gray-cloaked, regaling his listeners earnestly. He had reduced his bodyguard for the occasion to two hard-looking men who hovered at his back, restless-eyed.

Before him long tables were spread with gold salvers of food and platinum ewers of drink, which were being liberally dispensed by serving-lads and wenches in exotic costume. The light was failing from the high windows that looked on the courtyard, and tall candelabra had been brought in by servants and placed along the walls. Their flame-fringed tops made islands of radiance in the darkening room.

Conan turned away from one of the tables, under the lingering eyes of a serving-maid wrapped scantily in striped muslin. Drinking down the level of the wine goblet which she had overfilled for him, he strode among the celebrants. He wore a polished leather kirtle and a red silk shirt of Hundolph's which, though it had the proper girth of shoulder for him, was short; it left a handsbreadth of muscled midsection showing above his dagger-belt.

By the time he had crossed the room, his golden cup was nearly drained. He came up beside his captain, standing at the back of the chamber beneath the shadowed balcony, and spoke in wine-blurred tones.

"By Crom, if Ivor truly wishes to pay us, he need only melt down some of his tableware!"

Hundolph narrowed his eyes and glanced to the left and right to see if any had heard the remark. "I would not expect it. Lavish hospitality is required of every prince, and this one would be worth less to us without all his brac-a-brac." He winked at Conan. "Just see that none of it sticks to your fingers; his guards will be watching at the doors."

At that moment Ivor's expansive voice was heard raised across the room, and both men turned to watch him. The prince was standing with Brago, Drusandra, and Villeza amid a circle of onlookers. Now he flourished his cup and declaimed to them. "By such bold strokes are kingdoms forged. Your victories have vastly enhanced the security of our province, and will form the basis for even more daring action."

Ivor raised his handsome head and swiveled it, his glance sweeping the room. "But where is the most fortunate of my captains—my special pride? Ah, there you are, Hundolph! Come here." The prince beckoned, and faces around the hall turned expectantly toward the captain and his lieutenant. "For it is in honor of our victories of the past few days, and particularly yours, that this banquet is held."

Conan followed his commander among the staring guests and stood near him when the prince reached out to place a hand on Hundolph's shoulder. Ivor said, "On a day of brilliant victories, Captain, yours was the most signal. I salute you for it. It epitomizes the spirit and toughness that have come forth in our cause." He raised his cup to the listeners and gathered a scattered harvest of applause.

Hundolph muttered, "Thank you, my prince. Of course, I cannot claim all the credit."

"Ah, Captain, you are modest! Charming." The prince lowered his hand. "But then, a great part of leadership is the skill of choosing the right subordinates, such as your lieutenant here, Conan, is it? The leader of the advance party, if I am told rightly."

Conan nodded wordlessly. After a moment's wait Hundolph supplied a polite rejoinder for him: "And the planner of the attack, my prince."

"Indeed." The prince nodded to Conan. "Your plan resulted in a swift and cheap victory, greatly to your credit." Then he regarded the sullen officer more gravely. "How unfortunate, then, that the joy of victory should be marred by your unpleasant clash with my arcane counsellor from the East!" He glanced briefly about the hall. "Where is Agohoth, by the way?"

"Milord." One of the bodyguards at Ivor's back leaned forward and spoke into his ear in a rasping voice. "He sends word that he is casting vital star-readings tonight and will be unable to attend."

"Ah." The prince shook his head resignedly. "In any case, I hope that such regrettable conflicts of battle planning can be avoided in the future." His gaze again settled on the Cimmerian. "I trust that you agree?"

"The wizard was butchering harmless peasants," Conan declared. "Such mischief is hurtful to us, so I put a stop to it." He swigged down the last of his wine.

Hundolph hurried to add, "As you may know, my prince, two of our troopers were also killed in the village"—he spoke earnestly, as if to draw the prince's attention away from Conan—"a factor which added to my lieutenant's concern at the time."

In spite of Hundolph's effort to gloss over Conan's remarks, some of the knights and courtesans watching the discourse were muttering in consternation at the outlander's blunt tone of address. The prince's guards were watching with narrowed eyes. Now Ivor's look focused more closely on the Cimmerian's face, which was resolute, though slightly flushed with drink.

"Quite true, Captain. And yet my sources inform me that the wounds of the two dead men differed from the distinctive marks left on villagers by Agohoth's . . . amazingly potent spell." His eyes traveled to Conan's belt, where, in the absence of a broadsword, hung a dirk that extended almost to the barbarian's sun-bronzed knee. "So it is possible that their deaths were caused by something other than the wizardry—by fleeing Kothians, perhaps—or even by some of the 'harmless peasants' that you, Lieutenant, were so zealous in defending."

Conan gazed squarely into the aristocrat's face. "Since you call on the common people for their backing, I hope you know that the people hate nothing more than black sorcery." He shook his head disgustedly. "To turn that lizard-hearted priestling loose on them, and let him cut them up like giblets, would be the height of folly." He fixed his gaze on the prince. "Are you a fool?"

This time there was an audible gasp from the listeners. Even Hundolph seemed to believe that the efficacy of words was past; his hand wandered to the hilt of his dagger.

The prince, however, spread his arms to either side so as to restrain his bodyguards from moving against Conan. He did not give vent to any rage, but instead turned a tight smile on the Cimmerian.

"Our notions of policy may differ, Lieutenant."

His shoulders flicked in the merest hint of a shrug. "If so, it is of little moment to me. But I shall answer you in the following way." He turned his gaze over the company with a casual movement, as if to let them know that his self-control was unruffled, though a vein pulsed visibly beneath the unruly strands of hair at one side of his forehead. "Agohoth the wizard was sent to use as a weapon. Any such unfamiliar weapon must be tried out. I could have had no certainty of the tremendous power of this tool had I not tested it—at a slight cost." He lifted his hand before him, as if hefting the weight of a sword.

"Furthermore, a weapon is valueless unless it is entirely clear that its possessor is willing to use it." Ivor swept his hand down and aside impatiently. "Had I known the wizard's power, I might have ordered him to subdue the Kothian garrison quickly and totally instead of relying on your exertions, Lieutenant." His voice was honing to an edge of wrath. "Then the weapon would now be whole and undamaged."

Ivor stopped speaking, perhaps because he felt his anger leading him onto impolitic ground. Only after a long pause, with utter silence from elsewhere in the hall, did he resume—and promptly conclude. "In the future, I shall not hesitate to use the necromancer's powers wherever they are called for. And I shall expect anyone who does not want to be the target of them to stay out of their way."

With that the prince turned smoothly on his heel and moved a few steps off, where he made himself conspicuously available to others for conversation. His bodyguards, with ominous last looks at Conan, turned to shadow him.

Now the mercenary chiefs were left to draw aside and make noises of consternation. Villeza, reeling with drink, came to the barbarian's side and steadied himself with a hand on his shoulder, though

Conan's shoulder nearly overtopped the Zingaran's head. "Well-spoken, northman. That stinking magician has been nothing but trouble since he followed his donkey's tail to Tantusium. We should catch hold of him before the next battle and . . . oof!" His loud, intemperate rambling was silenced by a hardy slap on the back from Hundolph.

"Well-spoken, I would *not* say, Conan!" the old warrior grumbled. "I dislike fighting in crowds." A fine film of sweat was visible on his forehead.

Drusandra spoke more guardedly. "Yet Ivor's words did seem almost a threat to us. After we fight valiantly for him, instead of paying us, he tried to buy us off with a party—and now it sounds as if we may be discarded for his new sorcerous toy."

"But the power of the Turanian wizard-guildsmen, schooled in Khitai, is no toy." Aki Wadsai's voice was hushed with caution, and his eyes flashed bright in his dusky-black face. "Terrible stories are told of them. Such a man, if his auguries are good, can stand alone against a host!"

"It is clear that we will need to take precautions," Brago put in. "But here is not the place to discuss them. Tomorrow evening at my pavilion, perhaps."

The mercenary clatch gradually broke up. A chill had occurred, and the other guests at the party were no longer cordial to them, except to Drusandra, who always gained the attention of males, though she handled them ungently.

Yet the rich food and drink were an inducement to stay, and there were other diversions, including a dancing troupe that performed on the torchlit veranda. The full-hipped female lead, clad only, as far as the eye could discern, in filmy veils, swerved and leaped to thump of drum and clash of timbal, among spinning, high-kicking Zuagir warriors in feathered turbans.

During a lull in the entertainment Hundolph leaned

close and whispered into Conan's ear. "If I must stand about and wait for a dagger in my back, I would rather do so among rogues. I am off for the trooper's party in the market square. I suggest that you accompany me."

8

The Conspirators

Hundolph moved resolutely through the festive courtyard, half-dragging his lieutenant behind him. Conan's
tipsy equilibrium did not put up much resistance, and
he trailed passively behind his chief.

After giving brief notice of their departure to the
prince's concierge, Hundolph and Conan headed away
from the crowd and into the night's darkness toward
the row of tethered mounts at the back of the court.

But as they passed down a low stair at the side of
the veranda, a dark figure detached itself from the
shadows of a side doorway of the palace. It glided
straight toward Conan with a swiftness that made
Hundolph curse and his hand clank on the hilt of his
weapon.

Conan, too, recoiled—but then he rumbled out a
pleasurable laugh. For as the figure passed into the
fringe of the torchlight, it resolved into an elegantly
gowned woman—one of the noblewomen who had
been gracing the evening's festivities.

Her deep-brown hair was piled high on her head,
pinned with a glinting comb, and the red shawl which
had seemed black in the shadows covered bare shoulders and a fulsome body swathed in red velvet. The
evening darkness seemed to have been artfully deepened about her eyes, which glittered in the dimming

torchlight. Her berry-stained mouth bore a lax expression of intoxication and fleshly abandon.

"As I thought!" She surged up against the tall Cimmerian and clung to him like wave-washed kelp to a sea-crag. "It is the young trooper Conan, whom I spoke with earlier! But stay, sir"—she raised her eyebrows to him with thrilling effect—"surely you are not leaving so soon? There is much of the night ahead of us."

Hundolph relaxed, perhaps on seeing that both her pale hands were still in sight, stroking Conan's burly shoulders. There was scarcely a place on her body to conceal a weapon of any size.

Conan was amused and slightly astonished at her intimacy. "I'm glad you remember our talk, Eulalia." He let his hand clasp her back with comfortable familiarity. "But I was just leaving with my captain. What do you propose?"

"Oh, Conan, I found your stories so intriguing. I hoped we could continue our discourse at length . . . somewhere quiet, and more private. My chamber, perhaps. It lies just up these stairs." With a toss of her head she indicated the black doorway whence she had issued.

While the woman's hands and eyes still lingered on him, Coman turned to his employer. "Mayhap you could make your way safely to the troopers' brawl, Hundolph, while I remain here. . . ."

Hundolph grasped Conan by the arm and half-coaxed, half-hauled him away from his fancier. "Excuse me, milady, but I, too, must say a word in private to this young officer." He took Conan several paces across the paves and, with a heavy arm around his neck, hauled his head down to whispering level.

"You lout, it is not for myself that I am cautious! I have no fear of making my way through the city alone. But you—you have offended a powerful man!" Hundolph's agitation made itself felt through his heavy-handed, viselike grip on his lieutenant's shoulder. "Think you now to linger by night in his home and tickle one of his courtly trollops? If it be not a snare, and a fool's snare at that, then the risk is still utter madness. You had better come hence with me at once!"

Conan's face squared, showing less seeming of intoxication even in the darkness. He straightened himself up and shrugged the older man's grip from his neck. "Hundolph, I do not doubt my own fitness to handle what troubles may arise." His words were carefully chosen, spoken in a subdued and dignified tone, with only the slightest drunken slur. "I've talked with this maiden at length, and I find her . . . engaging. Therefore I choose to stay." He folded his arms across his silk-girt chest. "If, as my commander, you order me to come with you, then I must decide whether to obey."

Conan stood rock-steady and waited, half-illumined by the dying torches sconced on the veranda, and washed by the faint swell of music that now sounded from inside the palace.

Hundolph cursed in low-voiced exasperation. "Belabor me for a toe-biting idiot, to think of arguing with a barbarian—obtuse, drunken, and lovestruck to boot! Very well, I go alone." He started away into the night, then turned back and raised a lecturing finger. "But mind you, do not think to find me at your shoulder. I'll not be there to pull your cods out of the fire this time." He stalked off, pausing yet again to look severely at Conan. "Be back in camp by first trumpet if you still want your command. And be wary." His burly form dissolved into darkness, his further progress indicated only by the snorts of the tethered horses.

With a bemused smile Conan turned back to Eulalia. She stood alluringly, hand on one hip, beckoning with the other. As he started forward she backed toward the doorway, her sparkling eyes drawing him after her. Yet she moved with a new, brisk coyness and managed to stay just out of reach.

He quickened his stride and caught up to her in the blackness of the doorway. There his hand closed on a knot of smooth fabric at her hip. His other arm slipped around the firm curvature of her waist, and he swept her up against his chest.

His embrace crushed breath from her; he felt its warmth in his face and tasted its wine-sweetness as his lips pressed and probed in search of hers. She whimpered and twisted in his arms, her hands plying his shoulders in desire or resistance—for the moment he could not tell which, nor did he think to care. A red passion was blooming in his breast like the glow of a forge, fanned hotter by the gasping breaths of her mouth against his.

Then a gruff, incoherent shout sounded in his ear, and a hard fist smote his shoulder.

In an instant he had thrust the girl aside and lashed out bare-fisted against his attacker. The man was dimly perceived, a mere shadow in the deeper darkness, but Conan felt a solid bulk giving way before his lunge. He reeled a moment, sick and light-headed from passions that had mingled too fiercely in him.

Then metallic whispers sounded in the room. With a motion so practiced as to need no volition, Conan became one of two shadows that stood tense and moveless, the distance between them measured by two lengths of pale steel.

"No, wait! Do not fight." Eulalia's agitated voice was almost sobbing. "Randalf, sheath your sword. Conan, fear not. I have a light here."

The rasp of flint sounded, and a spark shone, trembling even more than was warranted by its frail newness. Then it settled and grew, becoming a flame in a dish of oil, which rested on a sill at one side of the narrow room.

The place was little more than a vestibule with two other doors besides the outer one, which was now closed. A stone stair slanted up one wall of the room and curved out of sight.

The red-gowned woman rested against the sill, flushed, dissheveled, and panting. Her bound-up hair had come undone and hung in a lank auburn curl at one side of her throat. Now she tried to refasten it, while looking first anxiously to the one called Randalf, then blushingly at Conan. "I am sorry. You were too . . . impetuous. I did not have time to tell you our real purpose."

Conan's voice came out husky with resentment. "What sleazy business is it, then?" He kept his long dagger leveled. "I have gone into low slum warrens with a woman before this to find a man waiting—and know ye, he never fared well at my hands. But I didn't expect to find such doings in a palace of foppish aristocrats!"

Randalf cursed and raised his sword, which he had let fall to his leg at the noblewoman's request. His speech came out harsh and tremulous. "I should have expected your way of courtship to be gross and barbarous, mercenary. But curb your slurs to my lady, lest I cut the slanderous tongue out of your head!"

Eulalia clutched his arm to restrain him, clinging close against his side. "No, darling, we deceived him!" She looked back to Conan, her face reddening again. "The lieutenant knows nothing of your claim to me."

Conan now examined Randalf with an intensified, dire interest. He was older than the girl, perhaps older than Conan himself, and growing stout at the middle; but he was fit-looking. His hair was cut level around his brow and shaved at the neck in the local rural style. There was an outdoor bluffness to his round-featured face, and his brown jacket, trousers, and boots looked like polished-up saddlewear. Conan pegged him as a wealthy farm squire.

He addressed the man dryly. "If your lady likes to play the sweetheart to professional soldiers, jealousy may be a vice you can ill afford."

Randalf gazed back at Conan with surly mistrust, and now he wordlessly reached around Eulalia to shelter her beneath the arm and hand that still held his sword.

"Forgive me, Conan." Eulalia's voice was steady and earnest. "We meant only to sound you out on certain topics. . . ." She glanced nervously around the chamber and went on more confidentially. "Political matters, which could not be broached in the open gathering. It was necessary that our meeting be secret, or its purpose disguised. I planned to approach you later, but your quick departure forced our hand."

"So your attraction to me was but a ruse"—Conan pretended to ignore Eulalia's renewed blush—"to cover up some sort of intrigue. But why separate me from Hundolph? I am his officer, and he is as solid a man as was ever hammered out on Crom's anvil."

"But could we finally trust him, Conan? We have checked the accounts of your clash with that archdemon Agohoth." The woman's voice now took on a note of political passion. "Tonight you placed yourself in open conflict with Ivor, but would your captain ever dare to do so? How staunchly did he back up your complaints to the prince?" She spoke with one arm around Randalf, her head raised now, her eyes flicking angrily in the lamplight. "No, I fear that like most mercenaries, his only concern is to line his own pockets by fighting for the highest bidder."

"Hundolph would not claim otherwise, yet he is a good man." Conan thumped his dagger into its sheath. "I presume to nothing more myself, yet you make me out to be some kind of rabble-rousing insurgent. I

merely spoke and acted my thoughts—as one who
has no love of sorcery or of cruelty to innocents.''

''Such thoughts are all too rare, but we know one
other who shares them.'' Eulalia glanced around nervously again. ''Come, it is dangerous to speak here.
He awaits us in his chamber.'' She eased out from
under her protector's arm and moved toward the
stair, taking up the oil lamp on the way. ''I lead, and
I will warn you back if I meet anyone. Randalf,
guard the rear.''

Conan followed Eulalia, watching her shapely calves
and sandaled ankles ascending the steep stair. He was
not easeful at having Randalf at his back, but the
man stayed far behind, trying doors to check for
spies.

They passed two curtained archways, and the noblewoman stopped at the third, parting the curtains
and leading the others forward into a short, narrow
corridor. There she went to one of four doors, pressed
its latch quietly, and peered inside. She entered,
beckoning the others through.

The room appeared to be a guest chamber, small
but well-appointed, with lavish hangings and an or-
nately carven sleeping cabinet. On a stool at the
center sat a man whose dress and bearing showed
him to be of noble station. At first he failed to look
up, for on the carpet at his feet frolicked a ring-tailed
yellow kitten. He toyed with it by trailing a knotted
ribbon along and watching the small creature leap
and tumble in pursuit.

The man's most striking attribute was his thinness;
as he leaned forward, his shallow chest and slightly
stooped shoulders showed that he was no man of war
or work. Yet he bore no look of illness, and was
even handsome in a boyish way. His middling age
was shown by the graying temples of his dark bushy
head, which looked ungainly large on his undevel-
oped frame. He was clean-shaven and well-groomed,

clad in a tailored suit of green velvet slashed with silver cloth at the chest and shoulders. As the visitors entered he looked up to them, his face retaining its bemused expression.

Eulalia bowed to him in a respectful curtsy. "Baron Stephany, here is the man I wanted you to meet."

"Oh, yes. Conan, the mercenary lieutenant." Stephany relinquished the ribbon to the cat. He drew his lean form up from the chair and stepped forward to clasp Conan's hand lightly. "Another man with doubts about the way our rebellion is going."

"I had no doubts until tonight," Conan said. "And Ivor may still come to see where his best interests lie."

"But it is not likely." Baron Stephany stooped to pick up the ribbon-wrapped kitten before settling back onto his stool. "Tantusium has been badly ruled for some time—since before the birth of any living man, and long before the rise of mighty Strabonus of Koth. It would be far easier for a new leader to follow the old, bad example than to invent a good way of kinging it." He lay his squirming pet in his lap and stroked it gingerly.

"We have followed Ivor because he has powers of leadership that I, for one, lack. He is a man of strength and action, and his words weave bright visions of the future. He spurs the imaginations of the people and rallies them to the national cause." Stephany shook his head thoughtfully. "Yet who can say what images play across the dark mirror of his inner mind? Some of us who brought him to power have come to mistrust those inner promptings. But please, Conan and my brave messengers, take seats, if you will."

Conan propped himself on the edge of a table between Baron Stephany and the door. "What you need in a leader, before goodness, is strength. If Ivor is the only one who can weld your squabbling factions into a strong force, then to weaken him is to court disaster. By plotting behind his back, you bring Strabonus's vengeance down the faster on your heads.''

Stephany nodded. ''Aye, Lieutenant, we are caught in the old paradox of rebellion—that the new regime must ever be harsher than the last. Yet there are factors that, as a foreigner, you could not know. If broadcast, they would mar Ivor's fitness in the eyes of the people. I shall not regale you with the prince's family history or that of the past rulers of Tantusium— we all have reason to watch the man carefully . . . but enough of that.

''In short, the situation we face is much like that of my pet here. An adorable little creature, is he not? Aii, but he bites like a fiend!'' Stephany winced as the wild-eyed kitten assaulted his forest-green sleeve, doing its best to shred it with every one of its claws and needlelike teeth. ''In fact, he was found and brought to me by the warden of my estate, and I have no idea what sort of cat he will grow to be—a tame, gentle house-pet, or a ravening hill-panther. I begin to suspect the latter.'' He rose from his seat and walked to a wooden cage standing on the table. Stooping over it, he thrust in his arm and withdrew it, scraping the clinging cat off inside. The creature mewled raggedly as it climbed the side of its cage.

The baron turned to face Conan while stroking his thin arm and his ravaged sleeve. ''Thus we watch and wait after every succession to leadership, to see what breed the new catch will be. Heretofore they have always been predators.'' He shook his head gravely. ''Tantusium cannot afford another such. To trade a far-off tyrant for a near one would be a sore bargain for our province.''

Conan pushed himself impatiently away from the table. ''Your notions of kingship are naive, Baron. You may as well sift for gold nuggets in a manure heap as look for a kindhearted man among Hyborian rulers.''

Stephany smiled ruefully. ''I fear so. And yet, if I could show you proofs of Ivor's unfitness—in particular, of his ill faith to you and the mercenary captains—would you act as my delegate to them and urge them to aid us?''

Conan shrugged. ''I'd have to see the proof first.''

''Then come here two nights hence—alone, at moonrise.''

Conan eyed the baron warily. ''And how am I to enter the palace? By drubbing the gate guards? Or is there some secret tunnel under the walls?''

Stephany flashed him a grim look. ''Believe me, Conan, you would not wish to venture into the bowels of this palace alone and by night. But here—my helpers will show you how to gain entry.'' He beckoned to Randalf and Eulalia, who were seated on a padded chest at one side of the room. The latter rose and took Conan's hand, leading him across the carpet to the curtained, balustraded window.

Drawing Conan up close to the balustrade, she stood with him a moment and took in the view—of a length of the palace wall, lit by torches socketed at broad intervals and tapped by the lonely footsteps of a sentry. Beyond it spread the huddled, angular roofs of the town. From the direction of the main city gate, noise and yellow glare gave evidence of the celebration in the market plaza. And outside the low line of the city wall, under the feeble starlight, could be seen firelit smudges of smoke rising from the mercenary camp. The night air was mild and flower-scented. Conan resisted an impulse to brace an arm around the girl, whose presence was warm at his side.

''Do you see that tall house with the carven gable that almost leans against the palace wall?'' Eulalia aimed one gilt-painted fingernail at it and continued in confidential tones. ''No one bides there but an old carter in a ground-floor room. Night after next, its door will be open, and a ladder will be in place from the roof ledge to the embrasure of the wall." She drew his attention to a point close under the window where they stood. "This door, where the causeway meets the palace, is not guarded, and the corridor connects with the stair we used." She turned and looked up at him, her pale, rouged face drawing back a little from their closeness. "Can you make your way without raising an alarm?"

"Aye." He nodded curtly to her and turned back into the room, to find Randalf standing behind them, nervous-looking and clearly eavesdropping. He shouldered past him and stood before Stephany. "Baron, you are too wise a man to trifle with me." Conan inclined his head to indicate the two by the window. "Those lovebirds may mean well—but see that they share your wisdom." He reached forth to clasp Stephany's hand, giving it a squeeze that made the man wince. "I'll see you in two eves."

9

Conan the Lieutenant

"Weapons ready—now step, slash, draw back! No, no, not as if you were hewing down a row of barley! Put some savagery into it!"

Conan's voice was beginning to croak from overuse, and his shoulders to droop with the weight of boredom. Before him several hundred farmers, herders, and town-fops waggled their wooden sticks halfheartedly in militia drills. All day they had shuffled through their paces on a narrow strip of hillside between the city and the mercenary camp. Now, though the afternoon was advanced, bright sunlight still rebounded from the white expanse of wall and scorched Conan's neck like midday heat.

Yet more wearing than any heat or fatigue was the frustration. Had he been called on to battle these well-meaning louts and single-handedly slay the lot of them, he could have done so while scarcely working up a sweat. But to teach them soldiery . . . that was something else again.

"Ho, stalwarts, that's enough. Now back to single drill. You, there, subdue this enemy straw-bag." Conan seized the tattered, rope-wound sack that dangled from a curving pole and shoved it at the first man in line, a gawky farmhand. The fellow made a great, clumsy stab at the oscillating dummy; then he dropped his wooden sword and hopped away, crooning and drawing splinters of the sword-hilt out of his palm.

"Next man!" Conan barked. "Remember, this sack is a battle-hard Kothian spearman, and he's hot after your gizzard!" A plump, crop-headed tailor's apprentice assaulted the bag, laying on a heroic rain of blows. An instant later he doubled over, coughing from the straw-dust his efforts had raised.

"Enough!" Conan threw up his arms. "Back to fencing—in pairs this time. A copper groat to the first man who welts his opponent's ear!"

As the sticks started to clack half-heartedly, Conan drifted downslope to where another two score recruits drilled under the lazy eye of Bilhoat.

Conan stopped beside his fellow thief-turned-officer. "I fear that these bumpkins will never stand against Strabonus's Seventh Legion."

"Methinks it just as well. It means that we need not fear being put out of work." The wizened man winked lizardlike at Conan and looked back to his charges, who were advancing up and down the field in straggling lines.

"And yet, if we could issue them real swords, they might learn something." Conan twisted his own sword and scabbard in its belt loop. "Half of swordsmanship is understanding the weight of the weapon."

Bilhoat shook his head. "Doubtless they now would be learning to chop off their own toes. Prince Ivor is wise to hoard away his keen Turanian steel for the nonce."

"Perhaps." Conan laughed. "And perhaps, if the prince were haranguing them from the city wall, they would show more spirit in their drill." He looked back to his recruits. "But I must go. My brats are quarreling."

Conan strode up the field to where two stablehands were rolling in the dirt, their sticks cast aside, goug-

ing at eyes and gnawing at ears. He hauled both men
up by the scruffs of their jerkins and hurled them in
opposite directions, giving the uphill one a boot in
the seat to speed him along. Then he addressed the
circle of gawkers. "That does it! Training is over for
the day. Go home!"

When the last of his charges had straggled away,
Conan stood waiting in the shade of a grape arbor.
After his example, it was not long before the rest of
the militia companies were dispersed. He fell in with
the other three officers and ambled along with them
toward the city gate.

"Ai, Conan! After a weary day of thumping civil-
ian backsides, I regret joining you in this venture!"
The speaker was a small, wiry Argossean with waxed
moustaches, who rolled a fiery eye at Conan as he
strutted up the road.

Conan laughed. "Ah, but Pavlo, remember, the
pay is thrice your former rate—not to mention the
prestige!"

"Horsecakes!" grumbled a rotund fellow who was
bringing up the rear. "Thrice zero is still zero. Our
captains have yet to persuade me that there will be a
payday at the end of this junket! And as for the
prestige . . ." The complaining man followed his
speech with a rude posterior noise, causing laughter
all around.

"Too true, Thranos!" Bilhoat chimed in. "Have
you noticed that since Ivor ordered the merchants to
give us credit, their prices have soared? Methinks I
have already spent my share of the booty of royal
Khorshemish!"

"The way you guzzle the grog, I doubt it not,"
Pavlo said to the other men's hoots.

"Ahead the city guard, men. Show them a bold
face." Conan nodded discreetly toward the gray-
cloaked soldiers standing on the customs terrace inside the gate who watched expressionlessly, exchanging

inaudible comments as the mercenaries approached. Conan muttered, "They are deciding whether to impound our weapons. Just let them try!" But the officer of the guard, eyeing their tabards of rank, signaled them past with a silent nod.

"Cursed street bullies!" Bilhoat whispered under his breath. "Always strutting around, considering how best to extort a bribe." The erstwhile thief expressed his opinion to the guardsmen's backs with a cocked finger.

"Ah, yes, they have been hard with us," Thranos said. "Especially in that broil two nights ago, when Varg and his drunken friends tried to go off limits in the town."

"If they put themselves in my way, I shall broil their collops for them." Bilhoat scrunched up his leathery face in a ferocious look.

"Aye," Pavlo agreed. "We might just roast their poxy town and serve it up to them on a platter." He cocked a wild eye at Conan. "This officer job is not so bad if it lets us go armed into the city!"

The men crossed the plaza and passed through a carven stone archway at whose apex was nailed a battered shield brightly painted with a picture of a red hawk swooping on a running hare. The public house inside was a gloomy barnlike room, smoky from a cookfire somewhere at the back.

The place was so thronged with idle men that it would have been hard to see its layout, but Conan knew it well. A stone counter ran atop a high curb along the back to separate the patrons from the casks of ale and wine, with only a narrow gate at one end for servants to slip through. Stone benches and tables were spaced about the room, set into the block floor and easy to swab down with buckets at the day's end. A second street archway opened in one of the side walls. All in all, a safe roistering yard for drunken soldiers, Conan thought—or as safe as any place might be.

The new arrivals caused a ripple of acknowledgment to pass among the loungers as they shouldered toward the back. But the jibing of friends and the raising of ale-jacks stopped well short of one rear corner of the room; there Zeno, seated with cronies from Hundolph's and the other companies, muttered to them and eyed Conan darkly. As an officer, he, too, was armed. One hand lingered restlessly on the hilt of his weapon as the other tipped a tankard to his lips.

"What are we swilling today?" Conan thundered. "Ale, is it? Four flagons here, Belda!" He clapped a silver coin on the counter. "And stand ready to nurse them back to health, for their lifeblood will soon be drained away!"

The bluff, motherly barmaid delivered the earthen cups and stood watching as their broad bases were raised slowly toward the ceiling. Patiently she collected, refilled, and returned them. The four men drifted away from the bar and stood scowling near a table until its occupants made room for them. Then they eased onto the hard benches.

"Ow indeed, but my eyes tire of the few and blowsy wenches that people this open quarter of the city!" Pavlo was watching a slack-figured maid with a giant flask in her arms threading her way among the idlers, expertly dodging pinches and slaps. "There must be comelier women in this town."

"Aye." Thranos nodded dolefully. "The town fathers have crewed the pubs and brothels of Tantusium with their unmarriageable daughters."

"But forget not the thrice-married ones, like gross Philiope at the Horn and Huntress!" Bilhoat plumped out his cheeks and belly in parody to a chorus of moans and rueful laughs.

"Heed Bilhoat well; he will be sleeping in her

arms tonight like a puppy!'' This remark, tossed by an invisible roisterer, raised a chorus of hoots and snickers.

Conan's neighbor at the bench, a swarthy ruffian, inclined his face drunkenly into the conversation. ''Some of those girl troopers are right easy on the eyes.'' He blinked and surveyed the company. ''Has any man ever had glee with one of them, I wonder?''

Bilhoat frowned. ''I would sooner try to love up a porcupine, the way those wenches bristle with daggers and barbs.'' He shuddered. ''Or an armor-plated dragon.''

''Hazard it not,'' Pavlo cautioned. ''Troopers have met with harsh repulse at their hands.'' The fierce little man addressed the company with a gleam in his eye. ''Why, only last night, after the revelry, I had to come to the aid of one poor stalwart, whom I shall not name. They had bound him up with his own pantaloons, by the heels, in a tree near their camp. And he was too drunken to loose himself!''

As his listeners' consternation broke up into laughter, Pavlo continued apart to Conan. ''Such is their method of retaliation. The victim never raises complaint because of the humiliation it would bring.'' Conan nodded thoughtfully.

''Nay,'' Thranos was saying, ''it is useless to pester the sword-bitches. I have heard tell of such women.'' He gazed around the company with a knowing look. ''They have no use for men—preferring one another's company in bed as well as in battle.'' His pronouncement was heard with nods and muttered assents from those standing near the table.

''In these times, women are mutinous against the rightful dominion of males,'' Bilhoat observed. ''I am told that they even sit the thrones of some kingdoms.''

''Indeed,'' Conan agreed. ''One year agone, I myself helped to install Yasmela as queen of the Khorajan border kingdom, not a score of leagues to the west of here." He gazed thoughtfully into the depleted depths of his ale-mug. "A more just or womanly ruler one might not find—though methinks queenship cools them down a bit."

"There is a whole city of wild women in southern Shem," an unseen listener proclaimed. "To make more of their kind, they capture Shemitish caravans and use the male prisoners lustily—but for only one night. Then they make living sacrifices of them, along with any boy-children, to their fierce snail-god."

"That does not surprise me," another replied earnestly. "Shemitish males are unmanly, and much better able to figure a profit than please a woman."

"What kind of slander is that, Nemedian rogue!" a voice thundered in the thick, sonorous accents of Shem. "Take it back, unless you want to choke on it!"

"Aye! We have had enough abuse from these northern clod-lumpers!" another drunken voice cried. "Any Shemite trooper is worth four of them!" The speaker was a slight, curly-haired man, but burlier sheepskin-clad shoulders backed him up.

"And just who are you calling clod-lumper, you desert goat?" demanded a fur-vested Brythunian. He ducked as a clay flagon shattered against the pillar by his ear. With a roar of rage he beckoned his friends into action. "Have at them, fellows." Around the room a flurry of quick motions occurred as concealed blades were drawn.

But as the Brythunian started forward, a heavy hand clapped onto his neck and stayed him. It was Conan's.

"Nay, Ulrath, it is not meet to brawl now." The Cimmerian spoke firmly, having risen from his bench to stand between the factions. "There would be useless bloodletting. Our daggers should be kept sharp for Kothian Imperials."

The red-faced Ulrath wheeled on him. "Keep out of this, Conan. These clannish sons of Shem have long been prodding for trouble, and now they have tweaked it."

Conan lowered his arm but stood firm, his glance taking in all the poised mercenaries. "I speak as an officer, and I am not alone." He nodded at his three seatmates, who shifted uncomfortably on their benches and reluctantly started to rise, laying hands on their swords. "Tribal feuds like these are a bane of the Free Companies and a sorry waste of time."

"He speaks true." Heads turned as another voice entered resoundingly into the argument. The interloper was Zeno, who pressed toward the center of the room with a couple of Hundolph's crew at his back. "How foolish to waste effort on such rivalries when there are graver matters to be aired. Such as lies! And the betrayal of one's fellows . . . and dire murther!"

His words caused a buzz among the troopers, driving the recent quarrel from their minds. Ulrath demanded, "What say you? What murder do you mean?"

Zeno regarded the company self-assuredly. He looked comely and hale, his bluff face framed by short locks of red hair. There was something in his stance of the swagger that drink can bring, and more in it of self-righteousness. "I mean the murders of Hundolph's man Stengar—an officer well loved by us—and of the fledgeling Lallo. A deed done against comrades under cover of honest battle, and then lied about to the captain. A crime of him who now presumes to command you: Conan—this Cimmerian savage!" His arm had risen as he spoke, to point directly at the scowling face of the accused.

An angry mutter of voices stirred in the room, but Conan's voice rose over them sternly. "A grave subject indeed, Zeno. Take care how you broach it, lest it lead to even more grisly deeds!"

"Hear him!" Zeno's eyes flashed in indignation. "The rogue threatens me openly! Do you own up to it, then? Know you, I saw the bodies, and it is clear that the men died of weapons-play."

"I have not denied the deed." Conan tossed his shoulders in an impatient shrug, while glancing about himself to make sure that no enemies were pressing close. "Nor did Stengar deny that he tried to kill me by stealth—as any of you know who have eyes or ears." He gazed defiantly about the watchers. "That score is settled now. But I am ready to tote up new ones, if any wish to wager their lives. . . ."

"Enough, upstart!" Zeno cried. "You scheme slyly—but you shall not continue to displace your betters. There comes an accounting!" He drew his sword and launched himself at Conan, who raised his weapon to meet the onslaught.

There was one chiming clash of steel, then a different cry was raised. "City guards! They have fetched the municipals! Look lively, dog-brothers!"

Most of the tavern patrons had not yet chosen sides in the new brawl. Now they found themselves herded before the score of pikes and shields that pressed in from the arch at the room's end. After letting fly a hail of drink-tankards, the roisterers could do little against the long weapons which prodded lethally forward. The cursing, retreating mob bore apart the two groups of armed officers.

The guardsmen cleared the room efficiently, working from archway to archway. Outside in the torchlit dusk stood a wedge of a dozen more gray-cloaks, preventing the mercenaries from reconvening their brawl or spreading turmoil beyond the plaza. As the taverngoers were ejected, they milled about briefly outside, shouting defiance at their watchers. Then they scattered, most seeking shelter in other bawdy establishments.

As Zeno came stumbling forth amid his bullies, he

was red-faced with outrage and still brandishing his sword. Then someone pointed out to him that its blade was broken off a handsbreadth from the hilt. He grimaced at it in amazement, then hurled it into the gutter. He cast about the milling plaza for his foe, but saw him not.

Meanwhile Conan led his three officers briskly toward the gate. Pavlo, nearly running to keep up with the larger man, was exhorting him, "False or true, you should not let such an accusation pass. He will continue to spread it behind your back, to your hazard."

"Aye, there's risk in it." Conan frowned down at the cobbles. "Zeno is sore jealous. I may yet have to slay him . . . but not tonight." He shook his head gravely. "I would not set troopers and guards against me just now, or call more attention to myself."

Bilhoat was fuming. "Wretched city guard-pigs, insulting real soldiers! We should order our fellows to seize the customs house and the weapon racks." He cast a fierce look at the gatekeepers as he swaggered past them. "Then we could harry them all the way to the palace!"

"Peace, vengeful one," Thranos intoned. "Mitra in his wisdom has decreed that we shall not go thirsty." He reached beneath his fur vest to produce an earthen flask that made a sloshy, promising sound. "Look what Belda was willing to swap me for a hearty goose!"

With happy exclamations the mercenaries clustered around him. They stopped for some minutes outside the gate, then passed on down the road with noises of laughter and ribaldry.

10

The Scented Pavilion

It was much later, when the swelling moon over-topped the city wall, that Conan found himself wandering alone and bemused through the silent mercenary camp. Having drunk and diced with his comrades before escorting the last of them home to their tents, he was faced with the problem of finding his way to his own sleeping-pad. And it was proving no small task, for his carousing had carried him to an unfamiliar part of the ever-growing camp, and his normally keen senses were befogged by liquor fumes.

Now moonlight sketched the madly various polygons of foreign tents on all sides. Time and again he tripped against invisible stakes and ropes, and once he trod on a man sleeping in the open air, to be roundly cursed in Akbitanian for his clumsiness.

He drew near some large octagonal tents. Though unique-looking and set apart from the rest, they gave him no clue as to his whereabouts. One was illumined palely by the flicker of lamps or braziers inside. He debated scratching on the entry to ask his way.

He had just dismissed the notion, when a voice hailed him from the shadow of a sky-grasping tree. "Turn away, trespasser, you prowl on dangerous ground. You will not be warned again."

The voice, though cold and flat, was unmistakably

female. Conan stopped and turned his head, peering into the leafy shadows to recognize the speaker.

As he did so, she resumed, and meanwhile her tone softened from the texture of rough steel to that of finished leather. "But hold; my challenge may have been too harsh . . . or too mild. I see that the intruder is Conan, protector of womenfolk."

Conan squinted into the darkness. "A title better applied to yourself, Drusandra."

The warrioress laughed almost melodiously, emerging a step from the shadows. "True, that is my role at the moment. And on every fourth evening—the only way a troop of women can get any rest in this rutting-ground of wild pigs." She nodded to the main huddle of tents a short distance away.

Conan kept his face and voice impassive. "I am told that you are an expert hand at the trussing of wild pigs."

"The trussing, aye," Drusandra nodded, smiling. "And the dressing, and mayhap the roasting too." Her eyes gleamed in the moonlight. "But you need not fear, Conan, for you have yet to offer us any grave offense." She was clad in a hooded cloak of a dark, concealing hue, which parted down the front as her erect posture shifted to a jauntier, relaxed one; beneath it Conan saw the glint of scale armor rather than her customary plate. She cocked one arm on a hip and said, "We shall not even ask what brings you wandering this way so late."

At her use of the word *we*, Conan looked warily about him. He was unnerved to find another dark figure lurking noiselessly behind him, much closer than he liked. It was Ariel, lithe and black-clad, waiting with her palms braced on the hilts of sword and dagger at her left hip.

"In fact," Drusandra was saying, "we could extend you an invitation. It has been long since a visitor honored our tent."

"But not long since one tried," Conan said, shifting aside to extricate himself from between the two armed women. "Captainess, if you have in mind some man-baiting trick, I warn you . . ."

"Nay, Conan, fear us not." Whether her words contained a veiled taunt or were merely prideful, he could not tell. "Your forthright dealing has won you a special place in my . . . esteem. And I think my tentmates will feel the same. True, Ariel, or not?"

When Conan glanced to the other woman, she deliberately averted her gaze and kept it fixed on the ground in silence. Her face was too deeply shadowed for Conan to read her expression.

"Come, then." Drusandra turned as though his obedience were assumed. She moved across the shadow-mottled ground to the low, canopied entry of the lit tent. There she paused and had a brief, muffled conversation with someone inside before spreading the embroidered flaps of the door and holding them apart. Beyond was revealed a cozy realm of diffuse, shimmering light.

"Why not, by Ishtar!" Conan muttered to himself, and strode after Drusandra. He stooped and passed close under her soft sleeve, which was scented by smoke and musk, and entered the pavilion. She followed him, Ariel remaining outside.

The tent's interior was adorned sparsely yet comfortably. Rugs and furs covered the floor, and quilts of silk and brightly colored wool marked the bed-pads along the walls. Neither furniture nor bulky cushions were present, but saddles had been placed to serve as seats and backrests. The tent was lit by oil lamps in four corners, so that no revealing shadows played on its sides. The flowery fragrance of incense filled the warm space.

The pavilion was occupied by eight of the mercenary women. Most did not react to Conan's entrance but continued what they were doing—honing and polishing weapons, mending clothing, or trimming hair to a comfortable length for a war-helm. Two sat cross-legged on a sleeping-pad, intent on some game played with ivory lots on a black throw-cloth. Another knelt beside a prone companion and massaged the dusky, oil-sheened skin of her back.

The women's state of dress was casual, with some clad only in shifts and others bare-breasted. They varied much in appearance, from a lanky blue-black woman of the southeastern jungles to a short, broad-shouldered, broad-hipped Hyrkanian wench. Most were cream-skinned maids of the Hyborian lands, and those were franker in returning Conan's gaze.

His blood was stirred by this sudden, intimate glimpse of females formerly known to him only as efficient horse-soldiers. He turned to Drusandra, who had stripped off her cloak and sword and laid them near the door; now she was slipping out of her unbuckled mail shirt, leaving only a silken shift that clung revealingly to her body.

After a moment's hesitation Conan unhooked his swordbelt and added it to the pile. Drusandra led him to a seat on a vacant pad amid the other women. He felt his face flushing more than seemed warranted by the warmth of the tent.

"A drink, O Cimmerian? Ludmila, take the remainder of my watch." His hostess kneeled over a brazier that smoldered at the center of the tent and poured steaming liquid from a pannikin. As she did so, a plump, curly-haired woman sheathed the sword she had been honing. She rose, donned a jazeraint jacket, and went to the entry, giving Conan a sultry, appraising look before she stooped to pass through.

Meanwhile Drusandra laced both cups with liquid from a flask beside the fire and turned back to him. "Here, Conan . . . Karpash spice tea with plum wine of Ophir—better than the mule-wash they sell in the town."

He scalded his mouth on the fuming, aromatic contents of the cup and grunted in polite but watchful agreement. "My thanks, Drusandra. I did not expect so pleasant a welcome."

"Few receive it from us." She settled cross-legged on the pad beside him and cradled her cup in her hands. "You can understand the danger we face from men as women making our own way in a world where many regard us as less than slaves, less than cattle."

"A man who abuses women is a cowardly snipe." Conan inhaled fragrant steam from his cup and regarded her. "And yet, once you draw sword on him, you cannot expect him to treat you gallantly."

"To abuse me, he had better be a brave snipe." Drusandra pursed delicate lips to sip the brew that he found impossibly hot. "But truthfully, Conan, long before many of us ever took up a weapon, we were injured by men. In married life, or in girlhood."

She lowered her eyes to the glowing, white-flaking coals of the brazier. "My own father almost died at my hands for the offense he offered my younger sister. It took all her strength, and all the pleading of my mother, to keep my dagger from his drink-stained paunch. That was after I had thrown him down the cellar stair." She kept gazing at a scene the coals showed only to her, then shuddered slightly. "After that I knew that I had to leave my family to whatever wretched peace our home gave them. I hired out as a soldier-girl. I learned my craft well, by fighting my own so-called brothers-in-arms more than I ever fought the enemy.

"And yet, I was not the only one." She tossed her blond mane to indicate the others in the tent, some of whom were harkening to her words and shifting their seats nearer their captain and her guest. "Everywhere I traveled I fell in with more embattled women—escaped seraglio slaves, desperate widows, fugitives from rapes and forced marriages.'' She looked around the group with a softer and more affectionate expression than Conan had yet seen on her face. Some of her listeners nodded or mouthed silent affirmation.

''Like my poor, dear Ariel, who never speaks a word—I heard her tale from a countrywoman of hers. She was an innocent Argossean peasant-girl, more than content to wed the head serf of the district, a strong young farmer. But on her wedding night, after all the feasting and quaint dances, the local squire's retainers snatched her from the hall and carried her off to the manor—for in those parts, by tradition, the squire has first claim to any new-wed virgin.

''As it happened, the lordling was an old, decrepit man. When he made perverse demands on her, she stabbed him with the knife she had meant as a love gift to her husband. Likely it was his age and unfitness that killed him, rather than the strength of her blow.

''Be that as it may, his death passed unnoticed. The household must have been accustomed to strange noises from the squire's bedchamber. Ariel was able to escape by a window and make her way to her husband's farm.

''But when she tearfully told him of her deed, he smote her and reviled her, crying out that she had broken tradition and brought ruin down upon his head. He tried to drag her back to the manor house. In desperation she struck at him with her knife and left him for dead in the forest.

''Months later, as an outlawed woman nearly mad with suffering, she fell in with us on our march to campaigns in western Shem.''

The chieftain's tale left a grim silence in the tent, which Conan finally ventured to fill. ''Sounds like a girl after my own heart,'' he observed. ''I could have done little better myself.''

At this the solemnity of the listening women dissolved. Drusandra laughed most warmly of all and pressed a hand on his shoulder. "It is ever easier for a man, though all the world be set against him." She set down her cup and laid her other arm around the smiling Shemitish wench at her side. "But it is to women that this soldierly band of ours gives comfort, though they have been deeply hurt." She fondled the short, dark locks of her neighbor. "Ofttimes they feel that they will nevermore trust a male. They hate men's roughness and their callous strength."

"I'm glad, then, that they seem able to stand me." Conan glanced around what was now a tight circle of a half-dozen women. They watched him with guarded interest while sipping tea and exchanging discreet talk; the masseuse was continuing her labors on another woman who knelt naked in their midst without modesty.

"Ah, Conan, they are at ease because they know I respect you," Drusandra said. "We trust you not to come back here with a horde of drunken swashbucklers to try to shame us. Such would be to your own peril, anyway, for we would carve the lot of you—" She stopped, shaking her head as if in exasperation with herself, and smiled. "But no, that is not what I meant to say." She leaned close to Conan, pulling her Shemitish companion sideways with her. "We are at ease with you because we are here together, safe in the bosom of our sisterhood. Do you understand?"

Conan watched Drusandra and did not reply, for he was not sure he judged rightly where her remarks were leading. He still felt somewhat disconcerted by her nearness, unused to regarding her as a woman rather than as a fighting officer.

The sword-woman slid her arm caressingly around Conan's linen-shirted back. "You know, most of us could not feel safe with a man . . . singly."

Conan nodded. "That I understand." He looked

around the intimate group of females, their faces flushed by drink and companionship. "I wager that most of my fellow troopers would not feel safe singly in this company."

Drusandra smiled. "Moreover, if one of us were to slip away to consort with a male, the others would feel betrayed. We depend on one another for our lives, so we dare not sacrifice our unity." She turned and bestowed a kiss on the face of the girl at her side.

Conan watched with mingled fascination and doubt. Some of the other sword-women's mutual pats and caresses were beginning to seem to him more passionate than sisterly.

Then he was surprised to feel a pair of cool hands kneading his shoulders and the back of his neck. They were, he discovered, those of a freckled northwoman in a clinging silk shift, who had moved up quietly behind him. Though she met his look of inquiry gravely, her touch was deft and pleasant, dispelling the tension of his watchfulness.

Meanwhile Drusandra had insinuated her hand beneath his linen shirt and was stroking the small of his back. "There is strength in our fellowship here, and there is also safety," she told him. Conan watched the Hyrkanian girl at his other side lay her hand on his bare knee; he felt her gentle fondling while Drusandra leaned closer to him, whispering, "For us, for now, this is the only way. Do you see?" She lay her head alluringly against his shoulder, her cheeks slightly flushed, her lips parted.

Conan could no longer doubt her meaning. His head was starting to swim and his body to tingle under the various caresses of the women. Above all he felt a delicious sensation of abandon—for he knew the warrior maids had him at their mercy, whether they wished to kiss him or pummel him. At this moment he scarcely cared.

In answer to Drusandra he reached an arm about her and drew her mouth against his. The others watched with lascivious eyes, some reaching forward to touch him. Passion blurred his vision, and the women's laughter and sighs faded in his ears as he was received among them.

11

Swords in the Dark

"What word, Brago? Have your men spied the emissaries yet?" Prince Ivor addressed the mercenary chief as he appeared in the gloomy archway.

Brago's hard boot-heels echoed on the floor of the council chamber. Halting before the waiting men, he dipped his head in a perfunctory bow. "Nay, my prince. They are deployed outside the city as you ordered, but the signal was to be a triple torch, and such has yet to be seen from the tower."

"Best hope that your dogs have not frightened them away." The prince swiveled on his heel and paced across the resounding parquetry. "Are you sure that the other mercenary captains know naught of the meeting?"

"Aye, sir. My men departed camp this noon, on the pretext of a training exercise."

"Good." Ivor ran fingers through his brown forelocks. "I still fear a trick. I know not what envoy Strabonus is sending, be it a page-boy or an Imperial legion, but if it is anyone of rank, we may gain a useful hostage."

The council chamber, site of the grand entertainment of two nights earlier, now wore a different aspect. Its gay trappings and plush furniture were retired, and it was once again a cavernous hall of state, lit by a pair of golden tapers on the prince's dais. By their glow the restless Ivor paced before Brago and a handful of men, while the far corners and vaulted heights of the room remained regions of shadow.

"And you cannot tell, O prince, what the king's message may be?" queried a lean, bearded man, one of two present in formal Tantusian military uniform. "Surely it is not of great moment, merely another ultimatum from our sworn enemy."

"Speak not too hastily, General Torgas." Ivor wheeled with an irritable toss of his gray-cloaked shoulders. "How should I know if it is of moment until I hear it?" He eyed the man narrowly.

"Likely it will be more threats," said the other officer, whose plumed helmet proclaimed him also a general. "Such are cheaper than real military action, and therefore more to tight-fisted Strabonus's liking."

The prince turned and gestured impatiently to one of his three bodyguards. "Go up to the tower, man, and assist the lookouts. Be sure that the main halls are cleared. Report to me immediately if you see any sign of . . ."

His words died out as he and the others became aware of ringing footsteps and the clank of weapons in the outer hall. They turned to see men trotting forward through the unguarded archway in two well-disciplined files—armed men in Kothian purple.

"Imperials! In the heart of my palace!"

Other shouts rang out simultaneously with Ivor's. "We are betrayed!"

"To arms!"

The first man forward against the intruders was one of the prince's bodyguards. He raised a long, cruelly tapered *spatha* blade that skilled slayers use to seek out fatal chinks in armor. But before he had gone three steps, the lashing discharge of an arbalest echoed in the room. The bolt passed through his chest and clattered off the wall near one of the great candlesticks, leaving a bloody spray on the white marble. The man was spun halfway around by the impact before tumbling across his sword, already lifeless.

In moments the prince was encircled by a double ring of steel—the outward-pointing blades of the defenders poised against the concentric hedge of swords, javelins, and barbed crossbow-snouts aimed by the dozen or more Imperials.

The two groups stood blade-to-blade a moment, tense and silent. Then the desperation in the eyes of the prince's men turned to amazement as they glimpsed the broad, dark figure who swaggered in at the doorway.

He was clad in purple and ermine, his helm and breastplate heavy with gold. His face, with its full nostrils and broad, grandly sloping forehead, was unmistakable, though the statues that represented it locally had all been smashed, and the coins reminted. Clearly visible was the resemblance to Ivor, though the latter's youthful countenance had scarcely flowered to the fullness of power and jaded sensation that this one expressed.

Two more soldiers flanked the king of Koth as he entered, stopping to close the great doors at his back. He strode forward and looked over the shoulders of his scowling men-at-arms with an amused, complacent expression. "My dear nephew! In spite of the ample notice I gave you of my visit, it seems that you have not prepared an adequate welcome!"

"Strabonus! How came you here?" Ivor made a brave effort at sounding haughtily outraged. "You deliver yourself to my throne room, the very locus of my strength!"

"Yes, as a fox delivers himself into the grip of his enemies, the poultry." The king smiled. "Think you, nephew, that I no longer have friends in Tantusium? Or that I do not know the secret ways of your city, and of this palace, where your father and I frolicked as children?'' He shook his head. ''Nay, Ivor. Your sentries in the countryside did not deter me, nor does your empty blustering now.''

The prince eyed him, his face pale and rigid. ''With a word I could have you and your men captured.''

Strabonus smiled. ''With a nod I could have you killed.'' He glanced around the gloomy chamber appraisingly. ''After which, I doubt not that I could fight my way out. If I needed to—for might I not find instead that all your die-hard rebels have suddenly reverted to being my faithful subjects once again?'' He scanned the tense circle of Ivor's defenders with a skeptical eye.

''Enough of your taunts, Uncle.'' On Ivor's forehead a fine film of sweat gleamed in the candle-rays. ''Clearly you have placed us both in mortal danger. Now, what is your purpose?''

The king turned away from his kinsman, folding his arms across his bulky chest. He said expansively, ''I have chosen to deal with you in person, Nephew, not only because it meets my needs of thrift, but in the hope of cutting through some of the stiffness and posturing that impede the formal channels. Between kinfolk especially, there is a certain understanding, a common interest that would be lost if we dealt through emissaries.''

Ivor shook his head impatiently, dislodging the unruly lock of hair on his brow. ''Rather the opposite, Uncle. Until now our blood tie has only been the cause of hatred and strife.''

''And yet we understand each other at least.'' The king shrugged. ''Decisions can be made in light of facts that only you and I know, regarding our backgrounds and our, ah, departed relatives . . . and certain pretenses can be dropped. Such as your inspired impersonation of a rabble-rousing champion of the common folk.''

Ivor narrowed his eyes. ''In truth, I have always defended them against your tyrannies. . . .''

''The better to inflict your own, I know.'' Strabonus looked around the line of his still-poised men. ''But enough sparring, and to business! Surely we can let these soldiers stand at ease.''

''Aye. We can fall back to the dais.''

Led by Ivor, but scarcely relaxing their watchfulness, the two bodies of men moved toward the end of the chamber. The prince took his seat on the edge of the throne, as if unaccustomed to the marble perch, while his retainers stayed close on either hand. Strabonus dragged the great chair's padded footrest forward to the line of his men, easing his heavyset body down on it with a grunt. His elite household guards stood with swords sheathed, pikes grounded, and crossbows angled up a few degrees from the lethal position.

''There, that is much better. My day's travel has been wearying. Now, nephew, in spite of my earlier jibes, I admit that it would be neither cheap nor easy for me to retake Tantusium and install a puppet in your stead. I simply do not have the military force ready to hand. I could sap your strength, yes, and deny you the benefits of westerly trade, but conquer you, no, at least not at the moment.'' The king straightened his ermine sleeves. ''And so, in recognition of the loyalty which you command in this part of the empire, and of my pressing commitments in other parts, I find it convenient to offer you terms.

''Therefore I propose that you be created a demi-regent and granted limited autonomy in Tantusium and its precincts, subject only to my own authority. Your domain can run from the Urlaub River in the west to the Drakken Hills to eastward and southward. As proprietor of a Kothian state, you will be under my protection and likewise bound to aid me in wars and insurrections.

"In return for this sovereignty, you are to resume paying tribute equal to one-half the former sum, annually." The king raised a hand to rub his steely-black chin. "Of course, for your own enrichment, your taxes will not be held to the former limits."

Ivor sat erect regarding Strabonus, his face showing something of bitterness and something of triumph. "And so, after all, you would have me as your satrap. Not necessarily a bad bargain, if it exempts me from your former intolerable restraints on my power. But tell me, Uncle, even if I were to agree, what would ensure my adherence to your treaty"—he glanced down the line of the king's men-at-arms—"once I am out of your crossbow-range?"

"A private word, Nephew," Strabonus said, beckoning with two fingers to the younger aristocrat. Ivor rose and, after glancing to make sure that his remaining bodyguards were flanking him closely, stepped forward and leaned down to hear the king's muttered words.

"In the event of further disobedience by you, I would be forced, through my agents in this city, to disseminate a true and full account of the death of your father." The king's face was inscrutable as his eyes searched out the younger man's. "Having been of a tender age at the time, you may not know all the circumstances, but let me assure you that, particularly in view of your pose of popular hero, it is not a disclosure you would wish. After all, the ways of his regime make mine seem enlightened. And though many have forgotten his dabbling in the arcane arts . . ." Here Strabonus's voice dropped to an impenetrable whisper as he leaned close to the prince.

Whether or not those standing nearest could hear the king's next words, they saw Ivor blanch and back away stiffly, to settle on the seat of his throne.

Strabonus covered the prince's discomfiture by speaking in a more public voice. "And so, kinsman, I urge you to accept my proposal, not merely to my face, as you undoubtedly will, but in your crafty heart. For the sooner I achieve the necessary quietude in this and a few other districts of Koth, the sooner you and all my subjects will be able to follow me to greater glories." He gazed benignly on those present, as on a group of attentive courtiers.

"Treasonous mouths may whisper that I am a harsh and grasping king. But do they not see that every tax I impose, every sacrifice I demand, is for the ultimate good of Koth? If I forge the Kothian army into the mightiest among the Hyborian nations, it is with an end in view; let those other nations tremble once they discern it. If I enlarge my treasury, or make my capital city Khorshemish the Jewel of the South, drawing to it the greatest resources of art, wizardry, and commerce, it is for purposes that may yet unfold to the world."

Ivor had recovered his composure, and now he spoke in the way of his own thoughts. "So, Uncle, you would withdraw your legion from Vareth province and remove the threat to my flank? I would require that." He brushed the heel of his hand across his brow. "And there are yet matters in Tantusium to be set aright before I can enjoy the full, natural scope of my power."

"Yes, yes, only a light garrison for Vareth, once your tribute is paid." The king nodded vigorously. "That legion is sorely needed in the West, in any case."

Another voice spoke from Ivor's side. "But, my prince, tell us—do you intend, then, to accept the king's bargain?" It was the bearded general called Torgas, whose flushed cheekbones bespoke his inner agitation.

"And what is your opinion, General?" Ivor eyed the man narrowly. "Fear not, you may speak freely."

Torgas gripped the hilt of his grounded sword with restrained passion. "My prince, here stands the tyrant we struggled so hard to throw off! By your own words he is a very devil of iniquity! I did not think our conflicts could be so easily reconciled . . . and I am not sure that your followers will lightly accept such a bargain. . . ." His voice trailed off into silence.

The prince rose from his seat to address all present. "The commoners, as always, will accept more than they know. And I—I intend to take full advantage of King Strabonus's proffered alliance. My control of the nobles and the army is, I believe, complete"—here Ivor's eyes lingered a moment more on General Torgas—"so the only potential threat to me is the mercenary rabble camped outside our city gate." He looked quickly to Brago among the men beside him. "With your notable exception, of course, Captain Brago. You know that I shall always honor my special treatings with you—but, frankly, I lack the funds to pay those other captains."

Brago stroked his blond moustache thoughtfully. "Not a healthy situation. They will not meekly ride away from your walls, you know."

Ivor nodded. "I had thought of seeking your cooperation in finding a way to dispense with them—for a substantial bonus to you, of course."

Brago nodded and smiled. "Such services are my profession, lord."

Strabonus laughed heartily. "A prince of my own line, to be sure, ever seeking ways to pinch a penny!"

Then a reedy voice said, "Perhaps I can offer assistance. . . ."

The entire party was galvanized at this utterance, which sounded from the shadowed center of the hall. The prince jerked his head up, and Strabonus pivoted in his seat to look on an ungainly, silk-clad figure who stood bowing diffidently with hands clasped against his abdomen. It was the sorcerer Agohoth.

"How came you here?" it was Strabonus's turn to demand.

"Emperor, and prince, pardon me, please. My training in distant Khitai has enabled me—when great events occur—I can pass where I will." Agohoth's head continued bobbing in diminishing arcs as he spoke. "The guards saw nothing—or at most a black and yellow moth flitting under the door." He waved nervously at the two soldiers who stood gawking with their weapons raised.

"Ah, Nephew, now I bethink me," said the king. He glanced to Ivor, from whom his troops still carefully screened him. "There is a wizard in your service of whom I have heard great things. This is he, doubtless."

"Yes. It is Agohoth, my ally from . . . an eastern land. A mage whose powers far surpass his age and his meek demeanor. I should guess that even you, Uncle, are vulnerable to his power at this moment. But come forward, Agohoth." Ivor spoke with an air of elation, as if expecting an advantage from this new quarter.

The wizard stepped toward the nobles, and the household guard moved to shield the king. But Agohoth continued to show great deference for Strabonus, halting a few paces away and bowing repeatedly.

"Emperor, I was so happy to hear—you and the prince have made peace. I have read of Khorshemish—its mighty wonders—my devout hope is to visit the city someday."

"A hope which I would be happy to grant, Agohoth," the king said. "I have always thought that Hyborians can learn much from the secrets from the mystic East. If your spells are as potent as rumor tells, then they might prove useful to me."

"Good, my sire! For it is the way of my sect to place ourselves in the service of great rulers—the greater the ruler, the more credit to us." Agohoth addressed the king, with never a glance at Ivor.

"Be mindful of your charge to my service, Agohoth," the prince reminded him curtly, "for I may not be through with you yet."

Agohoth looked to Ivor distractedly. "Oh, yes, Prince—I meant to say that, if the mercenaries are troubling you, I might try something—they have proven, ah, cumbersome to me in the past—and so perhaps in a few hours I could ready a spell . . ."

Ivor regarded him with raised eyebrows. "You propose to unleash some sorcerous terror on them?"

"Yes, sire, it could be done—sometime before dawn. It would be best, though, if other soldiers surrounded them. Some might escape, you see. . . ."

"Brago, your force is available for such a mission."

The blond warrior nodded briskly. "As long as my men are kept clear of the wizard's spells."

Agohoth nodded. "Yes. Ah, Prince, my urgent request is that when my service here is done, I might travel to the capital?"

Ivor nodded impatiently, "Yes, yes, when I have no further need of you, I will provide you with an escort to the royal court. That may be tomorrow, or sometime in the future. Assuming, of course, that my uncle agrees . . ."

Strabonus slapped his fur-trimmed thigh. "Why, yes, of course. Let me tell you, Ivor, I am thoroughly enjoying this little display of treachery. It proves to me that the royal blood runs true. I only wish that I could stay to see the disposal of your hirelings. But I must away this very hour." He shook his head regretfully. "Yet I would impose on your hospitality for one more thing, to wit, a small demonstration of this youngster's magicks. Would you do that much for your old king?" He turned his broad, dark face from Ivor to the wizard with a greedy gleam in his eye.

"Perhaps." The prince looked annoyed and nodded only reluctantly.

But Agohoth seemed positively eager. "Yes, a small summoning might be done. A sword-dervish, perhaps." He reached to his sash, where, instead of a weapon, a scroll was tucked, and he drew it forth carefully. "If one of you would hold this—my thanks." At the king's nod, one of his guards took the scroll by its wooden spindles and held it before the wizard's face. Meanwhile Agohoth stooped forward and squinted at the text through his crystal amulet, apparently reading the faint, straggling lines of characters in the impossible gloom.

Then he looked up at the king. "Sire, a special request. For this spell, all swords must be laid down. Right there—please, milords."

Strabonus looked to Ivor, who shrugged resignedly. The two men drew their swords, walked forward together, and laid them on the star-patterned tile. The other men of both factions followed suit, breaking ranks cautiously and grumbling as they went—but there was less complaint from the Imperials, for some of them retained spears and crossbows, including the two at the door.

Soon there was a low heap of swords on the floor near the wizard and his scroll-bearer. Agohoth gestured the last soldiers back with his free hand. Meanwhile he peered at the ancient document through his crystal charm and began to mutter in an oddly singsong way.

At first nothing happened. The king's troops stood on one side of the wizard and Ivor's men on the other, watching the empty space at the center of the chamber that seemed the focus of his gibberish. He was also making one-handed gestures, which looked like efforts to mold some shape out of vacant, shadowy air.

After long moments without apparent result, there began to be restless stirring among the watchers. A nervous guffaw sounded from one of the Imperial guards.

But as the noise echoed into silence, it was replaced by another sound—a faint, sibilant hissing, like the scales of a great serpent sliding across stone. As it grew slowly to audibility in the ears of the men, they became tenser and quieter than before.

Then the source of the sound became identifiable as that of steel on marble, for there were clinks and visible stirrings in the sword-pile at Agohoth's feet. Some of the blades were shifting, scraping the floor in a motion that began to be directional, as if the pile were stirred by a giant hand.

The speed of the movement increased along with the tempo of the wizard's words and gestures. Then, with a clashing and clanking that made the watchers jump back, the pile reared up into a vertical, man-sized column of swirling, dancing swords.

It hovered there a moment, a dust-devil of living steel, the jeweled hilts of the nobles glinting among the rest of the gleaming blades. Its sound was once again more hiss than clatter as the weapons caressed each other in harmonious movement. Yet the metal cyclone rode on sparks where its points snicked the stone of the floor.

At a sweep of Agohoth's arm the sword-dervish whirled off in a smooth curve across the gallery. Dashing toward one wall, it slowed just in time and veered away, the high curtains fluttering inward from the wind of its passage. Then it angled back and swooped toward the frightened onlookers. But before they could scatter far, the entity swerved into the center of the gallery and remained there, describing tight, swaying circles.

Strabonus turned to Agohoth, who had stopped reading and muttering. The mage had waved his trembling scroll-bearer aside, but he was clearly controlling the phenomenon with one hand that clutched rhythmically at air.

"Marvelous, sorcerer!" The king leaned close to the wiry-haired youth. "What next, then—what else can it do?"

"Majesty, the spell has one more requirement." Agohoth kept his eyes on the swirling steel, and he continued moving his hand as he spoke. "It is a war-sprite, living but to kill men." He paused awkwardly, stumbling over his words. "Before it will go away from here, it must consume—a life." He flicked a brief, expectant glance to the king.

Strabonus grunted. "A human victim, you mean." He knit his brow and looked thoughtfully at Ivor, who stood on the wizard's other hand. The prince started to draw back cautiously; his narrowed eyes showed that he had heard Agohoth's words.

Then the king smiled and nodded courteously to Ivor. You choose, his look wordlessly said.

The prince turned his head and whispered briefly to the bodyguards at his back, meanwhile catching the curious eye of one of his generals. Another officer, the bearded Torgas, stood silent between them with a look of dread in his eyes, mindful of nothing but the dancing sword-sprite.

Ivor's retainers nodded and sidled close around Torgas. At the prince's nod the three laid violent hold of him and hurled him forward, well out of the tight line of watchers.

The unsuspecting man gave a quavering cry while staggering and falling on the slick floor of the gallery. He scrambled to arise, but with his eyes riveted on the column of flailing blades a few paces away, he trod on his cape and slipped down again.

Meanwhile Agohoth gave a quick nod to acknowledge the prince's action. His dark eyes followed Torgas, flitting in his sharp-nosed face like those of a hawk. His hand made deft whirling motions that caused the hovering steel to move nearer the lone man.

Torgas had gained his feet and was facing the glittering specter while moving slowly backward toward his companions. They were starting to draw away from him nervously when, with a swift arc, the sword-dervish swept between him and his intended hiding-place. Its quickness terrified Torgas, who raised his arms and ran full tilt away from it, toward the guards at the door.

But his speed was not equal to the sword-sprite's, as a few more flicks of Agohoth's hand proved. In seconds the staggering runner was herded away from the door toward the opposite wall, and then promptly headed off again. Leaping over the corpse of the fallen bodyguard, he made for the shadows under the balcony at the room's far end.

Whether Agohoth had tired of toying with his victim, or whether he feared that the overhang of the balcony would give shelter to Torgas, none can tell. But he chose that moment to end the spectacle, as, with a forward sweep of his palm, he drove the sword-dervish onto its victim.

A scream, deep and soul-ripping, told of its effect, as did the milling *whirr* given off by enchanted blades suddenly meeting fleshly resistance. For a moment the fountain of silver steel became a fountain of red that sprayed forth in spiral patterns; then the noise and motion began to subside.

The blades moved to one side, disengaging themselves from a tattered mass which spilled to the floor. They whirled a moment more, their height dwindling and their motion slowing. Then, with a clatter of finality, they fell in a heap.

12

The Watchers

After a moment's uncomfortable silence in the great room, the onlookers ventured forward to see the aftermath of Agohoth's spell. With a word to Prince Ivor the wizard departed, passing out through the doorway like an ordinary mortal. The prince's bodyguards, at his order, took up the great candlesticks and bore them along to cast light on the scene; but as they drew near, one of Strabonus's elite veterans was already turning away from Torgas's remains with his hand to his throat and a sick, pale look on his face.

The others skirted the blood-slicked area of the tiles as they went to retrieve their weapons. On cleaning their blades they remarked that rather than being damaged, they seemed to have been weirdly sharpened to a new edge of hair-splitting keenness.

Then a shout rang out. "Look! Spies are among us!"

"Halt, you!" one of Strabonus's men cried.

"They may be traitors! Capture them!" the king raised his sword and waved both his own men and the prince's forward.

The guards rushed toward three fleeing figures, whose presence under the balcony had been disclosed by the approaching candlelight. One was female, and one was hooded in a forester's green cloak, and thus not recognizable. But the third was unmistakable—a giant of a man, black-haired, clothed piecemeal in a mercenary's mixed choice of armor—Conan, the trouble-making Cimmerian. "Take them alive if you can," Ivor added to the king's order.

The fugitives, well ahead of their pursuers, had reached one of the stairways that angled up under the balcony at either wall. Now the larger man practically hurled his two companions up the stairs, following more slowly himself while covering the rear. Then, of a sudden, he sprang to the top and out of sight, at the same moment that a crossbow bolt splintered on the steps where he had stood.

"After them! Hurry along!" were the cries as the guards pressed up the stairway. A moment later they were staggering and clinging to the baluster as the foremost of their number fell back on them, bloodied, driven down by Conan's fierce defense at the stairtop.

Repeated rushes availed the pursuers nothing against the outlander's strength and superior position, but then Ivor led a party up the other stairway, which proved undefended. Outflanked on the balcony, the astute warrior abandoned his position.

The guards poured up the stairs and onto the balcony toward the entry at its rear. Here a single door opened inward, with no bar on the outside, so it was an easy matter to fling it open, but across its threshold waited a panting, grim-faced savage whose bulky shoulders nearly filled the arch. Behind Conan the hallway stretched empty, with the other fugitives nowhere in sight.

The doorway was large enough for only one, and the Imperial who found himself in front tried to be cautious. He stepped to the sill and thrust his sword through, just energetically enough to test the barbarian's guard.

But a two-handed downstroke by Conan's weapon caught the crown of his helm with unequaled fury, and he was driven to his knees. Of the two spears which jabbed promptly through the door from behind him, one was hacked and split by the Cimmerian's sword, and the other was wedged against the door-jamb and splintered by the bulk of his armored body.

After that the pursuers stayed shy of the arch, milling indecisively and waiting for crossbows to be brought up. Finally one was jostled to the fore, cradled in the arms of a thin, olive-skinned arbalester. He meticulously selected a barb from the pouch at his thigh, placed it in the groove of the bowstock, and raised his weapon—only to find that the wild Cimmerian, having darted through the unguarded archway, was striking at him.

The edge of Conan's blade hacked into the varnished layers of the stressed bowstave. The archer flinched back, but in an instant the bow had ruptured, its fearful tension lashing the broken end across his face. He screamed and sank to the floor, clutching at his eyes with blood-streaming hands.

Other Imperials crowded into the doorway with angry shouts—but none dared press through against the free-swinging arc of Conan's sword.

"Come forth, dogs!" the barbarian challenged. "Is this the cream of Kothian soldiery? Step through, I say!"

But his taunts were vainglorious, and the soldiers knew it. In mere moments a second crossbow was raised, screened this time by the armored shoulders of two guardsmen. No command or warning was given.

Conan looked death in the eye, realizing that it could be smaller than a hummingbird. Through sheer, blind reflex he raised his sword at the moment of twanging release.

There was a jolt to his hand, and the sword-blade snapped in two before his face, miraculously deflecting the crossbow bolt. While its broken end clattered on the floor, men swarmed through the doorway. The foremost of them tripped Conan with a spear as he tried to run, and others surrounded him and laid into him with feet, fists, and weapon-butts.

"Take him alive, I say!" Ivor's voice rang over the drubbing. "I need to question him. What of the other two?"

"They arc long since fled, sire," the surviving general reported. "The Northron covered their escape."

"Then search the halls. But we cannot be sure of finding them, so seal off the castle completely." Ivor glared at his retainers. "I want no one to spread word of tonight's occurrences . . . understood?"

Strabonus laughed heartily from the doorway, standing behind a handful of his guards. "So already it begins, my young vice-king! At the moment of your triumph the bright unity of your cause is fractured. You reach out to grasp the glossy fruit, but it rots in your hand.

"Henceforward half or more of your subjects will be secthing in intrigue against you. You will play the ancient game of kings, with moves of stealth, treachery, and retribution. Nevermore in this world will you sleep peacefully or know a moment's innocent enjoyment." The king laughed rumblingly again while Ivor ordered the binding of the supine Cimmerian's arms with curtain-ropes torn from the walls.

"Such is kingship," Strabonus continued. "But you must weather it alone, for I have a weary road ahead of me this night. Our bargain is still firm, I take it?"

He waited for the prince's nod, which came curt and grudging.

"Good. Then send a trusted man along with me to learn my way of egress—or come yourself if there are none you trust so well." At the glare which Ivor shot him, the king chuckled again. Then he pointed at Conan's struggling form.

"As to that ruffian, I advise you to slay him promptly. He has the seeming of one who might cause trouble later on." He turned and moved back through the archway. "Ho, guards, we depart."

13

The Dungeon

Flaring torches, milling dark shapes, and harsh voices—Conan squinted through pain-misted eyes to watch the silhouettes of his captors bulking before him. Whenever he sensed a violent move against the torchlight, he clenched his body and ducked his head to avoid the blow that was coming—but always in vain. With arms bound tightly behind him and ankles hobbled a handsbreadth apart, he had no way to resist the beating they were giving him.

A straining grunt sounded in his ear. "Arrh!" Purple pain exploded in his abdomen as a fist caught him unseen from the side. He doubled over to hold his churning guts in his body, only to have a neck blow send waves of throbbing numbness down his spine. Then the bones of his skull were jolted by a steel-hard shock to his eye. He fell back against the stone wall.

"Now tell me, barbarian, who was with you tonight?" A strident voice moved closer, and Conan's thumping ears recognized it as Ivor's. "Who are your fellow conspirators? Not just mercenaries, of that I am sure." He felt fingers pinching his chin to prop up his sagging head. "Speak, you!"

"Ptuh!" The spit that dribbled forth from swollen lips onto the prince's silk cuff was pink-frothed with blood. Conan heard a curse, and a fist smote his cheek, driving the side of his head against the wall. A new volley of blows thudded into his body and he felt himself sliding, scraping sideways down the stone, to strike the floor amid a constellation of bursting lights.

"All this effort avails nothing," Ivor said. His voice wavered weirdly over the buzz in Conan's ears. "The wretch would rather bite out his own tongue than reveal anything to me. But it matters not, for I already know the answers to my questions."

A touch of steel chilled the skin of Conan's throat. "Shall I kill him then, milord?"

"Nay. Save him for torture." The prince's voice was now fading in and out, as if he were drawing close, then swooping far away. "Under my restoration, the ancient palace dungeons are being manned and equipped to deal with such offenders. Had I the time just now . . . but I must oversee Agohoth and Brago in destroying the mercenaries. Get him up on his feet."

Rough hands wrenched at Conan's bound arms, heaving him upright. Meanwhile a cautious-sounding voice ventured, "Sire, I have heard rumors of your unsealing the dungeons, and I wonder . . . are you sure that it is wise, in view of the stories that are told of them? There were terrors in the old days, and the people's memories are still vivid—"

"Nonsense." The prince cut him off. "I shall not let grand-dames' cacklings deter me from efficient rule. My household must reflect the full extent of my powers, and a palace without a dungeon is like a man without entrails!

"As to the stories—good, for they will terrify my prisoners all the more. Hmm, yes—a felicitous idea!" Now Ivor's voice indeed did draw close to Conan's ear. "We shall chain this renegade in the dungeon tonight, and by morning he won't be able to jabber his secrets to us fast enough!" The malign voice retreated. "Methinks his aversion to sorcery and matters supernatural has more in it of fear than of righteousness. Bring him away!"

Conan felt himself hoisted to his feet. Then he was shoved and dragged along, his hobbled steps measuring out a seemingly endless length of stone corridors and stairs. Torches floated about him, and commands were barked in his ears. Frequently he stumbled and fell, scuffing his knees and cruelly straining his arms, by which his captors jerked him erect.

Finally, in a cold, damp corridor that echoed with the sound of trickling water, they stopped and kept him pinioned before a massive door of green corroded metal. He heard the patient, probing rasp of a key in a lock.

As his head lolled back, his eyes fell momentarily on the keystone of the archway—a trapezoidal block that displayed the carven sigil of a sun half-risen, or half-set. With intermittent awareness he watched the play of torchlight on the strange emblem for a time; for some reason it made an impression on him.

Then sounded the querulous plaint of giant hinges, and he was driven forward once again.

The chamber that the torches revealed was an odd amalgam of the ancient and the new—the worn, treacherous steps that angled down to its floor, and the hoary, evil shadows of its vaultings, all patched by clean new stonework below. Piles of cut stone and tubs of mortar dust occupied part of the floor, while fresh timbers bolstered a sagging arch that opened onto deeper darkness at the room's far end.

Conan's captors shoved him across the uneven floor toward a side wall, where gleaming fetters hung against ancient stone blocks. Two men held him steady while a third clasped a tight, hinged shackle around his neck and threaded a chain through the hasp.

Then there were long minutes of jingling thuds as the men pounded a heavy copper rivet through the end of the chain to prevent its being drawn back out of the collar.

"That should hold him till morning at least," Ivor declared. "Cut his bonds and bear them away, lest he contrive to strangle himself. One man—you—will guard him. But close the great door and remain outside it; I want him to ponder his insurbordinations in solitude. Keep an ear cocked in case he begs to make confession before the night is out." The prince turned to the chained captive.

"And so, barbarian, wizard-thwarter, king-mocker, I leave you. Unless you want to purge yourself of treacherous knowledge, and mayhap deny a bit of nourishment to the ghouls that haunt these subterranean reaches." Ivor stepped closer. "Eh? What is your answer?"

Conan's answer carried him staggering to the limit of his chain, raking his neck against the rough metal of his collar. But the prince stayed calmly out of reach of his groping hands. He snorted his contempt. "We will away, then. Good night to you." Turning, he ordered, "Take the torches with us."

14

Prisoners

When the door squealed shut behind the prince and his guards, Conan was left in utter darkness, utter silence. The noises in his skull were suddenly a throbbing roar by contrast with the nothingness that closed in on him; he watched the lurid ghost-lights of his jarred eyeballs dancing against the all-enfolding blackness. Yet he felt his tremendous, wilderness-bred vitality slowly reasserting itself.

After long moments of dizziness he lowered himself carefully to the base of the wall, trying to spare the worst of his bruises and scrapes from contact with the rough stone. He waited again, letting his heart and his breathing subside.

Then, gingerly, he began to stretch and probe his body to learn the extent of the damage it had suffered. His groin, though protected by a leathern clout, was a nest of pain. Pain shot through his limbs at any extreme of motion. His chest ached, and he thought he could feel a broken rib beneath the linen shirt that his captors had left when they shucked off his armor. Counting his teeth, he found several loosened and one chipped to a jagged edge.

Still, the sheer mass of his muscle-laden body had stolen much of the force of his tormentors' blows. He had fared well—for that his thanks went out silently to Crom, Mitra, and many lesser gods.

But such otherworldly thoughts turned his mind to the rumored haunters of the dungeon. Ghouls, Ivor had said . . . a thrill of warning prickled the fine hairs of his neck and arms.

He tried to force his battered eyes and ears to penetrate the blackness about him. At the same time he smelled the darkness, tasted it, and sensed its cool currents. Savage dread welled up in his breast—not that there was any hint of superstition in his attitude, for he knew, positively and without doubt, that night terrors were real. A miracle it would have been indeed if such a cursed netherworld as this did not teem with them.

So he tried to subdue his heart and prepare himself calmly, as for the onslaught of any human foe. But it was impossible because of the unimaginable forms such entities might take. He could be set on at any moment; perhaps even now fanged and clawed things were creeping toward him in the dark. The barbarian clenched his aching jaw, striving to rein in his own treacherous imagination.

Finally he had to cast about for something to distract himself. Taking up the chain running through his neck shackle, he twisted and wrenched it between his fists, but to no avail. It was new, stout iron. To wear down even the copper end-rivet against the stone would take days of patient toil. The shackle, too, was sound, and the collar was so snug against his neck that the hingepin could not be attacked.

He climbed laboriously and painfully to his feet, biting his lip to suppress a groan. The chain ran from his collar to an eyebolt just in reach in the wall above his head. He turned his body around and around, twisting the chain to stress it.

It would not wind tight. A creaking, scraping sound, accompanied by the fall of fine stone particles on his face, told him that the eyebolt was turning in the wall.

With a sudden effort born of elation he hauled his weight partway up the chain, planted both sandals against the wall, and wrenched.

But the bolt would not pull free. The firm resistance it gave told him that rather than being old and loose, it was anchored by a flange or another eye on the far side of the wall.

He slumped back to the floor, sore and panting, railing mentally against the very gods he had thanked moments earlier.

He saw no way of escape. A mighty despair gripped him as he thought of his fortunes and those of his friends. Eulalia and Baron Stephany had escaped the prince's men—for the time being, at least—but Ivor had hinted that he knew their identities. Could they manage to escape the city in time to warn the mercenaries of their coming destruction?

Or, on the other hand, would they even try? His thoughts detoured into tangled, devious byways. With Tantusium on the brink of new civil war, might not Stephany decide that four thousand and more unruly freebooters were a threat better dispensed with? From what Conan had seen of Kothians, they were a crafty, treacherous race.

Conan thought of tawny-limbed Drusandra, of her supple sword-mates, and his rowdy old fellow-thieves. And of Hundolph—although their parting after the ball had been brisk, and he had scarcely seen him since, he believed the old captain still regarded him fondly. The notion of them all being consumed by Agohoth's sanguinary spells made Conan clench his moist palms in rage. In truth, it troubled him more than the prospect of his own torture, which Ivor had promised for morning.

The morning—his eyes tried vainly again to pierce the darkness. Would morning ever come for him? Would he know when it did, in this living grave? He listened intently for some sound from the guard who had been posted beyond the dungeon door, or for the noise of trickling water that he remembered from the outside hall.

No, there was nothing. But he thought his eyes could detect the thinnest, faintest vertical line where the door should be, as from yellow torchlight outside. Dare he cry out, then, and try to cozen the guard? Coax him within reach, throttle him, and use his sword to work away at the chain? A foolish plan.

Suddenly Conan's senses froze. There was, after all, a sound—though faint, intermittent, and elusive to the ear. It came from the opposite direction—that of the dungeon's deeper recesses. And it seemed to be drawing nearer.

As Conan listened, it gradually resolved itself into a slow, dry shuffling, that of rudimentary footsteps, feeble and halt. He thought he could detect a trailing rattle with every other pace, as of something dragging loosely behind. He opened his mouth wide, to diffuse the hiss of his breathing. He stood as still as he could, clutching his chain to keep it from rattling, hearing the steps draw closer.

Then a faint, dry voice, mere handsbreadths away, exhaled words at him, though to Conan's startled ear it scarcely seemed a voice. It could, after all, have been the sound of rats scuttering through old parchments, with whining undertones from the creaking of ancient dungeon doors. Yet the sense of it was clear.

"It is no use trying to hide, stranger. I can see you in the light from the doorsill above us."

Conan said nothing. While his heart hammered, his brain tried feverishly to supply images of the grotesque thing that could give utterance to those accents.

"Forgive me, stranger," the intruder muttered on, "I do not mean to frighten you. This mortal husk of mine is withered, but then, likely you cannot see it at all in this gloom. And my speech, I fear, is rusty with disuse. It has been a long, long age since I have had a visitor."

The uncanny whisperer came no nearer, and the voice seemed to issue from a modest height above the floor, about equal to that of a stooped old man. Still, Conan's skin tingled with the dread of the supernatural, and his own voice rasped as he spoke. "Ghoul, fiend, night-gant, whatever you may be— turn back from me, I warn you! For these hands have grappled with things of the pit before—and crushed the mockery of life from them!"

When the ancient voice resumed, it seemed to have slightly more timbre, even including a note of injury. "Abjure me not, stranger. And do not offer violence. I am just a man like yourself, a prisoner of these foul catacombs." A scrape sounded, as of cal- loused feet scuffing on stone. "I mean you no harm. I only want to keep company with one of my own kind again, after all the long years of loneliness."

Conan spoke in tones gruff with suspicion. "I know you're lying, fiend. For how could anyone live here long? The dungeon has been sealed off these many years. What would a man eat and drink?"

"Aye, there is truth in what you say." The el- dritch voice quavered now with a note of shame. "Perhaps I am no longer fully a man, nor fit for the company of world-treading men, for indeed, many years ago, after what already seemed a lifetime of captivity in the nethermost cells of this place, there did come an hour when the warders stopped passing in the hall.

"Gone, then, were the clanks of chains being forged, and the screams of the tortured, and all the other sounds that were to me as familiar as birdsongs and the banter of the street. Gone were the pots of gruel that had been my only, watery bread. It was clear to me then that the dungeon had been abandoned— and I along with it.

"Fortunately it was not long afterward that the weakest links of my chain, abraded over many patient years, finally wore through—and I was free!" The old man's voice rose with the word to a cackle of derision, then subsided promptly and apologetically. "Not free, you understand, of the dungeon, for there were seals and barriers installed that were far beyond my feeble power to break. But free to roam these dank corridors, and to survive! And I will not blame you if you think that, in surviving, I sank below humanness.

"For what was I to eat, I ask you, if not the crawling things that nested among the bones of my long-dead cellmates, and the scrawny rats that eat the crawling things, and the bats that sleep in the vaultings of the remotest chambers—although I have never been able to discover their route of coming and going. These and a thousand other unclean things have nourished me and kept me alive to this moment. And not an unhealthy diet it turned out to be—better than the gruel, I can say. . . .

"And water!" Here the speaker waxed enthusiastic once again. "Water I have had aplenty, for in the deepest corridor of the dungeon lies the ancient well of the citadel, a bit brackish now, it is true, but nourishing, and inhabited by strange eyeless fish that dart between one's fingers. When my feeble old hands can catch one of those fish"—his voice lingered dreamily on the thought—"that, sir, is a true delicacy."

Then the old one resumed his humble, matter-of-fact tone. "And so you see, stranger, that I, who know the ways of these rooms, and who, though halt and slow, am deft at the catching of small things, and who can see you clearly enough to know that you are now touching your neck to ease the chafe of your fetters—I have been able to subsist in this dismal world. And I can help you, perhaps, to do the same."

"And what of the ghouls that are said to haunt these nether places?" Conan asked, still dubious. "Know you aught of them?"

"Nay, sir, I cannot truthfully attest to finding any ghouls here." The old prisoner's tone rose once again toward levity. "For if I had found them, stranger, you can rest assured of one thing—I would most certainly have eaten them!"

The wheezing laughs that followed this remark sounded maniacal to Conan. Yet he could not restrain his own laughter, which, though mixed with shudders, swept aside some of his reticence toward the weird visitor. It almost seemed that the old man's years of suffering were all being wiped away by this one bout of hilarity.

"Very well, then," he grunted, his battered torso aching at the shock of his guffaws, "we are fellow-prisoners. Or if we are not, there seems little I can do about it." He leaned back against the cold stone of the wall. "What is your name, then, old one?"

The silence into which the wheezing had subsided was long in being broken. Finally the voice said plaintively, "Will you renounce me, stranger, unless I answer you?" Conan's unseen companion spoke with anguish that verged close on hysteria. "Can you blame me if I say—of a word that I have neither heard nor uttered for a score of years—that I do not remember it?"

"Forgetful, eh?" Conan sought to reassure his invisible friend. "Or close-mouthed. It does not matter. Tell me instead the event of your imprisonment. Like as not it was no crime of yours."

Dry, feeble sobs now, from one who had been tittering wildly a moment before. "It's no use! Better to ask me how to steal flies from spider webs, or where the cave-rats hide their young." The voice moaned brokenly. "My life as a man is finished, forgotten. It is all faded in the mist of the past. I have been here too long; I can tell you nothing of it!''

The fellow must be hopelessly insane, Conan thought. His voice became level now, with a note of challenge. ''Do you mean you've no thought of leaving here or returning to the world? If so, begone; I have little use for you!''

After an interval the elder one seemed to regain his composure. ''Indeed, yes, I have thought of leaving here,'' he said somberly, ''though I have forgotten what the sky looks like, and I know that I could never bear to gaze on sunlight again. But I would fain venture forth—by night, perhaps. . . .''

''Then fetch me some building-stones, or one of yon timbers, that I may break this chain.''

''It is simpler than that, my friend.'' The voice paused expectantly. ''But if I free you, you must promise that you will also help to liberate me. Do I have your pledge to that?''

''Why, yes, of course, man!''

''Then bide here. I will be but a moment.''

''What choice have I but to bide, old one . . .'' Conan began. But he fell silent as the shuffling, eerie footsteps resumed. This time they headed away from him with a slowness that seemed interminable, even painful. He listened, wondering what madness lay in the oldster's plan.

Yet he wasn't being gnawed by ghouls, at least. He raised his arms and tried to stretch some of the soreness out of them.

In a while the footsteps died out. Conan was once again left in a silent void. He looked up toward the dungeon door; the dim line of light there was unchanged. Either the guard had heard nothing, or he feared to respond to voices from the catacombs.

Conan began to wonder whether he would ever again hear from the old prisoner. Perhaps he had only dreamed the strange meeting, or been idly taunted by nightlings. He resumed his silent, alert stance, readying himself once more for the perils of the dark.

He heard a rustling, squeaking sound from overhead. A rat, he thought, as he felt tiny particles rain down on his upturned face—but then he remembered. He seized his chain in eager hands. The old man must have released the bolt from the other side of the wall!

He jerked the chain outward, and felt it give. A harder wrench, and it came free. He held the loose links high to keep them from clattering on the floor; then he lowered the clinking chain gently in a pile.

Savage joy coursed through him. Be it blessing or blight, in this fiend-haunted hole, he was free of the wall!

Still, the man-length of clanking chain was an unwieldy burden. He followed along the links to the uprooted eyebolt, a loop-ended piece of iron. The other end, whether it had been a second loop or a stud, seemed to have been rusted or sheared away. The bolt was hardly thicker than the rest of the chain; that was the important thing.

Kneeling, Conan hurriedly worked the chain through the hasp of his collar. The bolt, when he came to it, passed through with little resistance. Then he was able to spread the hinged halves of the collar and remove it from his neck.

Unfettered, he rose to his feet.

"And so you see, young friend, I have been able to do you some small service after all." The creaky-voiced one must have approached stealthily while Conan was busy freeing himself, for he spoke from near at hand.

"Many thanks for it, old man." Conan nodded into the dark. "And now for the guard! If you can somehow lure him to open the door, I'll brain him with a timber. . . ."

"Nay, nay, my friend." The elder one sounded

spryer and surer of himself now. "That avenue of
escape is closed to us . . . it is too heavily warded.
But come. I have bethought myself of another way,
one without a guard. It will lead us not only out of this
dungeon, but outside the palace itself."

Conan made no move to follow. "If you know of
such an escape route, why did you not use it years
ago?"

"Alas! The path was blocked by a stone too massive for my feeble strength. But I doubt not your
ability to move it, with those mighty young thews of
yours. Just follow me."

Still Conan balked. "It's black as the root-cellars
of Tartarus in here. I can see nothing but the ghost of
the doorway."

"Fear not, young one, I will lead you." The voice
was gentle and coaxing. "Just reach out straight
ahead and place your hand here, on my shoulder."

"All right, but if this is a trick . . ." Conan fell
silent, shuddering as his outstretched hand came in
contact with what felt like birdbones wrapped in
damp cheesecloth. It was well nigh impossible to
believe that such could be living flesh, yet beneath
the clammy, supple integument the interplay of bones
and ligatures could be felt. A frail, skeletal hand
clasped the top of Conan's as the decrepit body beneath started moving away from him, and from the
dungeon door.

"Careful, young sir, lest your grip should crush
my brittle old bones," the guide said. His shoulder
dipped with each shuffling step as he led Conan
across the uneven stones of the dungeon floor. "Yet
do not flinch away—your coming has been like a
wakening to me, calling back memories of the days
before they interred me alive in this drafty hole.
Stoop down here, for the scaffold hangs low across
the passage." Conan groped up and felt rough tim-

bers, which must have been those bracing the arch at the back of the entry-chamber.

"I said that I did not remember, but more and more now I can recall the world outside—a vast place, is it not? Blinding bright, but pleasantly dim and cool at night, and teeming with men and animals, and other kinds of life. Food and drink aplenty . . . and fabulous wealth!" The old prisoner must have been leading the way down a corridor now, for Conan felt an overarching wall on one hand. "Koth, yes, that was where I lived. A splendid place."

"And the city, Tantusium," Conan added, to spur his guide's memory.

"Ah, yes! The noble city, atop a ridge, like a falcon's lair! All the winding streets and lanes swarming with people, like a great rat-warren. Lit up at night with fires and smokes. I knew it well," the old man rambled on excitedly over his shoulder. "In my day I savored it all. For it all belonged to me."

Conan moved carefully to keep his footing behind the old one, whose lurching pace was increasing. "You were a ruler of Tantusium, then?"

"Yes. All was mine to command," the old one said matter-of-factly. "Peasants and nobles alike bowed to me, and scurried to serve my every need. That is why the chain around my ankle is of silver."

"Silver?" Conan bumped up against his guide, whose forward progress had slowed.

"Aye, silver. It is old and worn, and nearly parted, though it still vexes me greatly. You may have it if you have the strength in your hands to remove it."

"I'll make a try," Conan said. He knelt, tracing his hand eagerly from the old man's bare shoulder down the length of his ragged tunic, stiff with filth, to his bone-thin shank. The ankle was heavily calloused, and from it dangled a shackle and a dozen links that trailed on the stone. The fetter hung at an angle from the spindly limb and was worn half through.

Judging from its weight and texture, it was indeed silver.

Conan applied his massive hands to it, straining his sore arms, and felt the metal bend tearingly, then part in his grip. Gently he removed it and rose to his feet.

"A boon upon you, stranger," the old man muttered, turning back down the corridor. " 'Tis a release I have yearned for these many years."

"Wait," Conan urged. "Let me knock this fetter apart with a stone, and you keep half. You deserve it, and the silver may have helped you ward off evil forces all this time."

"Nay, you keep it. I want neither wardings nor wealth, for my old bones shall endure regardless. But come along, our exit lies down these steps."

Conan shrugged and tucked the silver chain into a fold of his leather clout. The old man, relieved of the dragging weight at his ankle, walked more quietly now, and a good deal more briskly. Either through his preternatural eyesight or his long familiarity with the dungeon, he was able to move unerringly through it. Conan, on the other hand, frequently stepped into wet holes or jostled against nitre-crusted archways. Hard-put to follow, he found further conversation impossible.

The way wound downward, along sloping corridors and stairways worn almost into slimy ramps. The darkness remained impenetrable to the barbarian's vision, and the air grew thick and stale. Furtive rustlings and scramblings sounded frequently on either hand.

At one point the old man led Conan into a chamber that echoed wetly; there he bade him kneel and drink. As Conan reached into the pond, cupping his hands, he could feel slick, living shapes writhing to escape from between his fingers. The water was tepid and slightly brackish in taste.

Finally, in a dungeon corridor where Conan's fingers had trailed for some time along an unbroken wall of native rock, they halted. "There is our exit," the old man announced. He grasped Conan's shoulder to press him forward. "There, straight ahead."

"Don't push."

On Conan's demurral the old one took his wrist in a surprisingly firm grasp, if a skeletal one, and led his arm forward and down. The Cimmerian felt his hand brushing a square-hewn stone with some kind of insignia carved on it in shallow relief. He kneeled to examine it with both hands; it was a hefty chunk, but set in masonry that seemed none too solid or craftsmanlike.

"There is the barrier. If the capstone is removed, our way will be opened. Long years it has balked me, but now, I think, my night of liberation is at hand."

Conan probed the masonry, looking for a grip. The carven sigil on the stone, his touch told him, was the stylized outline of a rising sun similar to the one he had seen earlier; an odd motif for a dungeon, he thought, but hardly worth puzzling over. The mortar around the stone was old and crumbling, and in a moment his eager fingers had brushed enough of it away to gain a purchase on the runestone's edge.

Squatting before the wall, he tugged at the stone, forcing it first up, then down, then sideways. Soon he felt it shifting in its place, and he began to work it outward. It came at first by hairbreadths, then more easily, with a heavy, crystalline grating. Some of the smaller stones surrounding it fell away, allowing the central one to sag forward. Through the cracks around it shot rays of silver light which, though pallid, were blinding to Conan's eyes.

"That's it! Keep at it, youngster! I can see the light of the world again. Its cruel brilliance is like fire on my parched old skin! But keep on!"

Conan gave a final heave, and the square stone wallowed forward amid loosened rubble, letting in a flood of light. Squinting through the aperture, he saw that it came from a near-full moon, which must already have been past the zenith and well down in the western sky. His eyes were dazzled by its glow. He turned his face back toward the interior of the dungeon, able to see only the vague surfaces of roughhewn tunnel walls behind him and a stooped, indistinct figure nearby.

"How strange it is—how invigorating!" the old prisoner marveled. "I feel the light, it seems to course through my veins like liquid fire. It brings back so much—the days of my strength, my youth . . ."

Still blinking, Conan was dragging stones from the masonry wall and shoving them aside. Then he leaned forward and thrust his head though the man-sized opening, to see what lay beyond. "Crom!" With a muttered string of curses he pulled himself back into the darkness. "Old man, you have led us to an escape route, all right, not only from our prison, but from this life! For do you not know—this is an opening in the sheer cliff below the palace! I see no means of going either up or down, especially for one of your frailness. . . ."

"Be not concerned, young one. It will be no trouble to me, now that my powers are returning." Indeed, the old prisoner's voice did seem suddenly more robust to Conan's ears; deeper now, and less rasping, it actually thrummed with strength in the confined space. "For I can pass where I will without impediment. My enemies think me dead! Now, as in the old times, I shall rove freely by night and take my food from the teeming streets." The speaker became grandiose. "The city shall again be my game-preserve—its residents, my cattle and kine. Once more the lowly ones shall learn to worship me, and to fear me."

Conan had grown used to ignoring the old man's prattle, but this speech was made with a force and certitude that he found unsettling. He peered above the silver patches of moonlight that glowed on his companion's ragged robe, up into the shadows of the tunnel where his face loomed, and the features he distinguished there were fuller and more dynamic than ever he could have imagined—a square jaw, not crumpled in toothless old age, but full-set beneath stark cheekbones. The elder one's eyes glinted from dark pits, and unkempt white hair straggled down the front of the man to well below the knees.

The face gazed imperiously down on him. "Of course, I regret the years wasted in these nether cells. But now, with all trammels and obstacles removed, I can embark on life—call it life for lack of a polite word—with a vengeance!

"Indeed, I have learned much during my sojourn here. I have consumed new life-forms I never would have taken in otherwise, but which will greatly enhance my shape-changing skills.

"For instance, the proper shape for this occasion—a flying creature, quick and sprightly, yet with senses far more attuned to night than my old, ungainly standby, the royal eagle. And yet it is just as fierce a slayer, or more so. Observe."

Before Conan's horror-stricken gaze, the shape that was his rescuer began to transform itself. Its filthy, tattered garment ripped and fell away from a swelling chest of glossy fur. Meanwhile the face that surmounted it deformed and blossomed unspeakably, and from behind the old man, dark, looming wings sprouted up.

Weaponless, Conan stood poised an instant between attack and flight. One course seemed as fatal as the other, for the monster was growing with a horrid vitality; already its fangs and wing-talons gleamed dagger-sized in the moonlight.

Whether his mind flashed through a chain of arcane logic, or whether he merely took the means closest to hand, he was never sure. But he clapped arms on the great carven stone that lay beside him and, with a straining and cracking of sinew and muscle, heaved it up and forward onto the titanic, loathsome bat-shape before him.

It struck with a crunch and a scream, and the shape-changer crumpled beneath it as any earthly beast would have done. But then the true, unearthly strength of the undead thing was revealed, as it writhed and began to drag itself free. It could be seen changing again in the dimness; its protruding parts moved and shifted in a mad sequence of forms, suggesting in turn the appendages of fish, insect, rodent, and man. Meanwhile it gave off a similar, sickening menagerie of cries.

Desperate, Conan leaped forward and threw his own weight onto the stone to keep the monster pinned down. He could feel the heavy block lifting and rocking beneath him as he clung to it. He grabbed up a smaller stone and savagely clubbed the head end of the wildly metamorphosing beast, but with little effect.

It was then that the stone's mystical properties became apparent—for it began to glow. At first only the sun-sigil was sketched by the warm light that differed eerily from the moonbeams falling around it. But then the block itself seemed to kindle with a hot radiance, as of a hearthstone in Crom's furnace. It became warm under Conan's hands, as though heated by a day's bright sunlight, and he sprang back from it and watched in dread fascination.

The supernatural radiance was accompanied by rising fumes and a sizzling, hissing noise; gradually these drowned out the shape-changer's horrid screams. Soon the floor of the tunnel was a seething inferno of reddish-yellow light, with Conan's shadow etched blackly against the masonry. The uncanny fire did not scorch him, but it consumed the monster, whose charring shape he could see writhing beneath the stone like a wisp of cloth in a white-hot furnace.

In the end the sound and light subsided. Nothing remained but the blackened runestone, resting amid soot stains and greasy ash.

Conan wrinkled his nose at the vile smell and muttered an imprecation; then, keeping well back from the remains, he turned and crept to the moonlit window.

15

Death Creeps by Moonlight

It was with fierce resignation that Conan, crouching in the gap of broken masonry, looked out on the night scene below him. The moon hovered bright over the Kothian countryside, its light silvering ridge after ridge of verdant, dew-moist hills. Yet to him the vista spelled death rather than freedom.

Below the shallow cleft into which the tunnel opened, bare rock sloped for two man-lengths. Then it curved away out of sight to a steeper drop—likely a sheer one, or an overhang. The surface of the stone looked weather-worn and treacherous. Stretch himself forward as he might, Conan could not see the bottom of the cliff. But he recalled that during his daytime explorations about the city wall he had judged the scarp under the citadel's west side unclimbable.

As he shifted his weight, a stone was displaced from the pile of rotten masonry beneath his feet. It rattled away down the incline, and Conan listened for a long, silent interval before hearing it smash on invisible rocks below. A fatal distance, to be sure. The shaft had probably been cut as an escape route in the event of siege, to be exited by means of ropes. But no ropes were present in the terminus of the long-abandoned tunnel.

What, then, were his alternatives? Behind lay the foul remains of the demon king, the black labyrinth of the dungeon, and the heavily guarded palace and town. If he turned back, there would be little hope of getting out alive, much less of warning his friends of their impending sorcerous doom.

Before him lay a cleaner death at least, and a thin chance of survival through a test of climbing skill. Long experience of scaling granite peaks in Cimmeria had taught him how much more dangerous than the climb is the descent—even when it is just a careful retracing of steps. To begin one's journey from the top, placing one's feet blindly along an unplanned route, seemed virtual suicide.

At this thought Conan laughed grimly to himself, for to make such a journey by night, even in livid moon-glare, compounded the risk; and to attempt it with a body racked by a savage beating put the enterprise well beyond the brink of madness.

And yet, as if to lure him, a few tents of the mercenary camp were just visible, eclipsed by the beetling stone scarp to northward. The absence of any turmoil there meant that the prince's reprisal was not yet unleashed. Perhaps there was still time.

The cliff, then. Without more hesitation Conan eased himself down to a sitting position on the tunnel rim. He slipped off his buskins and laced them to his neck, draping them well behind his shoulders. Then he swung his body around to face the worn stone. He lowered himself from the tunnel mouth, feeling for purchase with his bare toes.

The down-curving rock was rough and cold against his skin. At first there were no breaks in its surface, and the mere friction of toe-pads and palms had to bear his weight. Clinging thus to the slope, hugging his moon-shadow close, he crept down sidewise from the tunnel mouth.

He went slowly, moving one limb at a time, aware that a careless motion might send him flailing to his death on the rocks below. His sore, bruised muscles began to cramp with pain from the stress. Finally his toes found the relief of a small fissure, though it was littered with dust and pebbles, and too narrow to support more than the edges of his feet.

Trusting his full weight to the ledge, he raised his head carefully away from the stone. He craned his neck backward and down, and his expert eye measured the dizzy angles beneath him. The lower part of the cliff was broken by fissures and shallow buttresses of rock, until it leveled out among tall hummocks and giant boulders at its base. So there was a chance at least.

He inched sidewise along the ledge, clearing debris from it with his toes, until it began to trend upward. Then he halted, faced with the near-impossible task of transferring his grip from toes to fingers.

A moment of concentration to calm his erratic heart. Then he grasped a brittle wisp of weed that grew from a vertical crack in the cliff. Carefully he lowered himself to a crouch, his knees inching to one side down the rough stone.

The plant pulled loose, and the cliff began to tilt away giddily, but Conan's free hand darted out to gain a grip on the toe-ledge. His shoulder took his weight with a joint-popping wrench, but his plunge was arrested. He was left dangling by one arm, having lost a good deal of skin on the face of the cliff.

From there, chilled with perspiration, he had to start sideways. He worked his cramping hands along the fissure, inching his way into position; now he faced a treacherous vertical drop of more than his own height to the surface of a weathered stone outcrop. He relaxed his grip and plummeted.

His feet, striking the stone, caromed off it, as did his knees, with bruising impact, but by clawing at the smooth, curving rock with his fingertips he managed to keep from slipping on down the cliff. Hugging the rock, he hauled himself back up to the firm seat and rested a long, gasping time. He knew that if his descent were blocked now, he would never be able to retrace his path upward.

Arising, he inched down a slope and made a lesser leap to a second outcrop, and then to a third, each a challenge to his catlike balance and judgment. As the hope in his heart increased, it seemed only to make his limbs weaker and more unreliable. He could see the hillside below the cliff at a glance now, its shadows starkly etched by moonlight. But the distance was still great enough for the least misstep to leave a man dead, maimed, or senseless.

Creeping across the third buttress, he found a broad, shallow crevice into which he could lower himself by the outward pressure of his hands and feet. He used it deftly, making a swift descent down the sheerest part of the cliff.

Near the end of the chute tufts of grass were growing from crevices on either side. He used one for a handhold, grateful for the extra bit of leverage. Then he caught a glimpse of dark motion from the corner of his eye; he also felt an odd tingling. Looking closer, he saw a swarm of gray spiders spreading across his hand and up his arm.

He stifled his fear, but the mere thought of flinching was enough to undo him, for at that instant the friable stone under his foot gave way. He slipped, a moan quavering in his throat, and pitched straight downward.

An instant later he dashed feet-first into a pile of rock shards. From there he slid, arms and legs spread wide for stability, amid a rattling shower of debris, until he struck a half-buried boulder and began to roll. Then the slope pummeled him cruelly, with meadows, cliffs, and moon all rotating madly before his eyes.

With a jolt he came to rest in sparse stony grass.

Feeling the nerves in his elbows and knees still vibrating, he shook his head to clear away the dizziness. His whole body ached, but miraculously there was none of the urgent pain that would signal a serious injury.

He glanced over his dusty, abraded limbs. No more spiders were in evidence, and the silver shackle was gone from his breech, leaving only a sore spot where it had jabbed his groin.

He sat awhile, gazing upward. The cave mouth was nowhere visible in the moon-bright face of the cliff, but at its top loomed the walls of the palace. He saw no faces peering down, nor heard any alarm raised. The noise of his descent must have gone unnoticed.

As his head cleared, the realization that he was free and whole washed through him. He felt a rush of joy and, simultaneously, of urgency. He untangled his buskins from his neck and drew them over his bruised, abraded feet. Then he tottered up on still-shaky legs and headed for the mercenary camp.

He followed the faint, upward-trending cart-track that led around city wall and cliff. Scanning the top of the wall as he went, he stayed near the edge of the path, ready at any sign of movement to drop into the shallow weeds of the ditch. The wall curved here with the clifftop. On the short section that was in view he saw no torches, nor heard even the routine calls of sentries. He continued at a brisk pace, forcing his sore limbs to support his weight.

Soon the cliff dwindled and merged with the terraced slope. The crenellated bastion of the palace gave way to the smooth-topped city wall. Wall and path both straightened out here, and far down their length Conan spied movement.

He left the track and glided like a shadow over the brink of the first terrace, to continue advancing in the partial concealment it afforded.

Just ahead, on the nearer of the two towers adjoining the city's main gate, was a bustle of activity. The forms and faces of a half-dozen men were visible, lit from beneath by a bonfire on the tower. Though its flames were hidden by the parapet, a yellow-lit column of smoke rose straight up from it in the still night air.

As Conan drew near he recognized one of the men on the tower as Agohoth. The sorcerer's tall rawboned form was gesturing among the others, but not as if making magical passes. Rather, he was directing them in some task.

Several of the men wrestled an ungainly object to the parapet and, at Agohoth's urging, raised it to one of the crenellations. It appeared to be a large vessel of brass or other metal, for Conan could see its flaring mouth and bulbous sides gleaming in the firelight.

As he stopped to watch, the men tilted their burden forward. Out of it, over the edge of the tower, poured a sluggish gray fluid.

The stuff must have been more vapor than liquid, for it traveled down the side of the tower with eerie slowness, sending off curling wisps as it fell. Where it struck the ground it billowed and swirled a moment, pausing almost like a sentient, indecisive phantom; then it flowed forward past the bulwark protecting the gate, down the slope toward the mercenary camp.

From atop the tower the great urn still poured forth an undiminished stream. Agohoth leaned over the battlement and watched the phenomenon intently, mouthing commentary to those near him. Conan thought he could glimpse Ivor looming behind the magician.

No telling what sort of plague or poison the vapor might be; but Conan had no doubt that it was evil. He wished that he could somehow make his way to Agohoth and wrap his hands about the wizard's scrawny neck, but he dismissed the notion as futile. Instead, he carefully spied out the nearby terrain.

There were a few guards on the ground in front of the closed city gate, but they had eyes only for the creeping, gray man-high torrent, watching its sluggish swirls while staying well back from it. Those on the tower, too, seemed absorbed in the unfolding of the spell and oblivious to all else. Conan slipped away from the terrace wall and headed downslope toward camp, silent and unseen.

Yet, when he came to the edge of the next terrace, he had to freeze, for a man was standing there by a saddled horse. One of Brago's cordon, no doubt—he wore the tabard of the traitorous chief, and he stood screened by a shrub, facing the outermost row of mercenary tents.

Luckily no other sentries were in sight. Conan sank to a crouch and eased himself down the embankment.

A moment later there sounded a smothered cry, followed by the multiple crunch of vertebrae. Then the Cimmerian lowered the guard's lifeless body to the sod. He bent and stripped away the man's swordbelt.

The sentry's horse snorted and began to shy, but Conan seized its reins and dragged its head down. In a moment he had swung up into the saddle and was urging the beast forward into camp, shouting loudly enough to wake the dead and drunken.

"Dog-brothers, to arms! We are betrayed, and the camp is surrounded! Out of your beds, you slumbering swine!"

Bellowing at the top of his strength, Conan drove the horse recklessly down the lane of tents. The frightened animal staggered among crisscrossed ropes and stakes, and curses began to sound from disturbed sleepers. "Come forth, louts! Gird yourselves to face Brago's band! But beware the sorcerous fog!"

Moonlight made the camp a puzzleboard of dew-gleaming tents and shadows. Here and there wakeful voices began to murmur, and the few sentries who were abroad rushed forward at Conan's approach, then staggered back just as quickly from his headlong charge. When a terrace embankment yawned ahead, the barbarian raised himself in the saddle and drove his frenzied steed in a thundering leap down to the next level.

"Sword-women, awake! The prince has ordered Brago and the wizard to kill us!" As Conan pounded through the women's camp, he saw Drusandra already thrusting her sleep-tousled blond head from a tent door. He reined his mount back, its forelegs pawing the sky. "To arms! And warn the others—Agohoth sends a poison fog down upon us!" At the warrior-woman's look of comprehension, Conan wheeled his horse and galloped away toward Hundolph's camp.

"Hulloo, there! Out of the sacks, you sluggards!"

Where the strident Cimmerian passed, shouts and clanks of armor sounded in his wake; soon there were whinnyings, too, as horses were caught and saddled. While others began spreading the cry, Conan carried it back toward the upper part of the camp; but when he came to one of the central lanes, his path was blocked by a river of sluggish gray vapor. He reined in his steed in a flurry of dust.

"Beware the fog! It is Agohoth's sending!" he shouted to the men who were stirring nearby. The stuff flowed faster now on the slope, but it was also more diffuse, even translucent, in places. It cascaded down terraces in a ghostly flood and meandered among the tents, its wispy talons curling under the moon.

Conan saw a half-dressed trooper run straight through the fog a little distance away, with no apparent harm. Still, he dreaded to let the creeping grayness touch him. He turned his horse and guided it down a byway, to cut around the front of the probing stream.

A moment later, galloping down an alley, Conan's mount kicked up a low, unseen tendril of the vapor that was flowing between tents. He caught its smell—a strange odor that managed to be both foul and acrid.

"Hundolph, arise! We are betrayed!" The fog was already present in Conan's home camp, hanging in gray curtains between the grape arbors and spreading like a ground-mist among the upper tents. "To horse, man! Are you here?"

"Aye, Lieutenant." The captain's gruff voice grumbled from his pavilion. "I might have guessed it was you, howling like a plucked ape and rousing the whole camp! What madness is afoot?"

"Not madness, but darkest treachery!" Conan told the story as tersely as he could, to be greeted by a storm of curses and exclamations from the men who were arming themselves nearby. Meanwhile he dismounted from his stolen horse, which looked half-dead after its wild gallop under the barbarian's considerable weight, and gave it a slap to dismiss it. Then he set about saddling his own black charger. "Our only hope," he concluded, "is to get our horses under us and break through Brago's encirclement before this venomous fog destroys us." He tied buckler, lance, and ax to his saddlebags and mounted up. "Hundolph, are you ready yet?"

"Aye, Conan. But you should not be so rushed on a battle-morn." The captain's barrel-chest emerged from his tent, and he grinned to his lieutenant. "It's unseemly. Death is a patient lady; she will linger for you." Breastplated and helmed, he carried his bundle of weapons and saddle toward the corral, where a trooper was holding his horse.

"Hundolph, stay out of the fog!" Conan called as his friend passed into a spreading gray billow that was encroaching on the open yard. "It's the wizard's sending . . ."

The rest of his cry was lost in the tremendous sound that smote the hillside.

It started from somewhere above, with a roar and an eye-scorching flash, then raced through the midst of the camp like chain lightning. Fire ripped the air upslope, and the very soil seemed to be heaving in hellish agony. Conan watched the roaring chaos approaching and looked back to Hundolph, who stood to his waist in moon-silvered gray. One moment his mouth was opening to utter a curse; the next, flame blossomed around him and he was blasted aloft. Conan saw his ripped, crushed body hurled afar, over trees that bent low like grainfields lashed by a storm.

Then an even more violent blast occurred, and Conan was knocked sidelong on his staggering horse. The animal fell, and he feared it would roll atop him. But he found himself engulfed in something yielding and smothering—the fabric of a tent, enfolding both him and his steed. He struggled for long moments to free himself while the earth shuddered beneath him and flashes lit the sky.

Finally the panting animal fought its way upright, removing its weight from his leg, and Conan was able to throw off the scorched canvas. He jumped up to catch the panicky beast's reins.

He was standing amid a pattering rain of soil, debris, and dark drops that he somehow knew to be blood. The stricken field was dimmed by clouds of dust and smoke writhing before the moon. Fires flared here and there, but the worst of the sorcerous inferno seemed to be past. About him was a tangle of wreckage, from which issued moans of bewilderment and pain. Those men and horses who were not knocked flat were scattered through the night, and from the distance rose sounds of fighting—Brago's men closing in, he guessed.

Leading his horse along, he stopped and helped several of his fellow troopers to their feet, urging them to re-form the troop and prepare for combat. He did not linger over the wounded. When the able ones seemed to be getting things in hand, he climbed back into the saddle and spurred his mount downslope.

Among the windrows of canvas and foliage and the dazed, recovering victims, Conan saw grislier remains—whole and partial bodies of men and horses, some incinerated, some turned horribly inside out by the force of Agohoth's spell.

A filthy way to die—a dishonor to Hundolph, and Crom knew to how many others. Conan's face set in an expression that drew uneasy looks from some of the men he passed.

And yet the spell had not succeeded. As Conan rode on, the devastation around him grew gradually less. Soon he entered the lower, undamaged part of the camp, where men were still loading horses and readying for action. It had been, after all, mere minutes since he carried the alarm into camp; if he had not done so, the wizard might have let the firefog spread farther before igniting it, and perhaps gutted these companies too.

Now the flame and terror had spurred all to frantic action. Conan followed the cobbled road through a stream of horse and footmen. Many were girded for combat, but their movements seemed directionless. Conan looked for a central standard or a formation, and saw none.

As he trotted into Brago's camp, deserted now except for milling troopers, an approaching rider hailed him. "Conan! 'Tis no use going this way. The road is blocked."

"Ho, Thranos!" Conan's voice sounded subdued and gruff even to his own ears. "If the way is blocked, we had best unblock it—before Brago's men nibble us to death from the sides, or the prince attacks from the city.'' Conan proceeded past the slack-gutted mercenary, who reined his horse around and followed. ''What mean you, blocked?''

''Brago's best cavalry are straddling the roadway outside camp. All who try to pass them have been cut down. 'Twould be better to break out through the sides of the circle.''

''Is that so?'' Conan urged his horse forward, leaving his former fellow thief lagging behind. He rode past Brago's pavilion, which stood open and empty, and past several horsemen who waited indecisively by the wayside. The barricade at the edge of camp came into his view, and beyond it, outlined in silver moonlight, several mounted lancers in the roadway. He spurred his mount down the road more briskly.

''There goes Conan to try his lance!'' one of the onlookers called.

''A stout warrior—someone should back him,'' another voice said.

Unheedful of their words, Conan reached behind him in the saddle and drew up his buckler, jerking loose its lashing and slipping it over his arm. His free hand brushed the haft of his spear, but settled instead on his ax; this was a weapon with two broad, curving blades, heavier than his previous one. He grasped it by the head and drew it up out of its loop. Meanwhile the black stallion's heavy hooves thudded onward, gathering speed on the downslope of the road. Conan settled himself firmly into the saddle, looping the lanyard of the ax about his wrist, and slapped his mount smartly on the rump with the side of the weapon. The pace of the drumming hoofbeats beneath him intensified.

Ahead on the road, the waiting cavalry fanned out, and the centermost, largest warrior started forward at a gallop, couching his lance to a horizontal position. By his plumed helm and the wolf's face blazoned on his shield, Conan recognized the commander, Brago himself.

The horses raced toward each other along the white ribbon of road, hooves kicking sparks from the embedded stones. Conan bunched the reins in his bucklered fist and swung his ax up in readiness. Brago raised his shield to shoulder height in anticipation of the downward stroke of the ax, centering the honed steel tip of his lance on his opponent's heart. His eyes were invisible in the black-shadowed slit of his helmet, but below the nosepiece the moon showed up the curves of the blond moustache that fringed his tight, desperate grin. The distance closed with terrifying swiftness.

Then, with a thumping clang of flesh and metal, the horsemen drove together. Conan's wooden buckler smote Brago's lance up and aside, deflecting the point harmlessly. His own ax came in level and low, skimming the mane of his enemy's laboring steed.

The force of the barbarian's blow was rooted in his stallion's thudding hooves; it traveled upward, through the animal's muscle-corded fetlocks, through the hardened hide of the saddle-bindings and the rider's massive knees that relentlessly clamped the brute's ribs. The force was amplified by the sideward twist of Conan's body and the clench of his mighty arm, as the broad axhead drove in to meet the full fury of Brago's charge.

The blow struck the mercenary chief in his midsection, well below his raised shield, shearing in at the lower edge of his breastplate. The man's short, bellowing cry was dreadful to hear as the wind was hammered out of his lungs, but his fellow riders were more horrified to see that when the two horses staggered free of the impact, their leader's body tumbled from the saddle in separate halves, one falling to either side of his mount.

With scarcely a pause Conan wheeled to engage

another horseman. The rest of the cordon were quickly set upon by the stream of horse-soldiers who had galloped after the Cimmerian from camp. Some of Brago's followers turned away demoralized, while others stood fast. The clangor of swords rang in the night.

16

The Captains

"There is the murderer!"

Conan struggled up from a murky pit of sleep. His head felt smothered in musty wool, and his heart shuddered from the sudden awakening. Yet he must have been more ready than he knew, for he saw that his unsheathed sword was already raised in one numb hand.

He rose to his knee in the nest of rumpled furs that was his sleeping-place, laid between the roots of an overarching oak. Bracing himself against the massive trunk, he gazed on the ring of angry faces around him.

One of them said, "Zeno, have a scruple! The man has been dead asleep for hours—though how he could slumber at midday, through all this turmoil, I know not." The speaker glanced at the crouching barbarian, then back to the flushed red-haired warrior. "I say give him a decent interval to awaken and prepare himself before you start flinging accusations!"

"Nay! Justice has waited long enough!" Zeno pressed forward past the man's restraining arm. "Did the rogue give Stengar a decent interval? Or young Lallo?" The curly-haired mercenary was dressed to his neck in dusty leather. As he expostulated, his hand kept slapping the hilt at his belt, beating a tempo to his fury. "I shall not allow him time for

140

more treachery. Now he's gotten Hundolph out of the way, and he takes command of our troop as if it were his birthright!''

"A calumny!'' Conan snarled. "I tried to save Hundolph—and your worthless hide as well, Zeno!''

"Aye, that is so,'' a youthful soldier piped. "I was there. The barbarian's warning was in the captain's ears even as the firefog took him!''

"Well, I mistrust his overly provident warnings.'' Zeno's voice rang above the excited jabber around him. "I know only this: He was absent from us by night, 'midst the dark doings at the palace. And he was somehow privy to Ivor's plan for betraying us.'' His tone was heavy with insinuation. "Then he comes thundering into camp, bringing our sorcerous doom on his heels! I survived not by any help of his, rather, in spite of his so-called help, by my own wit and skill!''

Another voice rose from among the watchers. "And what of Brago? Conan slew him and broke the encirclement. Without his lead we would have been hedged in.''

"Nonsense! Mere glory-seeking! I myself led a band out through Brago's south perimeter.'' Zeno spoke to the nods of the men standing at his side. "The question is: How long will we let this barbarian continue to insinuate himself among better men, as he seems so curiously skilled at doing?''

Noisy controversy began to seethe in the crowd that had gathered around the oak tree. Once again, as in the confrontation at the tavern, a parting tide became apparent—some drifting toward Conan's side, others toward Zeno's. The Cimmerian, with thunderclouds gathering on his brow, noted that the dispute, if violent, was only local; for over the heads of the mob, on the rolling slopes of the hill beyond, he could see other mercenaries tending cookfires, making and striking camp, and saddling horses unconcernedly.

"The question, say I," an ancient, grizzled mercenary was opining loudly, "the question is: Who is to lead Hundolph's band now that the old pirate is gone?" He grinned around the group, wrinkling his leathery cheeks under silver stubble. "We have these two strutting-cocks here vying for the post. Now, say I, instead of fighting over it, we should settle it in the traditional way. And that is, let *them* fight over it!"

Cheers went up at this proposal, and the crowd immediately began to draw back, broadening the clear space between the two disputants. Into it Zeno strode, his weapon sliding from its sheath. "Good, then! True swordsmanship against brute barbarian bulk." He stepped into a crouch and swung his silver blade before him. "Forward, Cimmerian, if you dare! Let me see you try to break my sword this time!"

Silent, wrathfully swift, Conan rushed forward. His sword flew up and struck Zeno's with a mighty clash. Only the one clash . . . for the relentless force of the blow drove Zeno's weapon far down and aside. Then, instead of drawing back and fencing, Conan pressed forward bodily onto his opponent, well inside the arc of his weapon. The Cimmerian's sword fell unheeded to earth as his arms whipped around Zeno's trunk.

"Arrh! Grapple me, will you!" Zeno's cry came forth spasmodically as the great arms constrained his breathing. He kneed and kicked at Conan's groin while furiously sawing at him with his long sword. But the barbarian's leather jerkin thwarted both tactics. Conan drove into his struggling opponent, wheeling him around and working his own grip gradually tighter.

In moments Zeno's feet were scuffing the earth ineffectually, his whole weight borne up off the ground. Though not a small man, he was shaken in Conan's grasp like an antelope worried in the jaws of a lion. Yet Zeno did not give in. Clinging stubbornly to his sword, he kept reaching with his other hand for the dagger in his boot, but could not manage to grasp it.

Then one of Conan's arms swung up over his opponent's shoulder, and a huge fist clenched in the seat of Zeno's leather breeches. The victim was hoisted horizontal. Without so much as a grunt Conan heaved him tumbling through the air.

Dropping his sword to keep from falling on it, Zeno fetched up with a rib-cracking thud against a gnarled root of the oak tree. There he lay, face to the sod, gasping and feebly moving. Two of his companions hurried to kneel by him, detouring widely around Conan as they went.

"There. Does that settle my claim to leadership— for the time at least?" Conan glared around the group with dire challenge in his square-jawed scowl. He was answered by enthusiastic shouts and flourishes of the watchers' headgear. Then he moved forward among the men, who either smote him heartily on the shoulders or drew back cautiously.

He addressed the old grizzle-faced man. "Horus, take a roll of the troopers who are still with us, especially the petty officers. Leadership calls me elsewhere just now."

Conan moved clear of the men crowded under the deep shade of the oak and walked out into the hot sun. He saw that the haphazard encampment stretched across a grassy hilltop and down to the streamside below it. Hill and stream provided a little defensive benefit, but not much, especially against the kind of threat that Agohoth could mount. Hundreds of troopers loitered in the trampled grass tending their comrades' wounds, recounting the night's battle and the morning's flight, and repacking their gear.

Conan stopped by a kettle of water and raised a gourd to his lips, drinking deeply from it. He dashed a second ladleful into his face and shook the droplets aside. Then, smoothing his black hair with one hand, he strode forward to intercept a man he saw walking along a line of saddled horses.

The fellow was of compact build, wearing a cloak that was sunbleached to a whiter hue than his brown skin. Atop his head a steel helmet rose to a graceful point. Drawing near, Conan hailed him. "Health to you, Aki Wadsai."

"Ah, Conan." The desert chieftain spoke in Turanian, in which he knew the barbarian was fluent. "I bid you condolence for Hundolph's death. He was more than a captain to you, I know. A good friend of mine also."

"Indeed." Conan nodded in his turn. "But I ask you: Why do your men prepare to ride?"

The officer's brown eyes narrowed. "Ah, yes, I forget; you are captain now, in Hundolph's place—if the men will follow you." His gaze rested thoughtfully a moment on Conan's impassive face. "Well, my friend, I will tell you. We ride now because our commission is ended. Our ranks are—how do you Hyborians say?—thinned. I am lucky, for I still have nearly all my men. But we can never stand against more of the *djinni* of that fiend Agohoth." His dusky visage knit in a tight frown. "So we ride. Where your band will go, I know not. But my men and I will forage our way to eastern Shem, where there is always work among the city-states."

Conan raised his eyebrows. "Will you leave Ivor to enjoy his profit now that he has cheated us?" He regarded the chieftain calmly. "Can you live with that, Aki Wadsai? How will your men respect you henceforth?"

The desert rider's eyes narrowed. "All men respect me!" he said sharply. "All living men, by Tarim!" He spat to one side and gazed at Conan.

"I respect you." The Cimmerian nodded evenly.

"I know that you seek only honest victory and the best profit for your band. But I bid you, don't ride out of here yet. I want to meet with you and the other faithful captains. All except Hundolph survived the attack, did they not?''

"Yes."

"Then bide here awhile. I'll gather them." At Aki Wadsai's reluctant nod Conan strode away across the camp. He scanned the clusters of soldiers for more familiar faces; in a moment he spotted Bilhoat loitering with others of Villeza's troop.

On seeing Conan, the ex-thief detached himself from the group and came grinning to him. "So, you are still alive and whole, though spells and intrigues fly fast about your ears—and now you're savior of the Free Companions to boot! That's the Conan I've always known."

The Cimmerian nodded good-naturedly. "Bilhoat, I need to find your chief."

"Villeza? That's not difficult. He's in yonder tent, drinking himself into a stupor. Or into a rage—or both."

"And what of Drusandra? Has her company joined the camp?"

"Aye. I hear tell they've made their bivouac upstream, at the head of the fall. 'Tis a narrow gorge with a steep approach, and they've set a guard against any males who might come a-pestering." Bilhoat leered. "Still, some of the fellows were talking of making a fishing trip later. . . ."

"Advise them against it." Conan laid a hand on his friend's shoulder. "Bilhoat, I want you to fetch Drusandra for a meeting of the chiefs."

"I can give it a try." The Stygian looked doubtful. "I hope the sword-bitches won't string me up from the nearest sapling."

"If Drusandra balks, tell her I'll personally guarantee her safety in camp." Conan smiled wryly.

"That should make her mad enough to come down. In the meantime I'll be talking to Villeza."

Bilhoat turned and trotted away down the hill, and Conan set out in the opposite direction. On his way he was overtaken by Horus; the old soldier gave his tally of the survivors of Hundolph's band. "Conan, the men want strong leadership, stranded as they are in this land of their enemies," the graybeard said. "Most of them will stand behind you staunchly."

"Good, Horus. Stay with me for now, as my second."

It took a while for Conan to rouse Villeza from his alcoholic meditations. Then he had to make the grubby chieftain wash and dress himself. By the time they emerged from the musty tent into daylight, Conan saw Bilhoat returning up the hill. Drusandra and Ariel followed watchfully, hands on their weapons, amid whistles and raucous calls. When the blond warrior-woman saw Conan, she dispensed a brisk nod.

The captains and their seconds went to Aki Wadsai's pavilion, of which only the canopy and four posts had been salvaged from the embattled camp. A score of the desert troopers drove the loiterers back a discreet distance from the pavilion, then remained posted there on guard. When the party had entered the patch of shade and seated themselves cross-legged in the Eastern manner, Conan addressed the others.

"As leader of Hundolph's troop, I urge you not to disband your companies or take them out of Koth." He looked around the group. "Together we're a force to be reckoned with. We can win a just payment from Ivor—or else take the price of his treachery out of his hide."

"Aye, what a splendid idea!" Villeza cried. "We can extort the money by laying waste to the land. After all, there are enough of us to burn every hovel in these wretched hills, and then quench the fires with Kothian blood! We'll show these curs the sharpness of our steel!" His wine-soaked vehemence increased, overriding others who tried to speak. "The pickings may not be rich, but they're enough to feed and entertain us for a time. If we ravage by day and ride by night, Ivor and his cursed wizard won't be able to catch us."

"Never, you guzzling, rutting swine!" Drusandra had risen to one knee, her hand clasping her hilt. "If you think to ravish and slaughter the women of these districts, then try it at your own peril! I and mine will stand against you!"

"Hold! Be still, both of you." Conan's voice intruded sharply, then subsided just as promptly. "We will fight, it is true. But not against the commoners." He scanned the captains' faces severely. "Many of the locals have turned away from Ivor, and more will learn to hate him soon. It would be against our interest to kill our allies." He frowned. "No, we must strike directly at the prince and his forces—by scattered raids, or perhaps by siege."

"But, Conan, think of our losses of men and equipment!" Aki Wadsai was shaking his head impatiently. "With the havoc the firefog wrought, and the loss of Brago's band, our force is sorely weakened."

Conan folded his arms. "Hundolph's . . . that is, my band, still numbers near a thousand. Stragglers are finding their way here hourly, including most of Brago's former troops." He turned to the other captains. "Drusandra, your she-devils are all well? Good. And Villeza, your band suffered far less damage than mine."

"Thanks to you, Conan." The Zingaran gave a grandiloquent flourish of his plump hand.

"As to our supplies," Conan continued, "true, most were lost. For a time we'll have to forage, and yes, plunder, within reason. But there are local factions who will be eager to aid us. For one, I've had dealings with the royal family of Khoraja, which kingdom lies not twenty leagues to the west. I'll wager they'd be willing to fund an uprising against a neighbor as dangerous as Ivor—''

He was interrupted by the noise of riders entering the guarded space before the pavilion. He turned to watch two persons dismounting from well-lathered horses. A turbaned trooper scurried up to bow before Aki Wadsai. ''Sir, they wish to speak with him . . . the barbarian.''

Conan rose smoothly from his cross-legged position to greet the visitors. They were a man and a woman clad in travel-stained clothing that he recognized from—could it really have been only the previous night? His body ached at the memory of all that had transpired since. ''Eulalia, Randalf! You made your escape from the palace!''

''Yes, Conan.'' The noblewoman, comely in spite of her rumpled and clearly fatigued state, walked to him and clasped his hand in her slim ones; craggy-looking Randalf, his cloak crusted with dried blood too ample to be his own, stood close behind and gave a brisk nod. Eulalia continued. ''Baron Stephany also won free of the town with his retainers. But he's gone on to secure the defense of his estate. He is now in open rebellion against Ivor; he sends us to you as his emissaries.''

''You come at an opportune time.'' Conan turned to his fellow captains. ''Eulalia and Squire Randalf were with me in the palace last night while Ivor bargained with King Strabonus himself to betray us. Like me, they escaped by stealth and force of arms. They will attest that there is new opposition to Ivor in the countryside, and in Tantusium proper.''

''Aye, that is so,'' Randalf said. ''The poorest folk of the city are on the verge of revolt. Even the hillmen along the border of my precincts no longer support the prince. When they hear that he is reconciled with the king, there will be open skirmishing.''

"You see, Koth is far from united against us.'' Conan scanned the group. "These local factions crave our support.''

"More than that, Conan,'' Eulalia added. "The baron says that he and the farmers and herders backing him will provision any mercenaries who stay to aid us in our fight against Ivor.''

"But that is not enough,'' Villeza interrupted. "If we are to fight, we must receive the pay owed to us by Ivor, plus additional pay for the time it takes, plus booty. If your baron agrees to that, we'll level Tantusium for him.''

"I think I would rather fight this brigand sitting next to me than any traitorous prince.'' Drusandra glared at the Zingaran. "If I fight, it will be to aid the women and the good men, the powerless of the land—not to oppress them further.''

"Very well, woman, offer up your handful of sword-vixens for nothing!'' Villeza cried with righteous bluster. "Much good they will do the rebels. Myself, I captain sixty score picked men. They must get a fair wage, or they will not fight!''

"What can it gain any of us to fight if Agohoth's sorceries smash us to dust?'' Aki Wadsai finally spoke, shaking his head wearily. "All the plunder in the world could not pay for such a death. Our squabbling is for naught if it does not arm us against the wizard. To dawdle here meanwhile is folly.''

"Truly spoken.'' Conan regarded the desert chief. "I, too, have a healthy respect for the Khitan sorcerers' guild, which spawned Agohoth. You and I, having served in the East, know their power better than most men.'' He shrugged. "Still, such can be beaten—or else avoided. We can fight a running war and use false attacks to draw the sorcerer away from us.''

" 'Tis strange to recall that Agohoth was sent by

the emperor of Turan to aid Ivor in his rebellion.''
Drusandra spoke absently, as if musing aloud. "Now
that the prince and King Strabonus are allied again,
how will Emperor Yildiz like it? Perhaps he will
recall the wizard or have him killed rather than let
such a power fall into the hands of his rival.''

Aki Wadsai shook his head vigorously at this.
"Think you that Yildiz has the power to do so?
Agohoth is beyond his command now, answerable
only to his Khitan guild-masters—a separate and
shadowy force, whose way it is to serve both sides in
any dispute, the better to advance their own inscrutable interests.'' The chieftain paused somberly. "They
would like very much, I think, to spread their influ-
ence westward to the Hyborian lands. You all would
well be warned.''

"The wizard's fickleness will be no surprise to his
emperor,'' Conan said. "Mayhap Yildiz sent him to
carry discord and destruction to Strabonus's capital.''
The Cimmerian laughed. "If I were a king, I would
want him kept far away from my court—wouldn't
you?

"Nay, leave Agohoth to me,'' he continued. "Crom
knows, sorcery sets my teeth on edge as much as it
does any of yours. Yet I've faced it ere now and
lived.'' He paced between the emissaries and the
seated captains. "When lately I kept the throne of
Khoraja firm under the Princess-Regent Yasmela's
shapely hindquarters, I battled a sorcerer—an undead
spell-tosser who would have eaten this petty wizardling
without bread or salt. I commanded a host of ten
thousand then.'' Scanning the incredulous faces of
his listeners, he added lightly, "By a fluke it was, at
the command of a temple oracle.

"In any event, I vow to hold up my end of this
campaign. Stephany and the rebels will treat with
me, as you have heard, and if you will do the same,
together we can give Ivor a lesson in fair dealing. As

to the command of the operation''—Conan shrugged—
''we're all seasoned officers, and we should be able
to agree on questions of strategy.''

Villeza spoke up first. ''I'll fight beside you, Conan,
if Aki Wadsai will.''

''I, too,'' Drusandra said with a spiteful glance at
the Zingaran.

''Well, friend of Turim, what say you?'' Conan
watched the nomad's dusky, expressionless face.
''When our enemies join forces, we had better do the
same.''

The desert rider's head finally dipped in a nod.
''Very well, Conan.'' He rose to meet the Cimmerian's
grinning approach and handclasp, then flinched back
under the ham-handed, good-natured blow that thumped
his shoulder. ''But only if this Stephany and his
rebels will agree to favorable terms.''

Eulalia assured the desert chief, ''I know the baron
will be more than fair to you.'' She moved nearer
and turned the full force of her smile on him.

''But, Conan, we must not linger in this camp.''
Drusandra put a hand to the Cimmerian's sleeve and
drew him away from the emissaries. ''It is a deathtrap—
and inconvenient for the security of my troop.''

Conan stroked his jaw thoughtfully. ''Aye. We've
got to find a safe refuge within striking distance of
Tantusium. And before we lay siege to the city, we'll
have to deal with the wizard somehow. . . .''

After deliberations stretching well into afternoon,
the conclave adjourned. Aki Wadsai offered Eulalia
and Randalf the comparatively lush hospitality of his
camp, and the other captains and seconds dispersed.

Conan, his head still swarming with battle plans
and terms of payment, found himself walking back
toward his oak tree alone. He was grateful for the
silence.

But then, as he traversed a brushy area that was
already crisscrossed by the paths of the mercenaries,

he heard steps crackling in the weeds behind him. He wheeled, reaching for his weapon, reverting instantly to the lone savage in wilderness.

The follower was a few paces away and clearly recognizable, though long-shadowed in the rays of the declining sun.

"Zeno!" Conan stood ready, his sword undrawn. "So our business together isn't finished after all."

"Nay, Conan." The soldier, his hand lingering on the hilt at his belt, stood just outside fighting range. "In our duel today, you dealt me a humiliation that would be hard for any warrior to bear." His voice was low, almost hoarse. "Whether you are an honest man or a schemer, you would have been wiser to kill me."

"Perhaps." Conan watched the compact man carefully. Zeno's stance seemed slightly constrained, perhaps by soreness from the earlier fight.

"One wonders why you didn't."

Conan made no reply, watching him.

"I sought you out afterward, to avenge your insult. But there were too many troopers nearby. Then came your meeting with the chiefs—I watched from the crowd." The red-haired man gazed on Conan with something of determination in his eyes, and something of puzzlement. "We were too far off to hear much of what was said. But 'tis clear that for a raw northlander, you've gone far. Amazingly far." His expression took on something of respect. "Now, it would seem, you control not only Hundolph's troop, but all of theirs, too, whether they know it or not."

Conan frowned and jerked his shoulders noncommittally. "So?"

"So you have surpassed me . . . that is, surpassed what I would have done in your place." Zeno's brow knit in consideration. "I know that Stengar, though my friend, was a difficult man. I—I'm no longer sure of your guilt in that matter." He hesitated. "And it may be . . . that you have merits as a leader that I failed to see." He lowered his eyes. "In any case, I'm ready to offer you my service."

Conan nodded, looking him up and down. "You could make a good officer—if the men will still have you."

Zeno drew himself up to meet Conan's eye. "I don't think there will be any other challengers who can best me as easily as you did."

The Cimmerian looked at him, then smiled broadly. "Done, then." He moved forward and extended his arm to grasp Zeno's in the legionary grip, shaking it heartily. "You can be my lieutenant, along with old Horus." Zeno, to his momentary alarm, felt his shoulders clenched by the hands of the barbarian who had so recently been mauling him. "I'll be busy with the other captains and the rebels in the coming days. Much of the leadership of Hundolph's troop may fall to you after all."

Conan ordered Zeno to assemble the men, then parted from him to speak to Horus. The old trooper had overtaken them and watched their encounter from a cautious distance.

"Do you really mean to trust the Corinthian?" the grizzled one asked. "He will cherish his grudge and use his officership against you."

Conan shrugged. "His skill and loyalty will soon be tested. Tomorrow we ride at first light."

17

Blades of the Mountains

Hooves pounded the narrow valley of the Khorgas River. Where the stream's marge was a grassy meadow, the hoofbeats made dull, thudding sounds; where the path rose across a dry hillside, their noise was sharper, edged with the clatter of rock-shards and gravel. Above it all sounded the shouting and clanking of an ill-equipped army laboring to escape a stronger one.

Most of the river's course wound through farm and pasture land. The valley floor, walled-in steeply by hills, was dotted with serfs' huts and the occasional squirely keep. At one point, however, some ancient upheaval had raised a barrier to the river's progress—a sharp ridge of jagged, crumbling rock that jutted straight across the valley.

The river, with slow, inexorable patience, had worn its way past the obstacle by gouging into the base of the hill at the far side. Here the stream, easily fordable along most of its length, broke into cascades and deep pools. The road was forced to climb around the end of the shale outcrop, narrowing to a mere trail and passing treacherously close above the rapids before opening out again into a lightly forested valley.

This was the slope that rattled under the hooves of the last stragglers of the mercenary army—the poorest troopers ill-mounted on the slowest horses and donkeys, followed by a train of lightly laden sumpter animals. Then the rear guard: a dozen Shemites on limber southern steeds, armed with lances, shields, and steel caps. These deployed in a loose line, nervously watching the valley behind them, while their charges labored up the rocky trail.

As the last of the pack mules disappeared along the road, a scout came galloping out of some trees down the valley. In a Shemitish dialect he shouted, "Onward, cousins! They're yapping at my heels!" As he reached the slope he fell in behind the other riders, whose churning hooves were already raising a long plume of dust on the upward trail.

The next moment a hundred or more purple-clad soldiers burst out of the trees below. They were coming at a brisk gallop, strung widely across the field in pursuit—Kothian Imperials, the sun bright on their steel armor. As they reached the broken ground, their paths converged and their pace slowed. They milled uncertainly at the base of the slope for a moment. Then, promptly upon the bellow of an officer, the formless mass extended forward in a single line, starting up the trail where the mercenaries had vanished.

The steep part of the road was narrow and tortuous, forcing the riders to string out even farther. And when the foremost of the Kothian detachment reached the level stretch of valley above the cataracts, they didn't plunge onward into the scrubby pines. The young officer leading the party could plainly see that the tracks of the fugitive army disappeared there— but what would happen, he thought, if their quarry had turned at bay somewhere just ahead? Better to wait for more men, he decided, and then to approach in force. It would take time for the remainder of the advance guard to follow him through the defile. He ordered a pair of scouts forward, deploying the rest of his horsemen defensively as they arrived, in a line curving across the trail.

When less than half the Kothians had come up, the senior officer, Commander Tosc, joined them. He had been directing the pursuit of the rebels since his patrols had reported their campfires early that morning. He ordered the men forward, pointing out acidly to his junior that since the mercenaries had not troubled to defend the slope, they would hardly be likely to set up a defense in the valley. The soldiers moved forward in a broad front between the stream and the hills.

But after advancing a few dozen paces into the trees, the Kothians came upon the bodies of their scouts, knocked from the saddle by arrows, each man feathered by a half-dozen shafts. They eyed the brush around them with a newfound mistrust. Then they were thrown into disorder by the sound of raucous war-cries to their rear, accompanied by a great rattling of stones.

Spurring back toward the defile, Commander Tosc found the pine-crested shale ridge above the stream swarming with mercenaries. The ambushers fired arrows and hurled rocks down on the part of his force that was spread out on the narrow trail; some pried chunks of stone loose with their spear-shafts and sent them bounding down the slope. One great shard of cliff was dislodged by the efforts of a dozen men who, placing their backs in a crevice alongside it and linking arms, pressed it away from the slope with the strength of their legs. The officer watched the monolith slide downhill amid a slather of rubble, carrying several horsemen and a portion of the trail into the river with it.

The Kothian commander galloped toward the ridge in the midst of his troops. As he went he observed the failure of the Imperials who tried to charge the position. Either they were unable to drive their horses up the steep slope, or they were prodded out of their saddles by spears when they finally reached the mercenaries. He veered back toward the road. Cut off from the bulk of his army, Commander Tosc saw no way of reestablishing contact. He barked orders at his men and led them in a sweeping charge toward the forest.

But now the valley floor was alive with defenders. A flight of arrows skimmed the foremost of his riders from their mounts; he saw his junior officer go down, choking on blood from an arrow in the throat. The archers fell back into the wood, still firing and letting the scattered trees dissipate the force of the Kothian charge. The mounted men tried vainly to chase the footmen through the brush, taking casualties all the while and losing their sense of direction.

Then came a new threat, heralded by hoofbeats, splashes, and the shrill of hunting horns. A hundred mercenary horsemen forded the stream above the cataracts, driving into the Kothian's unguarded flank. At last the cavalry fight was joined, but on sadly unequal terms, for the Imperial troops were depleted and scattered. Yet they fought valiantly, desperately. One of the last to die was Commander Tosc, scythed down by the broadsword of a roaring barbarian on a coal-black stallion.

"Huzzah, Conan!" a Shemite officer cried, reining in his blood-spattered horse beside the Cimmerian's. "A noble rout! We've won, providing that the rest of the Kothian legion doesn't come swarming over that ridge."

The warrior laughed. "Nay, Elael. It will take them many hours to clear the road. Days, perhaps, to get their supply trains through."

The Shemite grinned, exposing vacant places among his teeth. "And I thought you a poor general to let the main strength of your army get so far ahead of the stragglers. A ruse, I see now, to buy time to ready this ambush!''

"Aye." Conan nodded matter-of-factly at the man's praise. "It left you in a tight place, racing with the slowest of our army against the swiftest of theirs. But you did your part. Now we can move our force unhindered deeper into the hills."

Captain Villeza had drawn up his steed on Conan's other side. "What about setting up a defense right here? We could hold this valley until the crack of doom."

"Nay." Conan frowned. "Strike and run, that's our game. We don't want to be caught in a pitched battle." He regarded the swart man coolly. "Though short of supply, we can move swiftly. If we press on across the Khorajan border, we may find allies. And no Kothian general is likely to follow us into Khoraja without direct orders from the capital."

Villeza grinned, the black stubble of his chin bristling. "Very well, Conan. You go on at your general's game. Even if you've already managed to get a Kothian legion snarling at the seat of our pants, you seem able to handle it." As the Cimmerian turned his steed and cantered away from him, he lowered his voice and addressed the Shemite guardedly. "But I would wager he's not told us his true reason for wanting to go to Khoraja."

After putting things in order at the rear, it took Conan hours of riding to reach the border. In the course of the ride he passed the supply train and the forward elements of the army and so was one of the first to arrive at the frontier. The valley was narrower here, hedged in by gleaming mountains rather than hills, and the Khorgas River had dwindled to a singing brook.

Conan tethered his horse among a handful of others in a meadow bright with wildflowers. Stretching his saddle-cramped legs, he strode up a steep causeway that led to a square military tower emplaced on a rock promontory at the base of one slope. The bronze door stood open; inside were Zeno and a half-dozen troopers. They stood at the narrow windows, appreciating the view of valley, road, and approaching mercenary army that the tower's lofty position commanded.

"There were eight border guards," Zeno said. "They galloped off as we rode up. By your order, we did not pursue them."

"Good. Keep the tower undamaged, and bide here to cover our rear." Conan walked to a battered wooden wardrobe at the back of the gallery, opening it and exposing green winter cloaks of the Khorajan guard. "If legionnaires should approach, don these and try to turn them away by blustering about Khoraja's royal sovereignty. If they cross the border, fall back before them. We'll set our defenses farther up the valley."

Zeno nodded. "There are baskets of arrows in the loft. We could hold them off for days if you like."

Conan smiled and shook his head. "Nay; I want to keep every officer and man. I'll be needing you soon."

He retrieved his horse and continued with the mercenary vanguard through meadows and woods to a place where a reedy lake blocked most of the valley's width. On its farther side he ordered camp to be made. The troopers cleared a short perimeter of land between the lakeshore and the slope, erecting a log wall behind a flooded ditch.

But when Aki Wadsai rode up and spoke of placing defenses along the side of the camp that faced Khoraja, Conan dissuaded him. "If the Khoraji want to drive us out, their mountaineers will attack from the slopes," he assured him. "Fixed defenses will avail us little. Like it or not, we're relying on their goodwill."

18

The Reunion

It was later, when cookfires were akindling and foragers returning with deer, pigeons, and fish for the evening meal, that word came from the Khorajans. It was in the form of a four-man guard riding haughtily on matched white horses. They were only lightly armed, and dressed in the livery of the royal court. The herald dismounted and addressed some of the officers.

Drusandra told Conan as he came up, "In the name of King Khossus and the nobles of Khoraja, they say you are to go with them. I gather that a royal personage awaits you somewhere not far from here. They won't say just who, or where." She looked him up and down. "I didn't know you were welcome in such lofty circles."

"Nor did I." Conan turned toward the lakeside, where his war-horse was grazing.

Villeza confronted him as he returned with his saddled mount. "Some of us should go with you." He looked disgruntled at not having received a royal invitation. "How do we know it's not some sort of treachery?"

"For myself, I fear no treachery. I mean to treat openly with the Khorajan royal household." Conan swung smoothly into the saddle. "And if it's betrayal by me that you mean . . . you'd be in more danger coming along than in remaining here with your troops and mine.''

Villeza considered the point soberly a moment, then nodded. ''Very well, Conan. You go, and we'll await you. But only till noontide tomorrow.'' His voice was firm, yet he kept it too low for the ears of the waiting escort. ''After that we may just fight our way out of these mountains—whether through Koth or Khoraja, I cannot say.''

''Aye. I'll return by then.'' Conan guided his horse into the midst of the four guardsmen, and they rode away up the valley.

There followed a brisk ride along steep, winding mountain trails, through the sun's declining rays and the chill shadows of dolomite peaks. Though wild and scenic, the terrain was wearying for Conan after his day's travel, and he was relieved when he caught sight of a new glimmer of alpine waters and the angular shape of a lake castle.

It was situated on a stony promontory of the shore-line, behind a wall strengthened by two round towers. On passing through the moated gate and entering the yard, Conan was surprised to see that the side of the compound facing the lake was unwalled, opening onto verandas and piers where pleasure-skiffs and galleys were moored. The manor house itself was a luxuriant marble edifice, falling back in balustraded layers to a central dome.

Conan dismounted and, leaving the escort to care for his horse, went through the tall open portal of the manor. He found himself in a high-ceilinged chamber with walls of gray marble veined with pink. Two filmy-gowned serving women hurried forth from a side door with basin, cloths, and a stool. Sitting down on its embroidered seat, he let them lave his bare, dusty legs and arms in scented water.

But then, hearing two notes of a familiar voice issuing from a doorway at the back of the chamber, he rose abruptly. He shook the anxious wenches off him and strode barefoot toward the sound.

On passing through the gilded archway, he stopped. Before him was a lavish sleeping-chamber open to the lake and to pink-tinged sunrays that shone in from the western sky. A narrow finger of the water was let into the room itself, cut into the very bedrock of the floor in an oval, marble-lined pool. There, wading unclothed under the eyes of a young male servant in a gold-trimmed tunic, was Princess Yasmela, Princess-Regent of Khoraja.

"Conan! I didn't expect . . ." Yasmela blushed, but did not avert her face or move to cover herself. The servant, though no warrior, stepped forward awkwardly to defend his mistress. Conan's gaze was drawn to the princess's body, which hovered like a pale blossom over the water. Nevertheless he started to yield in a moment to the frantic tugging of the two serving-women behind him.

"Wait, it is all right. Let him stay." Yasmela's voice resonated sweetly in the chamber. Water splashed lightly on the tiles as, with unhurried poise, she stepped out of the pool and took the drying-cloth from her servant's arm. "You may go," she told him. "And you two women also—but see quickly to our meal."

The servants vanished from the room, and Conan walked forward toward the princess. "Yasmela! I've missed you, girl. Come, let me clasp you. . . ."

As his progress toward her accelerated, Yasmela raised the scanty towel to cover her body and stepped behind a table of carven onyx. "No, Conan, stay back. This isn't the time. . . ."

The warrior halted abruptly. He leaned toward the princess across the end of the table, his knuckles pale against the dark glossy stone. "Aye, woman, I'll not maul you." His look became dour. "But thrice-blast it if you mean to tease me as you did from month to month at your court . . .''

"No, Conan, I promise you! I have yearned for you, as you must have done for me all that time. Only there is much to be said, and much business to be settled."

Conan could find it in his turbulent breast to believe her as she stood there draped in flimsy linen that was nearly transparent with moisture. There was much of her remembered warmth in the look she gave him, and no hint of the coy self-absorption that had later replaced it. Now she vouchsafed him a smile.

"A spy told me of your role in the Kothian rebellions, Conan. It ought not to surprise me, I suppose. After all, you led the armies of my own country ably enough."

"Aye." Conan folded his arms across his chest. "But this time it hasn't happened by the whim of god, or priest . . . or princess." He gazed steadily at her. "It has been by my own labor, and by the natural unfolding of events—and the spilling of blood."

"And now the prince of Tantusium has made peace with his Kothian majesty, yet you remain in open rebellion." Yasmela shed her towel demurely and walked to a carven chair, from which she took up garments of silk sewn with many small, iridescent feathers. The skirt she tied loosely about her lithe hips; the jacket she donned nimbly and fastened with one pearl button, leaving her breasts alluringly free beneath it.

With the attentiveness of a hungry cat Conan watched her feathers glinting. "Aye, that devil-bitten Ivor has sold us all to a Zamboulan brothel, and royally. What think you of the snipling?"

"Ivor? I have not met him, but how well I know his type from my own court!" Yasmela moved back to the table and rested a knee on one of the stone chairs, regarding Conan. "I grow so weary of these petty, proud nobles. They balk at every initiative from the capital, loudly declaiming about honor and freedom, when all they really want is power—power to deplete the land and lord it cruelly over their peasants. Why do common folk never see that the reigning monarch is their real friend in restraining these petty tyrants?"

Conan shrugged. "I've met King Strabonus of Koth too. Between the two sorts of tyrant, there's not much choosing."

"Well, perhaps. Even my royal brother, Khossus . . ." Yasmela sighed and gazed confidingly at Conan. "Since you freed him from the dungeons of Ophir, he's not been the king I'd hoped. He grows daily more absorbed in pageantry and protocol, and nightly fonder of lotus wine and imported dancers. Meanwhile the real affairs of the country are left to be settled by courtly scoundrels and intriguers." The princess sank lightly into a chair, folding her arms beneath her feather-trimmed decolletage. "For the welfare of our house I am forced to take matters ever more in hand. Although my skills in such things are considerable, I have no official power under his rule. I broach vital proposals subtly, letting him imagine they're his own ideas." She shook her head in exasperation. "And he has no inkling of it, Conan. He talks frequently of selling me in wedlock to fat Shemite kings for advantageous trade treaties!"

Conan listened patiently to Yasmela. Now that the well-remembered curves of her body were covered, though scantily, it was easier to observe the beauty of her face—her hazel eyes, the fine olive paleness of her features. Her dark hair flowed up and back from her brow, its damp ends hanging in wet curls, flicking her shoulders with each motion of her head. She was a prize indeed, and had once been his. Yet as she spoke of the cares of her rank, her words recalled to him all the reasons why he had decided not to return to her side.

"Yes, in truth," he answered to her last complaint. "Khossus spoke of the need of finding you a suitable husband when he was telling me why I could never . . . hold real power or rank in Khoraja."

"Or wed me, Conan?" Yasmela gazed up at him with unwavering eyes. "I fear that such is still the case. But perhaps—"

She stopped abruptly as footfalls sounded from the chamber entry. The three servants appeared, carrying food on blue crystal salvers, placing it on the table between Conan and Yasmela. A rainbow heap of exotic fruits, garnished and spiced; a hot, fragrant round of golden bread; and a trussed gamecock glistening in sauce. Wine-flagons and utensils were laid before them, and the menials hovered nearby, cutting and doling until the princess impatiently dismissed them.

"I can trust these servants to protect me, but I would rather not speak my heart before them," Yasmela said. "I should have brought my faithful Vateesa along! But I need her ears in the palace during my absence."

They dined in silence for a time. The princess merely teased at her food, watching while Conan raked large portions across his platter and reduced the fowl to a wreckage of bones and string. While they sat, the sunset's rays deepened. The lake outside became a placid mirror of a sky shading from deep blue to crimson, pierced jaggedly by black reflections of mountain peaks.

When the barbarian finally pushed away his ravaged plate, the serving-maids reappeared. They lit reed lamps and cleared the table, replacing the wine-pitcher with a crystal carafe of a paler southern vintage. Yasmela dismissed them and arose, moving toward a broad couch at one side of the room; Conan followed around the end of the table, bearing the wine with him. The princess let him be seated first, then settled herself a chaste distance away on the silken pad.

"You have not changed, I see," she said. "You're still the barbarian, simple and direct."

"I wouldn't say the same of you." Conan lounged back on the divan, cradling his full flagon, and leaned sidewise to observe her. "You've grown and ripened some since I knew you."

"True." Yasmela blushed at his remark. "I've had . . . consorts since you left. And learned something of the ways of power." She met his gaze. "And I've learned to value your honesty, and the virtue of direct action."

"Well, then." Conan started to ease himself closer to her on the sofa. But seeing her stiffen slightly and shrink away, he stopped. "No doubt your lovers have been highborn, courtly men, suited to your royal station."

"Oh, Conan! If I have to endure the attention of more princely fops, I shall go mad! They posture so, and flatter me so glibly, but always to press some hidden scheme or intrigue. It's gotten so that I feel starved for an honest word or touch!"

"Aye. I remember the feeling from trying to wend my way among the servants and eunuchs at your court. It was like being mired in a tar-bog." Conan twitched his shoulders uneasily. "That vexation was a great part of my decision to . . . leave such things behind."

"And give me up." Yasmela nodded, finishing his thought. "And yet, your strength and directness could still be of value in a court like Khoraja's. I think that kingdoms are best shaped and held by men of simple, unwavering beliefs."

"Indeed, if I had the royal rank and pedigree to be heard or seen there." Conan frowned thoughtfully.

"Perhaps if I chopped down Ivor and crowned myself king of Tantusium, then I would be a fit suitor for a Khorajan princess." He tossed the dregs of his wine down his throat. "By placing yokes on other men's necks, I might prove myself worthy of noble company."

"I doubt whether even that would appease my brother and his sniffy-nosed counselors." Yasmela smiled. "And yet, men like you know how to deal with obstacles greater than that." She reached out and touched the deep-brown skin of his hand with her own paler one. "Conan, would you consider returning to the capital with me, to second me in palace affairs in a discreet way? There could be no official rank, of course, except perhaps captain of mercenaries. But I promise to afford you every . . . privilege."

"To be your bone-cruncher, you mean?" Conan frowned. "Your chief spy? That is not my way. And how long would your royal brother tolerate such doings?"

Yasmela cast her eyes down sullenly. "Khossus is out of touch—dangerously so. He's not a fit ruler. He would have to be . . . circumvented."

"His gullet slit, you mean." Conan leaned forward earnestly and sought her eyes. "Yasmela, I never thought to hear . . ."

"No!" The young woman's almond-sharp nails stabbed the back of his hand as she grasped it. "He would not have to be hurt, merely put aside. In time you and I could rule openly, and he would have to learn to tolerate it."

Conan drew her close to him to soothe her restlessness. "And what of the courtiers and the people of Khoraja? Your brother's prejudices only mirror theirs."

Yasmela tossed her head impatiently. "What is your great mercenary army for, if not to silence such complaints?"

Conan pondered a moment, then shook his head.

"It is an impossible plan, Yasmela. You shouldn't even think of inviting such an army as mine into your capital."

"Oh, no?" Her face was only inches from his now, her agitated breath brushing his cheek. "If you didn't have such an arrangement in mind, then why did you lead your force here and consent to see me?"

Conan gazed on her exquisite skin and raised one hand to play in the deep-brown curls at her neck. "To strengthen my hand in Koth. I meant to propose an alliance of another kind. . . ."

"Oh." Her face moved yet closer to his so that her lips brushed his cheek. Her voice was breathy, almost inaudible. "An alliance of another kind, then." She pressed her body against his while he clasped her in a fierce embrace.

The two could not have been more different in character and background, nor in physical form. He was large and rugged, akin to the sparse, sturdy pines of the northern forest, while her delicate, luxuriant efflorescence was that of an orchid from the steamy tropics. Each was splendidly adapted for survival, each in a different way—and yet for a time they were consumed in each other.

The night passed still and mild, with only the sheerest of curtains needed to screen them from the lazy airs that brushed the lake. When dawn's light tinged the peaks above the far bank with gold, the two awoke and stirred awhile together.

Then Conan rose, padded across the stone floor, and plunged head-first into the cool pond. His dive sent waves marching along the marble inlet, and he followed them, swimming just underwater with powerful strokes, far out into the lake. In several minutes he returned, hauling himself from the pool and scraping his skin dry with a knife-edged hand. Then he went to join the silk-robed Yasmela at a table which had been spread in his absence with fruit, bread, cheese, and other simple, excellent foods.

The two ate silently for a time, communing only by their looks and by the light pressure of their thighs laid side by side in the stone seat. Finally Conan said, "We can meet often thus, Yasmela." He reached past her for a pomegranate and began to husk away its leathery skin. "For know you, my mercenaries need a safe roost within striking distance of Tantusium. And we're short of supplies since Ivor's treacherous attack." He pressed a torn piece of fruit to his lips and sucked away the delicious drops. "You and your brother should equip our band, even throw in some skirmishers of your own. We can harry the princeling at will and return here now and again to . . . restore ourselves."

Yasmela turned her face away from him. "Then you still refuse to consider the course I spoke of last night—of coming to the capital with me?"

Conan shook his wet black mane. "Nay, girl, such intrigues aren't my way. I have accounts to settle with Ivor." He extended a hand to the princess, offering her a chunk of the pomegranate's crimson-beaded flesh. "And let me tell you, the gain in this affair could be much greater. . . ."

She pushed his hand away, with the fruit it offered. "Pursue your greater gain then, Conan, but without me. I cannot allow your troops to make war on neighboring kingdoms and then scurry to mine for shelter. Nor can I counsel my brother to permit it." Her eyes flashed to his, then away. "If we should become too great an annoyance to Koth, King Strabonus will send legions against us. Win or lose, there would be no gain in that."

"Strabonus is busy keeping his own empire together." Conan stroked Yasmela's shoulder and leaned toward her, seeking her gaze unsuccessfully. "He's not likely to widen the struggle. And our combined forces could repel an attack easily.''

Yasmela twisted her shoulder out from beneath Conan's hand. ''Whether or not that is true, such a conflict would jeopardize my goals at court.'' Her fair face was set in an expression direr than a girlish pout. ''What would be easy, quite easy, would be to denounce your mercenary army as invading brigands. The whole force of Khorajan chivalry would be set against you in quick order!'' She turned to meet Conan's eyes, and her look had calmness and resolution in it. ''And that is what must I promise you, Conan, if your army is not out of Khoraja by tomorrow!''

The barbarian looked away from her and scowled at the fruit rinds awhile. Then he smote the table with the heel of his hand. ''Devils trounce and truss you, woman! Can you not see the wisdom of a partnership? Is it not clear to you what a vile neighbor Ivor will make if you let him consolidate his power?''

Yasmela sat with her hands clasped on the table before her. ''By departing to eastward, over Eribuk Pass, you can avoid your Kothian pursuers. They will not dare to violate our borders yet.''

Conan cursed again. ''You knew all along you'd be telling me this, didn't you?'' He reached to her and, gripping her delicate jaw between thumb and forefinger, turned her face up to his. ''Did you ever truly think my presence at court would aid you in your royal schemes?''

At the sight of the tear that crept from the corner of one of her dark-amber eyes, he let go her chin and arose from the table. Padding away on bare feet, he walked to his clothing, which the servants had cleaned and left folded on a side-table. Brusquely, wordlessly, he dressed himself, while Yasmela's eyes watched him from the shadow of her downcast face.

After buckling on his swordbelt he strode near her

again and stopped. Once more he reached down to her chin, turning her moist face up to him. Then he bent to place a kiss on her forehead. "I think you will fare well in your maneuvers among the nobles, Yasmela. Continue being careful and resolute."

He released her and walked on out of the room and through the echoing vestibule. The main door of the manor stood open and unattended, and although there was no escort outside, his horse was saddled and waiting at the foot of the steps. He mounted and rode toward the gate, which a stocky old porter drew wide for him.

The splendid scenery of the ride back to camp served only to deepen Conan's melancholy. The morning sun now lit the far side of the mountain valley, and each turn of the trail revealed new cliffs and cascades gleaming among the pines. Overhead the sky was brilliant blue with small white puffs of cloud, and it mocked the doleful thought that he might never return here.

Then his ear caught the jingling and clopping of hooved beasts somewhere ahead. Conan turned his horse off the path and down through the trees toward the sound. Finally he spied its source, moving along a cross-trail below him. It was a pack train of at least two score mules.

A few moments watching told him that there were only five Khorajan soldiers conducting the beasts. He spurred his mount back to the trail and down its more gradual slope until he intercepted the mules at the road fork. Then he trotted his horse up the trail toward the head of the train, eyeing the animals covetously. They were too heavily laden to shy much at his passing, decked with pack-baskets of provisions, tents, and weapons.

Of the two men leading the caravan, the more seasoned and scarred one was the officer. He eyed Conan without alarm, keeping both hands relaxed on the reins in his lap. At the Cimmerian's challenge he scarcely raised an eyebrow.

"Your destination?"

"The same as yours, I think." The officer nodded his head down the forested valley. "The mercenary encampment below."

Conan narrowed his eyes, letting his hand come to rest on his sword-hilt. "And is it customary for Khoraja to send tribute to trespassing armies?"

The officer smiled as broadly as his military bearing would allow. "This is a special consignment, by order of the Princess-Regent, who has many loyal followers in the army. If questioned by my superiors about these goods, I would have to say that they were looted from us by brigands." The man glanced confidingly to his subordinate, and then back to his questioner. "I do not know the purpose of these gifts, but in no case would I deny them to Conan, hero of Shamla Pass, and savior of my country."

"Aye." Conan laughed. "I thought I recognized you from the Spear Companies. Mayhap we diced together once at the Stuck Boar . . . ?"

Falling into earnest conversation, the riders continued down the valley.

19

Wolves of the Hills

On all sides the hills stretched wild. For many leagues before and behind the army they spread in huddled ranks, as if marching eastward in more regular formations than the loose road-order of the mercenary companies themselves. There was something weirdly inscrutable about these serried guardians of Koth's southern border; amid their brushy, eroded slopes it was easy to feel insignificant and lost.

Perhaps this accounted for the sullen, apprehensive mood that had settled over the men, Conan told himself. Here were not, after all, the gleaming mountains of Khoraja that teased the eye like the flanks of recumbent women. The way through this strange land was steep and winding, and the day's march had served to remind every trooper that a hundred hillocks of a hundred cubits height are just as wearying to cross as a single peak ten thousand cubits high.

Or perhaps, on the other hand, it was the weather that darkened the men's mood. Since morning the clouds had gradually thickened; now they rolled overhead like gray millstones, seeming almost to scrape the rounded tops of the ancient hills and threatening to grind to powder any foolish mortals who ventured in between.

"Curse and double-curse these wretched roads," Villeza muttered from the saddle of his mount, which plodded just behind Conan's. "Why do they climb every hillock and plumb every gorge? They must have been cut by blind men, to meander so!"

"I've heard that ancient roads sometimes veer from the straightest path in order to pass near eldritch shrines and hallowed places." Drusandra's doleful look as she delivered this comment showed the same oppression of spirit that was evident in the others.

The Zingaran shot her an apprehensive glance. "Indeed, sword-woman? Are there many such haunted spots around here? For myself, I begin to doubt the profit to be had from this expedition. Why should we let ourselves be chased through Ivor's hinterlands in the forlorn hope of collecting a few gold miters?"

Drusandra shrugged and glanced to Conan. "I trust that this march will be more fruitful than our junket to Khoraja, at least."

"Khoraja furnished us with tents and cookpots for our campaign, and mules to carry them," Conan pointed out.

"True." Villeza nodded. "And now that we've recouped some of our losses, it might be well to divide up the sorry remainder and head south for better pickings." He glanced around at the hulking slopes and shivered. "These hills are . . . infernally hard going."

"Hard for us, harder yet for our enemies. It is well." Aki Wadsai alone, of all the officers, did not act tired or disgruntled at the day's march. Rather, he seemed at home in these lower, drier regions. He urged his horse a little ahead of the others, and in a gruff local dialect he addressed the Harangi guide who rode at the front of the army. "You hillmen expect the rough country and the crooked roads to foil invaders, I think."

The fur-jacketed guide twisted in the saddle of his small robust steed and answered in speech that Conan could scarcely follow. "Many are the armies that have tried to chase our raiding-parties into these hills. Many are the foreign carcasses that feed the wolves and bears and eagles of the land for our hunting sport.'' The squat man grinned back along the length of the mercenary train, showing strong brown teeth. ''Foreigners always come here to their peril.''

Villeza glanced back down the road, where the double column of riders wound out of sight around a stony slope. He squinted at Conan. ''What did he say about foreigners just then? Can we trust these hill-monkeys?''

Aki Wadsai put on a careful smile when he replied to the guide. ''Fortunate is it that we come as friends—to fight a common enemy. Happy we will be to find a safe camp in your hills, whence to strike against hated Koth.''

''Aye.'' The guide frowned and bristled at the memory of ancestral feuds. ''The wretched Kothian sheep-kissers.'' He nodded vigorously, making the brass point of his fur-lined helmet waggle. ''You will find a strong camp here. My chiefs will lead you to a safe place.''

''I think I see one now.'' Conan had topped the rocky shoulder of the hill with the others and was gazing on a striking view that unfolded ahead, that of a sharp ridge looming against the clouds.

It was a long, jagged height that reared before them like the crest of some great beast, steeper and rockier than the surrounding hills. Yet its nearer end, spreading out ahead of and slightly below them, formed a level mesa that looked both habitable and defensible. This plateau was roughly triangular or wedge-shaped, like the head of a salamander, elevated above the surrounding canyons by cliffs on two sides; on the third it merged with the loftier slopes of the razorback ridge. There was an approach to it via a sloping promontory of stone that angled forward and down from one side near the front of the ridge;

this steep, natural causeway passed close up to the mesa's corner and looked as if it would be easy to defend by means of projectile fire.

"See, there, those trees tell of a spring at the base of the rear slope." Conan raised an arm to point out the feature to his fellow captains, who were gazing at the panoramic view as their horses started on the downhill trail. "An army could bear a long siege there."

"My troop will take the back end of the mesa, near the water," Drusandra said, urging her mount forward among the men's. "If there is an attack, we can hold the crest against infiltrators."

"A wise plan," Aki Wadsai agreed. "But remember, what we have to fear the most is the sorcery of that hellion, Agohoth."

"What about those rock outcrops in the middle? Are they natural, or the sarsen-stones of some ancient race?" Villeza knit his olive-skinned brow and regarded the two unequal prominences of pale stone at the center of the mesa, aligned parallel with the ridge. "Such dolmens have an evil repute."

"They're too large to be put there by men," Conan declared. Then his attention was drawn to Aki Wadsai and the guide, who were expostulating beside him.

The Harangi seemed upset by the officers' interest in the mesa, and he looked around at them, rolling his eyes. "It is the Zamanas. A bad place." He grimaced nervously, turning down his mouth in a fierce frown. "Only fools would want to camp there."

The desert chieftain nodded deeply at the man to calm him. "Aye, warrior. Perhaps it is not for us, then. We'll take up the matter with your chiefs."

While Aki spoke soothing words to the Harangi, Conan brought his steed close alongside Drusandra's. "Still," he muttered to her, "the Zamanas Mesa would make a fine place for us to turn at bay."

As the road carried them down the far slope of the

hill, the strange-looking vista remained a long time
before their eyes. And the officers and men in the
van of the army had much occasion to look at it, for
the darkest afternoon clouds had gathered about the
eminence, and a thunderstorm that had been building
for hours was finally unleashed there. Visible smudges
of rain swept the flanks of the ridge while threads of
lightning played about the jagged teeth of its crest. A
few bolts even licked at the twin monoliths in the center
of the mesa.

Only as the troopers descended, and the surrounding hills rose to eclipse the view, did the storm
seemed to abate, with thunder-crashes rattling less
and less often through the gorges.

The guide took the mercenaries off the apparent
road, across an expanse of sloping rock that would
show invaders no tracks, and down a steep side-
canyon. Arriving at the bottom, they followed a turbulent stream that was already swollen with the burden
of the recent thundershower. Its course led them up
before a buttress of native rock that had been made
loftier by rude stone walls. While the lead contingents of the army dismounted to wait along the dark
narrow stream-bank, a log gate was raised to admit a
few officers and men to the hill village.

The plastered-stone dwellings on either side of the
single street had rounded conical tops, from whose
roof-holes columns of smoke meandered skyward.
Scraped hides were strung along the exterior walls to
dry, giving off a ripe smell. Village men and women,
most armed with long blades at their fur-trimmed
belts, stood boldly in the doorways and watched the
strangers ride past. Several times the saddle party had
to slow or stop while straight-backed pedestrians passed
insolently before them with unhurried steps.

Finally the riders dismounted before a stone lodge
larger than the other buildings, whose roof was formed
by multiple domes. A nodding servant ushered them

into its gloomy, many-pillared interior, where fur rugs were spread and a central fire flickered. Firelight glinted on the curving swords at the belts of a dozen or more Harangi warriors standing by the room's side walls. Beyond the firepit sat five figures draped in furs and gleaming metal harness.

Old and wild-looking men they were, their grayblack beards and hair cropped in varied patterns. As the visitors took their seats on the floor at the nearer side of the fire, the chieftain in the center, a flatnosed man with long gray braids, addressed them in barbaric Kothian.

"Why do you come to these hills? The hetmen of the Low Villages have told me that you seek our aid."

Aki Wadsai raised himself slightly on his folded knees. "Aid, yes, and refuge. We want to join you in warring against Ivor, prince of Koth, and we need a safe camp from which to strike against his forces."

A younger chief to the right of the flat-nosed one spoke irascibly. "We Harangi are raiders, not soldiers. We might assault a target with you if the plunder is good, but we will not march with your force."

Aki Wadsai nodded. "Such help could be valuable."

The first chief said, "As to camps, there are suitable strongholds deep in the hills." He scowled fiercely. "But if we receive you, how can we be sure that you foreigners will not turn on us, steal our cattle, and pollute our women"—he paused—"and boys," he added, looking severely at Drusandra.

"Honored one, we would rather swallow knives," Aki Wadsai said. At the old chieftain's narrowed gaze, he explained, "Only because we know that such a course would be foolhardy unto death, here in the homeland of the fierce Harangi warriors."

Villeza leaned forward and added, "In any event, chieftains, we do not intend to stay long. Either we shall strike a mortal blow soon at the satrap of Tantusium, or we leave your lands and seek profit elsewhere.''

The flat-nosed one straightened his gray braids down his gold-buckled chest, considering. "So the attack you plan will be soon? Where are we to strike?''

The other mercenary captains hesitated, and Conan spoke. "The plains to eastward of Tantusium. 'Tis a rich area, but the Kothians can afford to keep only a medium-sized garrison there, at Vareth. Most of their troops will be held back to garrison the capital.''

The Harangis looked thoughtful a moment, then nodded to one another, conferring. "Yes, a fine district, with much plunder,'' the centermost chief could be heard to say. Then he looked back to the captains, seeming well-pleased, and said, "Foreign friends! An alliance between us might be productive, I think. Now, as to the question of a fortified camp—''

"We know where we want our camp,'' Conan interrupted him. "The hill called Zamanas.''

Conan's own fellows seemed just as startled by this demand as were the clatch of chieftains, and on both sides muffled remarks were exchanged. To Villeza's heated protest Conan whispered, "Consider, man, if they dread the place so, at least we won't have Harangi thieves and cutthroats creeping into our tents!''

Then Flat-nose turned back to Conan. "You are strangers to our hills. Would you wish to make your camp in a place . . . of ancient and evil repute?''

Conan hitched himself up to his knees and looked gravely across the licking flames of the firepit. "Chiefs, we are an army, not as nimble as your bands of raiders. Yet we, too, must be ready to strike swiftly. Here, after only one day's march into your hills, we will find it hard to field a force in Koth.'' He clasped his upper arms in his hands and swept his gaze among the chieftains. "Zamanas is close at hand, with strong terrain—the natural base for us."

The head chief conferred briefly with the man on his right, then spoke. "Such a choice is a matter of the spirits' will, and can be disclosed only by a shaman. Come." He gestured the others to arise and began laboriously to climb to his own feet, aided by servants who ran forward to his side. The leaders filed toward the door, flanked by armed Harangis, and walked forth into the street of the village.

It was still light, although the overcast sky seemed eager to speed the twilight. Harangi women and children looked up incuriously as the party emerged. Not stopping to mount a horse, the limping old chief led the procession up the rutted lane and around a corner into a narrow alley. There, at the back of a cul-de-sac that ended against a rock cliff, was the only wooden building the visitors had seen in the village. It was a small ramshackle structure of rough and twisted planks, through whose crevices the light of a blazing fire could be seen. The exterior was decked with animal skulls, fetishes of fur and bone, and bundles of roots, all hanging from pegs driven into cracks between boards. Before the hut was an area blackened by many fires, but cold now.

To the foreigners' surprise, the old, braided chief fell to his knees in the sooty earth before the hovel. He cried out, "Father, oh Father! Come forth, we beg you, and grant us your blessing."

The first time, nothing stirred within the hut. But when the cry was repeated a shape could be glimpsed through the crevices, moving before the fire. Then the ragged curtain that served as a door was jerked aside, and there emerged a half-naked man whose nether parts were wrapped in grimy fur. Though shrunk and wizened, he looked junior to the one who had called him "father." He had only one eye, the other being absent from its caved-in socket. He stepped forth and stood a moment, regarding his supplicants sternly. The expectant stillness that followed his appearance was broken only by a rustle of thunder from the remote hills.

Aki Wadsai whispered to Conan, "These Harangi shamans are to be watched. This one has plucked out his right eye and given it a full funeral so that it may gaze on the spirit world."

The chieftain remained kneeling before the holy man and rattled out a rapid stream of dialect, presumably telling of Conan's request. While speaking, the braided man raised his arm once toward a pale bluff that loomed farther up the valley, beyond the town roofs, and Conan realized that this must be the nearer edge of the feared mesa. Then, in the midst of the chief's narrative, the shaman jerked his head sharply toward the Cimmerian, his single pale-blue eye fixing him with a piercing look.

When the chief was finished speaking, he struggled to his feet with an air of great obeisance and limped back, head bowed, to take a place amid the others, where they had fanned out across the alley.

The holy man walked forward with a bowlegged gait to stand close before Conan and stare up at him. "You are the one who would take his night's rest on the heights of Zamanas?" He spoke in fairly good Kothian. "A northern barbarian. Is your fear of supernatural powers, then, even less than your fear of smaller barbarians?"

Conan kept himself from recoiling at the man's excessive nearness and smell. "I'm wary of magical forces, old one. I've been brought close to death by them."

"Indeed. Your enemy, the prince of Tantusium, employs a mighty sorcerer, one who devises your doom at this very moment."

Conan nodded solemnly. "Aye, the Khitan Agohoth.

He has the power to command unliving objects and the elements, with gruesome results.''

"A dangerous man." The holy man squinted his single pale eye. "Yet sorcerers have plagued Tantusium ere this. The father of the princeling Ivor was himself a dire mage—a shape-changer, it is said, and a ghoul—until he was endungeoned to ease the shame of his brother, Strabonus of Koth."

"I knew Ivor's sire." Conan nodded. "I slew him myself some days ago, beneath the royal palace."

Conan's companions made surprised sounds at this disclosure, but the old shaman only nodded curtly, as if a mere confirmation of his knowledge. He chuckled softly. "And now, somewhere in your barbarous brain, lurks the notion that this Agohoth might find it harder to hurl his spells against one of the Harangis' ancient hallowed places?"

Conan shrugged wordlessly before the old man's cycloptic stare.

A long and thoughtful silence ensued while the shaman turned to regard the distant brow of the mesa. Then he brought his soot-smudged face back to meet his questioners. "I warn you, Conan Skull-basher, not to take such a step lightly." The old man knit his features into a tight frown. "There are many kinds of magic touching our world. Many kinds of evil. Few of them are obedient to your petty schemes."

Conan stood impassive.

"But then, if you are rash enough to bear the risk, go ahead." The shaman shrugged dismissively. He turned to the flat-nosed chief, said two curt words, and went back into his cabin, leaving the soiled curtain swaying behind him.

"Come," the first chief said to Conan. "My men will lead you to Zamanas. May the hill-spirits protect you as babes in your folly."

20

The Mesa

Days later Conan stepped through the low portal of the eight-sided pavilion, closing the flap behind him over the murmur of sleepy female voices. Few mercenaries were abroad in camp, for it was still early morning. He nodded to Sidra, a chestnut-haired Gunderwoman standing guard near the octagonal tents; she favored him with an insolent, worldly smile, then went back to her vigilant stance, clutching her shield and the sword-hilt at her waist.

The troopers seemed to have accepted Conan's practice of spending nights in the pavilions of the warrior-women, though he knew there were widespread whispers and jests about him. As he strode toward the main part of camp he called a greeting to one dissheveled trooper who had wandered into the bushes to relieve himself. The man looked from him to the women's tents with astonishment and suspicion.

There was more bustle near the center of the mesa, where the razorback ridge did not loom so high as to block the early sun. Men were skylarking there, talking and basking on the rocks, approaching one more idle day with boredom and a little mischievousness. They greeted Conan with jibes which he studiously ignored.

The men's earlier fears of the Zamanas Mesa had faded during their sojourn here. The ride from the village had proved easy—even after their Harangi guides halted at the stream, claiming that no man of their tribe had crossed it in living memory. The stone causeway Conan found to be a gradual slope, cleaner of brush than the surrounding hills, communicating with the mesa via a last scarp that would make the place easy to defend.

The plateau was broad, level, and well-drained. It was formed of eroded pink stone that was markedly different from the shale of the surrounding hills. But on its top were soil, trees, and forage for animals. There were no caves or ruins where danger might lurk—only the two pale, unequal monoliths rising at the mesa's center. And these, on close examination of their tapering, rounded shape and iron-hard composition, appeared to be formed by nature rather than by human artifice.

So, after the first day's hunting bagged them a venison feast, with nothing untoward occurring to jar their comfort, the troopers were lulled into accepting their new, pleasant surroundings. While the days passed, they rested and repaired their harness; the skilled gamblers grew rich, and were in their turn robbed or knifed, and Conan began to worry about his men's idleness.

He took his breakfast of boiled groats from his own troop's kettle, which steamed over a bed of flaking coals. While he gnawed dried figs to round out the repast, Aki Wadsai came to him with a greeting.

"Tarim's boon, Conan." He squatted near the Cimmerian in the poised, fastidious way of a desert rider. "Is there no word yet from the rebels?"

"Nay, Aki Wadsai. We should send another rider in case the last one met with misfortune on the road—or with temptation."

"Aye." Aki Wadsai frowned. "The courtly maiden,

Eulalia, said she would send word of their fortunes. I hope the prince has not crushed them.''

Conan nodded. "It would seem that the Kothian legionaries have lost our scent. A shame; I would have liked them to follow us here. Perhaps they've gone to Tantusium to help Ivor quell his trouble.'' He shrugged. "In any event, our rogues are getting restless. We'd better see some action soon. . . .''

They were interrupted by shouts from Conan's quarter of the camp, near the front of the cliff. The Cimmerian arose and vaulted to the top of a rock hummock to gaze in that direction, thinking that the cries might signal an approach or an attack. Instead, he realized, men were calling for a rope.

"Some of my mountain apes are in trouble," he told Aki Wadsai. "I should see to it before it turns into mayhem.'' The other captain understandingly waved him on his way.

Keeping his gait to a brisk walk to avoid drawing more of a crowd, he went down to the cliff-edge, where a group of mercenaries loitered. Some were laughing and hooting as they looked down the side of the cliff; others watched in evident concern. One of the latter saw Conan and ran over to him.

"Sir, the northman, Gandar, climbed down the cliffside and met with some misfortune. He was going to catch us a fat lizard for our lunch, but now he cannot get back up.'' The straggle-bearded man blinked at Conan. "He acts mad or mazed. We need a rope—''

"That's him, is it?'' Conan interrupted. "Or is it one of the rescuers? Why is he shouting like that?''

Conan was watching a long-limbed fellow, a Vanirman by his look, who crouched in a shallow cavity a few score paces down the slope of the mesa's rim. He was barefoot, clad in pantaloons with one of the legs torn and bloodied from a scrape and flapping loose in the gusty breeze. He clung there like a feral thing, seeming to shout and rave at the blank rock wall before him. The sense of his utterances, if sense there was, could not be heard over the distance.

"I know not what ails him. A snakebite, belike." The bearded man looked up nervously at Conan. "He is a nimble climber, and he went far down the cliff out of our sight. Then he crawled most of the way back, raving like that. But now he will not budge."

"I'll find out what the matter is. But keep those gawkers from kicking down rocks or falling on top of me." Conan removed his buskins and his sword and lay them aside, then padded down the rough, weathered stone. "You there, Gandar!" he shouted. "Stay put, and fear not! I'll come help you."

He ran down the rock until the slope became too steep, then turned and faced the stone in order to go crabwise. He was drawing near the afflicted man, listening intently, but the fellow's northern dialect still combined with his frenzied gabble to make his words indistinguishable. Conan saw him taken by a wild fit of some kind, clawing and scrabbling against the stone in a pantomime of frantic climbing, without going anywhere. The cliffside before him was streaked with blood from his lacerated knees and hands.

Then there was a call from above. One of the mercenaries had procured a rope. Now he hurled it down the cliff, the thick coil unwinding as it fell. It was a good cast, and the last coils struck the Vanirman across the shoulder and back.

"Gandar, the rope! Hold the rope and wait for me," Conan called to him.

But the fellow never heard. Instead, he gave a shriek and tried to throw the line off himself, struggling with it as if it were a biting, coiling serpent. As he screamed and thrashed he rolled backward out of the depression in the rock. In a moment he was tumbling down the cliff, gaining speed as the slope dropped away beneath him. His screams finally faded as he pinwheeled out of sight.

"Crom!" Conan started to curse, but then he stopped and changed his imprecation to a silent prayer for the dead. The fellow's antics had cost him his life, and Conan hoped it would deter others from similar exploits. Still, there was something eerie about the death.

Turning and going back up the cliff, he tarried awhile to speak with the chastened men at the top. There was little more that they could tell him of the event. The consensus of opinion seemed to be that Gandar had seen some hobgoblin on the cliff that had frightened him to madness. Conan remained noncommittal about this, and finally turned away in ill humor.

Lookouts had passed the word of approaching riders, and by the time Conan returned to the council fire, the envoys were already arriving: Baron Stephany himself, astride a magnificent silver-gray stallion, escorted by the trousered, travel-worn Eulalia and a half-dozen armed rebels.

"Conan! A splendid camp—what a view you have!" The baron reached down from the saddle to grip the Cimmerian's outstretched hand. "I knew this meeting would be of import, so I left Randalf in charge of our preparations. But I brought along my most trusted aide." He indicated Eulalia, who gave Conan a hug and deluged him with questions.

While they spoke, Conan eyed Stephany. His slim form, sheathed in green riding-clothes, no longer looked so frail or studious. He was at home in the saddle, as was the tame forest cat that perched on his saddle-bow. The creature had grown since Conan had first seen the baron toying with it in the palace, and the stripes of its tail had spread farther up its supple, tawny back; yet its growth was by no means complete. Throughout all the greetings it sat placidly, taking in each new sight with impassive yellow eyes.

Other mercenary officers arrived, along with a party of mercenary women, and the baron became the special object of their attention both because of his fine steed and his strange pet. For a long while Drusandra and her sword-mates stood clustered around the nobleman, while he smiled down indulgently and let them touch both his horse's silver mane and, more gingerly, his kitten's fur.

When Stephany finally dismounted and tethered the catamount, he approached Conan. "Tell me, how do you gain cooperation from the hillmen? I myself was wary of them, being the first Kothian noble to venture into these hills for years, except at the head of a punitive raid."

Conan gazed at the baron matter-of-factly. "I gain their trust by not being Kothian. And I have their promise of help in ousting Ivor."

"Impossible!" Eulalia interrupted from her place at Stephany's side. "They would burn the city and turn every countryman against us. The battle would end in chaos."

"Likely." Conan shrugged. "But I plan to keep them away from Tantusium. I'll use them as a diversion from the main attack."

"Against a Kothian stronghold, you mean . . ."

"Aye—Vareth."

The baron nodded. "A possibility. The Imperials stationed there should keep them occupied."

Eulalia broke in. "But we'll have to warn the villagers, lest they be butchered alive as captives in the hillmen's games."

"Don't send the warning too openly, or too soon," Conan admonished her. "There may be spies among your rebels, and the Kothians should be taken by surprise. I don't want the Harangis slaughtered or betrayed." He caught Stephany's eye. "I have plans for them."

Eulalia told the mercenary officers of events in the

capital. "Ivor is learning that his new unbridled power only means fresh, unchecked opposition. The people are stunned by his sudden accommodation with Strabonus. They balk at all his new taxes and restrictions." The noblewoman smiled cynically. "And he, fearing to arm his subjects, has dropped his plan for a militia.

"Once he demanded that Strabonus withdraw the Imperial legion from Vareth; now he begs the king to reinforce it. He shows his ugly side by making harsh reprisals, but each outrage only strengthens our following."

Eulalia, too, had toughened in recent days, Conan could see. Her mode of dress was consistent with fast riding, and her skin showed less powder and more sun than it had at the palace revelry. She seemed to thrive on it; the firm tone of her voice and the mobility of her body and face betold her enthusiasm. "The rebel cause remains strong," she concluded. "What the barons and squires would not take from King Strabonus they will not take in deuces from a greedy princeling."

"And what of the sorcerer?" Villeza asked. "Hasn't Agohoth been able to scourge the troublemakers into line?"

Stephany leaned forward to answer. "Ivor has yet to unleash him. I think he fears that sorcery, used in the heart of the province, might strengthen our following even more." The baron frowned. "My worry is that he may send the sorcerer against my holdings, or those of the other fractious nobles, to make an example of us. We must strike promptly and avoid being weakened thus."

"But hold . . ." This time Aki Wadsai raised the question. "Is it meet to speak of attack? Surely Ivor will have no qualm at using his magician against us if we put ourselves in his way? Isn't that what he waits for?"

Conan smote his knee resoundingly and stood up. He stepped forward to face the others. "Enough fretting about Agohoth! I'll deal with him myself, by Crom!" He glared around the company, and none stood to gainsay him. His gaze settled on Aki Wadsai, who returned him a slight, earnest nod, as if to record his oath and accept it. Conan shrugged impatiently. "Just plan the attack, and make it soon! My troopers grow unmanageable."

Later, during a lull in the talk, Conan walked over to the monoliths. The mercenaries seemed unfazed by the word of Gandar's death. A horde of ruffians were noisily trying to dig up the stone columns with pikeshafts, on the theory that there was treasure buried underneath them. Pavlo, their leader, was standing atop the shorter of the columns, which was as tall as three men; he directed a gang who were trying to pull it down with ropes.

"Leave off that!" Conan roared. "You, Argossean, down from there! No more horseplay." He strode among the men, who backed cautiously away. "Make ready your kits, dogs. We'll be on the road by morning."

21

Harriers from the Hills

The hillmen rode by night. Overhead cold stars gleamed, while on all sides sounded the scuff of hooves overlaid by the jingling of harness and the mutter of barbarous speech. In the distance male voices were raised in unison, chanting songs that had been cherished by the Harangi tribesmen since the immemorial days when, according to legend, they had ruled the broad eastern plains.

Conan guided his horse as much by the sound of the riders around him as by the sight of them; for his view was limited to an occasional weapons-bristling silhouette, or the glint of starlight on a spiked helmet or shield-rim. Mentally he checked the direction of the horde's movement by the position of the stars, and was reassured; the chieftains must have been using the same method, for amid all the hundreds of Harangi horsemen was only one torch. It came into view now and again when Conan topped a rise—a tall, smoky standard made from the skull and antlers of a stag, set in bronze.

It had been a long ride—down from the hills at the head of the mercenary column on the previous day, then away from his own army and off with the hillmen as they poured out of the canyons into the open, vulnerable countryside. The Harangi had covered distances swiftly by day, and they flowed through the darkness like some shapeless creature that gropes blindly for its prey in murky sea-depths. Conan had changed mounts twice, overburdening one of the smaller native steeds for a while with his robust weight. Now he was back on his sturdy black in anticipation of a fight.

Conan's ear caught a commotion ahead, and in a moment he glimpsed its source: a single rider breasting the throng, moving toward the torch-standard and the chieftains riding abreast beneath it.

"Hyuh." The Harangi war-chief who rode near Conan snapped his reins and headed toward the standard, gesturing to his retainers to keep their station on the left flank of the army. But Conan spurred out from among them and trotted up close beside the hillmen, his massive war-horse effortlessly pressing past the smaller steeds and riders.

"What is it, Hwag of the Red Cliffs? Has one of your scouts found the enemy outpost?" Conan used the smattering of Harangi dialect he'd picked up in recent days.

The hillman did not turn around. "Why do you want to know, outlander?"

"I'm here to make sure that your wild wolves attack the right quarry." Conan stopped speaking, straining his ears to catch the phrases that were being tossed loudly among the hill chieftains.

"In truth?" Hwag answered with a sneer in his voice. "I thought you were a hostage sent along to ensure us against the treachery of your Kothian friends."

Conan frowned. "Aye, perhaps that too. But I shall be leaving you ere long to join the rebel attack—and to handle certain other matters."

The Harangi tossed a suspicious look back at him now that they were both splashed in yellow torch-light. "My chiefs must decide that. You will not

leave the band without their consent.'' He turned
back to watch the parley.

The chiefs were barking out orders to their hetmen,
and Conan tried to catch the gist of what was being
said. But there was no need to wonder, for a cry was
suddenly raised by Hwag and the others, and it spread
through the throng with rapid and frightening ampli-
fication. *"Viridiya!"* Forward!

And as the cry vibrated on a thousand throats, the
mass of horsemen began to accelerate. At first from a
walk to a trot, with Conan's stallion drawn irresist-
ibly along by the movement of its kindred beasts.
Then to a run, amid the swelling rumble of hoofbeats
and a din of savage yells. And then the entire horde
was thundering in a wild, bone-jarring gallop across
roadless meadowlands.

In moments the torch-standard had been left behind. The riders were charging through star-frosted
blackness with only the ghosts of earthly shapes visible on any side.

The rhythm of hooves and the jolting of hard
saddle-leather beat wildly in Conan's consciousness.
He began to feel a mad, suicidal exultation at racing
through the night toward an unseen enemy, entrust-
ing his life to the tremendous power of the herd.
Vainly he peered into the black abyss ahead. His
jolting brain conjured up phantom forms that menaced
him for an instant, then vanished in the flying turf
and dust of the stampede.

He could sense the smaller, nimbler Harangi steeds
and riders flowing past him on either side. Once when
his mount negotiated a shallow depression in the
terrain, he was nearly flung out of his saddle by the
lurching change in the animal's gait. Yet he never
doubted that the hillmen could survive the rush, for
they were consummate riders who could cling to their
horses as if stitched to them.

His own steed was beginning to labor—and he

himself to wonder how long even the mad Harangi could continue this gallop—when some of the choking dust seemed to part and the blackness before him started to take form. There was a smoky glow and a horizon line with man-shapes laboring along it. Then the scene crystallized.

It was the wooden wall of a fortified legionary camp, seen over the backs of the swarming riders. Torches were being brought to the parapet, and the sentries were looking down on the attacking horde with alarm—perhaps at the fearsome yells that rang from the throats of the Harangi on all sides, seeming to wash up against the fortification and rebound from it in palpable waves of sound.

Yet the wall looked lofty, and the gate was closed. Conan, as he plunged desperately toward the target, could not help wondering what these horsemen planned to accomplish against it. By now he had been left among the last of the Harangi horde, and so he had a full view of the assault—the foremost riders veering left and right before the barrier, unleashing a volley of darts, javelins, and arrows that knocked down some of the defenders from atop the parapet. Then a denser wave of horsemen washed up against the wall, hurling ropes tipped with jagged weights that caught in the wood. These latter riders wheeled their horses directly before the stockade while others still surged in around them.

The grapple-lines were not for climbing, Conan realized; rather, the hillmen, displaying expert horsemanship, threw the weight of their steeds simultaneously against the ropes, wrenching outward. With an audible straining and cracking, the timbers of the stockade began to give. One sentry threw his arms up in surprise and tumbled backward into the fort as the footing was jerked from beneath him. Others clung precariously to the wall where it sagged forward.

More horsemen hurled ropes as their fellows pressed

in to engage the Kothian regulars atop the flanking
wooden towers. The short thick bows of the Harangi
twanged like lute-strings, and long spears jabbed at
the men on the parapets. Conan saw hillmen leap
from the saddle or climb on their fellow-horsemen's
shoulders to gain purchase on the wall. Some were
beaten back while others managed to drag themselves
to the top.

Now the inexorable rush brought Conan forward in
his turn. He was surprised for an instant to find
sword and ax clenched in either fist, and a savage
yell throbbing in his throat; then he thundered among
the milling horsemen, with the stockade looming
overhead. He felt a wild urge to hack and chop at its
very timbers for lack of a human foe.

Then he saw a breach opening up in the hated
barrier, between upright wall sections that were being
dragged down by the Harangi. And his war-horse
must have been even more frenzied than he, for
without any urging the animal made a mighty leap
and launched itself into the narrow, V-shaped crevice.

Then came madness—a din of screams, a forest of
pikes and torches that waved about Conan but parted
ineffectually before him—for none of their wielders
could have expected the giant horse and rider that
dropped onto them out of the sky. The black stallion
wallowed a moment across crumpled human bodies,
trampling and biting like a hell-fiend, while Conan's
weapons lashed left and right with terrible effect.
Then man and horse were through the massed defenders and turning to beset them again.

But by now a wide segment of the wall had fallen
flat, and screaming Harangis were charging in over
the uprooted timbers. The Kothians could not stand
between them and the raging Cimmerian, so they
parted away to both sides. Conan pressed in against
one flank and helped to drive them relentlessly back,

until he had to turn to meet a fresh wave of defenders fleeing their burning tents.

In time the last of the Kothians took refuge in an old stone keep at the back of the camp, to which the fort's wooden walls had been added to house the legion. The royalists fought without hope but doggedly, for they expected no mercy from the wild hillmen. The latter set about knocking down the gate of the keep with timbers ripped from the walls. As the steady drum of the battering-ram echoed through the fort, it was clear who the victors would eventually be.

Came the time when, although the battle-din still echoed through the compound, no Kothians were left alive in the outer yard, and many of the Harangi were busily engaged in stripping bodies. Conan had paused in the fight when he felt his horse wheezing cruelly beneath him, and he dismounted to see its mouth dripping pink foam. He led the animal to a drinking-trough whose water was only slightly bloodied.

While the animal rested and drank, Conan went to accost a hillman engaged in stealing five wild-eyed horses from the Kothian officers' stable. Choosing the largest, the Cimmerian snatched its tether from the man and stood glaring at him; the fellow started to protest, but then shrugged and led his other prizes quickly away.

Conan saddled the fresh horse and tied his stallion behind it. As he mounted up, cheers and the rending of wood sounded from the back of the compound. The door of the keep was finally yielding.

The Cimmerian jerked the reins, heading out through the broken wall into the body-littered fields, where a bright half-moon was climbing the eastern sky.

22

The Night Riders

None of the Harangi made any effort to stop Conan, though his route took him through the nearby village, which was prowled by loot-seekers and apparently empty of inhabitants. One hillman raised his curved sword and called out a salute to the Cimmerian as the first warrior through the breach, but none else paid him heed. By the glare of a burning dwelling he saw the milestone of the eastern road and started along it.

From a cluster of stables and sheds at one side of the lane sounded feminine screams overridden by gruff Harangi laughter. Conan glanced warily to the unlighted structure, then frowned and looked away, hardening his heart to one more eventuality of war. The pace of his steed did not falter.

Then the scream was repeated, and something remotely familiar about it tingled the hairs at the back of Conan's neck. An instant later a frail shape darted out of the black mouth of one of the sheds, followed closely by two burly forms. Conan threw off the reins of his trailing horse and spurred the Kothian steed to intercept the runners.

"Halt! Wait!" Conan barked in Harangi, but the warriors did not look back at him. He overtook them swiftly and wheeled his horse between the men and their fleet-footed quarry, swinging down from the saddle in a simultaneous dismount. "Halt," he said again, facing the pursuers. In Kothian he called over his shoulder, "Eulalia! Stay near the road!"

The Harangi had paused, but now one of them started forward, cursing and reaching for his sword. Conan lunged out with blinding speed, clubbing him on the side of the neck with a balled fist. The man staggered and sank to one knee. His comrade hung back dubiously.

They stood at an impasse for a few moments. Then the felled Harangi tried to arise, clinging to his fellow-warrior's coat and arm to steady himself; the nervous man tried to shake him off, fearing a renewed attack by Conan. As the two were thus engaged, Conan moved off to gather in the reins of his horses and lead them away. He kept a wary eye on the men until he was well away from them.

Then, walking along the narrow, rutted track, he began to call quietly. "Eulalia! Where are you, girl?" Hoarse from battle-shouts, his voice sounded gruff against the trill of crickets. "You can cleave to me now. The danger is past." He scanned the moonlit weeds on either side of the road, but saw no movement. "What are you doing here anyway? Yester-eve I left you safe in the midst of an army."

An exasperated noise sounded somewhere just ahead of him; then the noblewoman's slim shape rose wraithlike from a cluster of weed-stalks by the road. "Conan, I had to warn our folk in the village!" Her voice surged in defiance, though her face gleamed teardamp in the moonlight. She moved near him where he stood and hovered uncertainly, her arms clasped across her bosom. Her riding-skirt was gone, and her long embroidered blouse left her legs bare from the middle of her thighs to the calves of her low boots.

Conan looked her searchingly in the face. "Stephany sent a courier to warn your allies of the attack."

"Yes, but I went with him. I had to be sure it was done, and done rightly." She frowned with determination. "Else the heads of our people might have been piled higher than the housetops."

"Your own stubborn head was at no small risk." He reached out an arm to clasp her shoulder.

She flinched at first, then stood steady under his hand. "Yes, but it was worth it. As it happened, the courier was overtaken and slain by outriding Harangi, who consider all Kothians their enemies. I escaped, though it killed my horse to get me here ahead of those hill-demons. Then, trying to find another mount, I was cornered by the two you saw." She shuddered under his touch.

"Come, we've tarried too long," Conan said, glancing behind him. "I've a task to perform." He drew her toward the horses. "My black will scarcely notice your weight—if you can ride bareback." He looked her up and down. "Or better, climb into the saddle with me. You must be chilled."

Conan mounted the Kothian steed and drew Eulalia up behind him, and they started along the road. From the saddle Conan could see a few hillmen moving before the flames in the town. But the two near the shed were gone, and there was no sign of pursuit.

Then, after the buildings fell away behind them, they passed a walled villa with Harangi steeds tethered outside. From beyond the spike-topped wall, flames and human screams rose skyward. Conan glanced back at Eulalia inquiringly. "No warning for them?"

Her face was set in a frown. "No. Most were the families of royalist officers—or villagers who consorted with them. Agents of Kothian tyranny who deserve no better." Though her voice was sharp, the clench of her hands on his shoulders felt anguished.

Once into open country, Conan spurred his mount along to make up time. The trailing battle-horse had regained some of its tremendous vitality and now, without the burden of arms, armor, or rider, was able to pelt along at a brisk pace. The road was level and firm, and Conan leaned low in the saddle, hugging the mane of the Kothian steed and letting the animal run out its fear of fire and war. Eulalia clasped her arms about him and silently clung to his mailed back.

It was a long gallop under the staring moon, and in the course of it the land lost its flatness. The gently rolling western plains began rising in a series of ridges; on the remotest of them, somewhere far ahead, perched the city of Tantusium. The long upward slopes and steep descents of the road slowed the riders' pace to a walk, making it easy to speak.

"Conan, you keep craning your neck to scan the road ahead. We are still far from the city—whom do you expect to see?"

"Who else but the enemy, woman?" The Cimmerian shot a glance back to her face close behind his shoulder. "Since we made sure that the prince would hear of the hillmen's approach and think it our main thrust. If he sends a sizable part of his force from the city to meet the threat, then this is their most likely route."

"I see." Eulalia's voice sounded pensive, and her hands hugged his chest more snugly. "There is risk, then, in taking this road."

Conan nodded, making the black strands of his hair bob in her face. "A risk, and an opportunity."

After a moment the noblewoman spoke thoughtfully. "So this night's feint and the morning's thrust will determine the fate of our rebellion."

"Aye. By tomorrow Stephany's rebels should be fully committed—if he's bargained with me in good faith." Hearing his saddle-partner drawing in her breath to protest, he spoke on quickly. "And if we fail to take the city, I'll not be able to hold the mercenary bands here much longer. It's only hard profit that keeps a troop of Free Companions in the saddle, and the whole purse looks to be riding on this throw of the lots."

Eulalia's reply came only after a long pause. "And yet, if we do take the city, our trials may only be starting. How do we know that your troops won't sack the place and ride roughshod over our plans for reform? Do you even have the power to make such promises, Conan of Cimmeria?" She leaned forward against his shoulder to glimpse his face, her breath warm at his ear. "Of course, our troops would fight yours if they tried such a thing."

"If you doubt that I can control my troops" —Conan's frown darkened the side of his face that she could see—"rest assured, I shall not let them wallow long in Tantusium. I have other plans. Just pay us as agreed, and you need fear no betrayal. As to your rebel dreams"—he shrugged—"they, too, serve my end, for I may need your realm as an ally in the months to come.

"Nay, girl, the obstacles before you are few, if not small: Ivor the satrap, his grasping uncle Strabonus, their combined armies, and their sorcerous mascot Agohoth."

Eulalia shivered. "The last alone could send us all to our graves."

"Aye, but remember: The Khitan loves royal power. He battens to it like an eel to a carp. If we kill Ivor and weaken Strabonus a bit more, the mage might just worm his way into the graces of some other monarch and forget your little province altogether." Conan nodded reassuringly to her. "Or something else might befall him."

Eulalia sighed. "How strange it seems, after our long struggle and all our careful planning, that our fate depends on someone like you." She paused, then decided that she should explain her remark. "A foreigner, I mean, an adventurer. Someone who might ride off tomorrow and never be seen again. Not . . . a nobleman."

"Aye, not of the blue blood. Ever my failing."

Conan nodded grimly. "Matters it not how much noble blood I've spilt, or waded through?"

Eulalia made no reply. They rode forward in silence over the crest of the next ridge to see the moonlit road winding among hillocks and copses in the next valley.

"It's too dangerous to go on," Conan said. "We could be caught by surprise at any time. We'll have to stop and wait."

He chose a place where the road skirted a broad expanse of forest. They rode into its near-blackness, among low-hanging fronds and snapping twigs, to a place where a meadow opened palely ahead. There they dismounted, and he tethered the horses.

Then he took a stout bow and a fistful of long arrows from his saddle-gear. "Wait here till I return. There is a fur robe to wrap yourself in. If wild animals come foraging, climb up into the saddle." He started away, then turned back to her. "And should you hear me shouting oaths to Crom, ride off and save yourself."

She grasped his arm. "Oh, Conan, I cannot stay here alone!" Her voice was low and urgent. "I am a town girl, not a creature of the forest like you. The night-terrors would be too great . . . take me with you!"

"Very well. But stay quiet!" He placed his arm about her, and they walked back through the forest gloom to the roadside. The white ribbon was still quiet, and Conan went to its edge to look up and down its length. Clamping the borrowed bow between his legs, he carefully bent and strung it. Then he nocked an arrow to it, sticking the others upright in the mold beneath an ancient tree, and they settled down, waiting.

The night dragged on without event. Time and again Eulalia started to speak, with Conan hushing her. They listened till their ears felt starved for sound, yet were rewarded only by the occasional creak of a limb or the desultory flutter of a night-bird.

It was easy to doubt the purpose of crouching here, watching shadows of gnarled tree-limbs creeping across the road. Conan begrudged every moment lost from the ride to the city—why languish so when glory and doom would soon be parceled out on another fighting-field?

Then he felt a light caress at the back of his leg, where his steel-stapled armor skirt left it exposed to the mild air. He turned his head to see the pale oval of Eulalia's face hovering near. As he watched she leaned forward to brush her lips against his, with the warmth of her bare thigh pressing him.

The familiar passion surged in his chest, the same that had been aroused once before by this face, this soft body. But now he held it back, like the reins of an overspirited horse. He felt blood swirling up into his brain, making him dizzy. Eulalia became ever bolder and more passionate, passing her slim hands beneath his armor to caress him.

Then their rapture was broken by a sound: the distant tattoo of horses' hooves, backed by a deeper tone. It was thrown up a few moments by the road, then quickly muffled, as if by a curve. "Hear that!" Conan whispered, thrusting her away from him and snatching up his bow. "Several riders at least."

He tensed and watched the road where it emerged from a copse, while Eulalia settled into a crouch beside him. "Hush, now," he said, to still her gasps. Then he seized her by the nape of the neck and thrust her head to the earth. "Your face is too pale—keep low!"

The riders were upon them more at that moment, with hoofbeats that could be felt shaking the ground— four horsemen wearing the plain gray mail of Tantusium. "Ivor's not with them; he would have brought a larger guard." Conan drew his bowstring taut as the soldiers galloped past in pairs. But he did not aim until a dark shape rattled into view. "As I hoped," he muttered.

Agohoth's wain rolled forward, drawn by a matched pair of gray coursers. Its ebon canopy hung far out over the front, flapping loose at the sides. In its interior shadow Conan was almost sure that he glimpsed the familiar aquiline face, the large pale hands grasping the reins, but then the movement of the curtain obscured his view.

As the eerie car approached, he aimed where he thought the charioteer would ride. It rumbled past and he released the arrow, following its flight straight to the black cloth.

The vehicle did not slow or turn, and Conan's next arrow never sped. He listened to the rumble of the wheels receding. Then a rear guard of four riders galloped briskly past, and the party was gone.

"Did it hit?" Eulalia's hand was on his arm, her face intent.

"Yes, I think." Conan frowned uncertainly. "But it may have passed straight through the wain's canopy without even being seen. Or mayhap the thrice-blasted driver is sitting dead at the reins."

"I pray so!" Eulalia looked nervously down the road, where the hoofbeats had died away.

"In any case, we know Ivor has sent the wizard away from the city. Our ruse has bought us time." He tipped the woman's face up to his view. It looked wan and frightened. He planted a kiss on her forehead. "But come—we'd best be away from here without delay."

23

City Fight

Morning dawned clear along the road to Tantusium. As the eastern sky shaded from pale gold to paler blue, the riders beheld the city itself on the crest of the far horizon, and then rediscovered it across the swell of every hill and the unfolding of every curve. It grew gradually from a mere dark silhouette, pricked yellow by watchfires, to a spreading, mottled warren of roofs and walls, an ancient nest of human hopes and iniquities ready to stand yet another trial.

The place was enjoying no tranquil dawn, as the watchers could tell. Dark smokes rose from behind the white outer wall, and masses of antlike figures swarmed on the slope before the city. Increasingly the rattle of many-throated shouts carried to Conan and Eulalia over the steady thrallop of the horses' hooves.

Then they found themselves passing among stragglers and tardy recruits of the besieging force. Most were farmers and foresters, armed with axes or scythes, joining the road at intervals from field and path and trudging for the city. Eulalia hailed each one joyously from the saddle as she rode past, but Conan galloped on in silence. He gave only a brusque nod when they came abreast of familiar mercenaries riding with the tail of the baggage train, so intent was he on the action ahead.

Then, on overtaking a makeshift vehicle formed of long, crossbraced timbers mounted on wheeled caissons, he bellowed, "By Crom, what are these ladders doing in the rear?" He paused to harangue a quartermaster riding near the head of the dray-team. "Get them up to the walls quickly. All other traffic is to make way for you, by my order."

Soon the familiar terraces of the old camp thudded beneath their horses' hooves—and then the tract that had been churned and scorched by Agohoth's sorcerous blast. Pale-green grassblades were already springing from the soil fertilized so richly by soldiers' blood and ashes. Here were tethered many horses, tended by elderly or maimed troopers. On the next terrace were lines of mercenaries and Kothian rebels waiting to be ordered into the city assault.

Pavlo and a few others raised a cheer when Conan rode up, but its echo among the rest of the troops sounded weak and dispirited. Conan dismounted and gave his horse to one of the mercenaries for unsaddling. He turned to Eulalia, only to find that her lover, Randalf, sheathed in the fine plate armor of a knight, was already lifting her down from the saddle and into his tight embrace. Conan turned abruptly away and headed up the slope.

The highest terrace, just out of bowshot of the city wall, contained regrouping forces and wounded men. Nearly all of these were mercenaries, who, as the prime battle-hardened companies, were spearheading the attack. Conan strode to a group of officers and drew Zeno aside. "How goes the fight? I hoped to be here earlier."

The curly-haired lieutenant gazed somberly at Conan from beneath the raised visor of his helmet. "It goes ill, Conan. We tried a rush at first light—here, because the fire from the towers is too heavy near the gate." He gestured to the curving white wall that loomed all the higher above them because of the height of the ridge. "Stephany was wounded, and we were driven back. Afterward we sought to bring arrow fire to bear on the parapet—without success. The height gives them thirty paces more range than ours." He glanced to where the other mercenary captains were quietly conferring. "Aki Wadsai supported us in the assault, but I think his men are unused to fighting on foot. And Villeza has been holding back his force."

The Zingaran, sensing his name in the air, turned away from the other officers and walked toward the two, frowning. "I think your troops should bear the brunt of the attack, Cimmerian. After all, we are here at your suggestion"—he glanced at the waiting forces downslope—"and at the pleading of your Kothian friends."

Conan nodded curtly. "Just be ready at my back, Villeza. And be not overly cautious." He turned away from the Zingaran's insulted look and faced Zeno. "Where is Stephany?"

"There, Conan."

He followed his officer's nod toward a line of men who lay in the shadow of the terrace wall. He dismissed the lieutenant, turned, and strode toward them. At first he gazed in alarm at a soldier whose green tunic was heavily crusted with blood from a bashed-in face, but then he located the baron, seated on a saddle-blanket behind some loitering men. One perforated greave of the aristocrat's fine silver armor was removed. The broken, bloody arrow lay in the grass nearby, and the wounded man was tightening an herb poultice about his calf. He looked up at Conan and smiled apologetically. "A nuisance, this. My studies have not included much of war. But I hope to be back in the fray soon. . . ."

Conan shook his head. "Better to stay alive, Baron. You're needed more in peace—if ever it comes to their weary province." He waved aside the older man's protestations. "But what of the rebel forces inside the city?"

Stephany sobered, shaking his head. "They cannot capture the gate for you, Conan. They are ill-armed, and Prince Ivor knows he has enemies within the walls. They can rise up when we enter the city, but not before."

Conan pondered these words as he gazed at the slope before him. Its grassy expanse, he saw, blossomed fletched arrow-shafts like wildflowers. They grew as if magically, even from the scattered, motionless corpses. At the top of the field was the undamaged wall, with heads and shoulders of pikemen staring down. A group of archers stood at one place along the parapet, idly vying with one another in long-distance bowshots at the attackers. Further to southward were the twin towers, swarming with defenders, that flanked the gate. As he watched, a catapulted stone arched up from below to strike the nearer one and bounce off harmlessly. Beyond the towers rose the heights of the citadel.

Yet here, after all, was just a whitewashed masonry wall, tall as five men and made of small stones only, as Conan well knew from his sojourn in the city. Such a rampart could be breached or undermined by slow, patient toil under turtleback sheds. But the threat of wizardry allowed no time for such labor; the city must be carried today, if at all. This very morning!

"We made the siege ladders to your specifications." Stephany was indicating the long, caissoned timbers that were now being trundled onto the level terrace. "There are more of them lying before the wall."

"Aye." Conan shook himself out of his reverie and bent down to take up the baron's shield, painted with its silver cat's-head insignia on a green ground. "I'll need to borrow this." Turning, he raised it on his arm and started toward the roadway. "Troopers!" he thundered. "To the ladders, and follow me!"

On all sides the ranks began to stir as men gravitated toward him. One soldier called to a friend, "If we're going over, best to go with Conan!" and his remark was echoed down the ranks with increasing enthusiasm, "Conan . . . aye, Conan will lead!" A general surge began among the crowd of armored bodies.

Passing near the clustered officers, he shouted again, "Bowmen forward, to give covering fire! And pass the order down the lines to harry the walls from all sides."

He reached the caissons and stooped under one of the timbers, raising the shield strapped to his arm so as to shelter his head and shoulders as he grasped the heavy, T-shaped base. Powerfully he straightened his legs and back beneath the burden, and mercenaries and rebels rushed noisily into place behind him, vying to share the weight of his ladder.

With lusty shouts that merged gradually into a spirited work-chant, the troopers set out upslope with the ladders. Conan led his dozen men up a tumbled place in the terrace wall while the other ladders lined up, snakelike, to follow. Meanwhile men swarmed up the slopes on either side. Archers trotted forward, some crumpling to earth beneath the force of arrows and slung stones. But when the survivors came to a range where they could strike the top of the wall, they slowed to a walk and began to nock and release their shafts with a deadly rhythm.

The defending archers concentrated their fire on the ladder-bearers, who were partially protected by their shields and the stout, cross-barred timbers. The slope before the wall was steep and long, and the bearers' steps faltered often, as did their chanting song, when arrows struck the leg or the groin of one of their number. Conan labored forward, feeling the ladder racking his shoulder ever more heavily as carriers fell from beneath it and the others stumbled over their bodies.

But of the unburdened warriors passing on either side, a few stepped into the gaps to help. One of these was Drusandra, as Conan realized when he heard her voice behind him. "I'm falling in with you, Cimmerian, in hope that you'll bear most of my share of the weight." Giving him a poke in the nether quarters, she added, "Your bulk makes a handy buttress to hide behind." Her humor in the midst of slaughter was inspiriting, and he felt the ladder surge ahead with her arrival.

Conan marched the troopers almost to the base of the wall, doing his best to pretend that the clattering rain of projectiles was not falling. Slipping out sideways from beneath the wide foot of the ladder, he grounded it firmly amid the litter of stones and arrowshafts. "Raise it up now! Briskly, briskly!" Stepping back to the center of the pole, he laid hands on one of the projecting rungs and heaved it upward. With a score of arms thrusting simultaneously, the narrow end of the timber swung high into the air. The bearers moved forward into a tight knot, pushing upward. The ladder passed over the apex and swung down against the sloping wall, with Conan dragging backward to keep it from striking too hard and rebounding.

By the time he was ready to climb, a pair of mercenaries had already swarmed up the rungs ahead of him. Drusandra was poised to go next, but Conan shouldered past her and set his feet to the roughhewn wood, crowding the uppermost men from behind and taking up the space of two on the ascent. He felt the ladder sag and settle with the weight of bodies piling on beneath, and he thought he could feel the tremor of ax-blows from above.

As he climbed he felt arrows glancing lightly from

his armor; he wondered at their weakness until he realized that they were spent or rebounding shafts from his own side. The projectiles of the defenders were more deadly, as he soon saw; for he heard the dull clang of rock striking the helm of the man above him.

Stone and man both plummeted past Conan onto the climbers beneath, knocking some of them loose with yells and a clattering. Then, as he raised his shield-arm to the next rung, an arrow drove between his mailed sleeve and his silk shirt, gashing his skin painfully. He jerked it free and continued upward, an oath bursting from his lips.

The ladder overhung the wall by half a man-height. As Conan reached the top the remaining mercenary in front of him died, pierced through the throat by the pike of a gray-cloaked defender. But the trooper clung to the pikeshaft with both hands and bore it away with him as he toppled away to the side. Two more pikes bit into the timbers as their wielders started to thrust the ladder away from the walls. Feeling his perch arching giddily out into space, Conan reached across the top rung and splintered one of the straining pikeshafts with a stroke of his ax. The weight of the ladder was too much for the other man to bear alone; he faltered and let it come crashing back against the wall. This impact overbalanced Conan, who tumbled forward onto the rampart.

As he struggled to regain his feet, a blur passed over him; it was Drusandra. In a moment she was leaping over the body of one pikeman and fencing the other back over the edge of the rampart.

Conan grunted thanks to the sword-woman and raised his ax and shield to drive back two more encroaching defenders. With that the section of wall was clear, and mercenaries were swarming onto it from the ladder.

The rampart was wide enough for two, and Conan

took the lead with Drusandra, shouting curses and boasts, pressing toward the gate-towers against a thickening knot of defenders. Their progress was stalled at last by two swordsmen of Ivor's royal guard, backed by two more who struck from between them with pikes.

Conan jabbed and flailed in vain with his ax, staying clear of the deadly blades and points; but then an arrow flew up across the waist-high battlement into the armpit of one gray-clad swordsman. Conan seized the chance to club him crushingly on the helm and kick his staggering body back across the pikeshaft of one of his comrades.

Leaping past the wounded man, he got close enough to the encumbered piker to chop his head half off his shoulders with a mighty stroke.

Meanwhile Drusandra's darting blade had found a crevice in the other swordsman's belly-armor, and he sagged down in agony before her. More guards rushed to aid the last remaining pikeman—then another siege-ladder struck the wall behind the defenders, and they turned in confusion.

Conan and Drusandra cleared the rampart at the head of the second ladder, driving forward until the narrow way was again clogged with defenders. Meanwhile fresh invaders fought their way down ramps and stairways, scattering the guardsmen and chasing them into the lanes of the city. New ladders spewed men onto the wall to outflank and overwhelm the defenders, and soon the gate-towers loomed close.

Then a fresh alarm was raised in the alley below. Stable doors flew back to disgorge a party of townsmen who ran forth brandishing clubs and swords. Seeing Conan's green-and-silver shield embattled on the wall above them, they raised a cheer, shouting, "Stephany! Life to the baron! Down with Ivor!"

Milling in a disorderly crowd, they headed toward the city gate. Looking ahead to the gateyard, Conan could see swords clashing in the morning sun. Their clangs sounded faint above the nearer battle-din.

"The rebels are under arms!" he told Drusandra, who had just stabbed and chased back a hatchet-swinging opponent. Then he drew out of the fray, letting Ariel and another of Drusandra's women press forward to take his place.

Casting about him briefly, he dashed back along the rampart, shouldering past arriving troops. He collared Bilhoat, who had just stepped down from a ladder. "Lieutenant! Send for Stephany, if he'll come! Bring him up on the wall to be seen by his followers. But shield him well!"

"Aye, Conan." The wizened ex-thief looked doubtfully down the ladder, which was acrawl with the backs of climbing soldiers. "I'll try." He looked up to say more, but Conan was gone.

He had rushed back to Drusandra and Ariel, who were pressing the fight relentlessly along the wall. "Take heed, sword-wenches!" he shouted. "The defenders are falling back into the tower!" Indeed, gray-liveried men were darting through the arch of a stout brass-bound door at the place where wall and tower met. Now the two guards who opposed the sword-women gave back faster, in hopes of reaching it before their frightened fellows shut them out.

But Conan, to all the watchers' surprise, sprang onto the narrow parapet and dashed forward along it, raising his shield high against arrows from the tower. He danced nimbly over the sword of one embattled guardsman as it lashed out once, twice, at his ankles, and then, to cheers from beneath the wall, he gained the vacant space near the tower. Leaping down from the parapet, he pelted for the door.

The last few guardsmen through the arch saw him coming and began to swing the heavy panel shut. In spite of his closeness there was clearly no hope of reaching it in time.

It was then that Conan, giving vent to a mighty bellow, halted his rush and hurled his ax.

It struck no one; rather, it thudded into the thick edge of wood between the brass-banded hinges, effectively blocking the door against closing. One of the tower-guards sprang into the doorway to work it loose, while Conan drew his sword and resumed his charge.

Now arrows rattled down from the tower-top, striking sparks from the stones of the rampart. Miraculously none struck Conan; however, one nested in the back of the guardsman retreating before Drusandra. As he crumpled, his despairing companion turned to run, only to be hamstrung by Ariel's darting sword. That left the way clear for all the besiegers on the rampart to stampede forward over the fallen bodies.

Meanwhile Conan's sword had found the man in the archway, near-nailing him to the door. The battle-frenzied Cimmerian had trouble wrenching his blade free, and when he finally succeeded, it was driven out of his grasp with a mighty clang. A paving-stone had been dropped from the tower-top, passing a hairsbreadth in front of him and cracking the flagstones at his feet. With a savage roar he stooped and lifted the rock chest-high, hurling it forward into the aperture of the doorway. It banged past the edge of the door and fell with clanks and screams into the confusion beyond.

Then a forest of friendly blades blossomed around Conan, and he was borne forward through the arch on an irresistible surge of bodies.

The din was terrifying in the darkness of the tower, where armored fighters hacked and hammered at one another. The fiercest resistance was along the spiral stair leading to the tower-top, but Conan found his

way among the struggling men to the downward
stair. Descending, he passed into one of the lower
chambers, where the great sliding bar that sealed the
city gate stood unguarded.

"I'll join you, Cimmerian," Drusandra's panting
voice echoed from behind him. "That fighting up-
stairs is not my style. I hate having my toes trodden
on." She passed inside, as did Ariel next, who turned
to watch the doorway.

"Crom! A heavy toothpick it is, by my hilt!"
Conan eyed the gate-bar, a squared tree-trunk that
passed out horizontally through the tower wall. He
hove his weight against the cross-dowel at its near
end, shoving until his buskin-soles skidded on the
paves. The great timber creaked but did not notice-
ably shift.

"Let me try my strength," Drusandra said, laying
hands on a metal crank that protruded from the wall.
It turned readily, and the bolt began to trundle its
length into the room.

Conan flushed with embarrassment, but clapped
her shoulder good-naturedly. "Say nothing of this,
and I won't boast of who was first on the wall."

"Nor will you say in what posture, I'll wager."
Drusandra winked at him. "But I will." Then, laughing, they set their backs to the windlass in the middle
of the floor, starting heavy chains a-rattling through
stone apertures. As could be seen through the arrow-
slit before them, one portal of the city gate was
swinging wide.

Shouts and hoofbeats from outside told of the effect, as the besiegers saw the opportunity. Conan walked
down to the lower level, gathering up a half-dozen
fighters along the way, and drew out the bar of the
ground-level door. As he cautiously levered it open,
he saw a wave of mercenary horsemen already
sweeping through the gate. And beyond them, against

the far wall of the plaza, were a party of Ivor's guards. They were in the process of abandoning their post in the second gate-tower and fighting their way back into the town streets. Conan strode out onto the customs-porch.

"Aki Wadsai!" he called to the foremost of the horsemen. "Follow yon guards!" He pointed to the fugitives. "Press them close, and clear our way to the citadel!" The desert rider waved assent to him and spurred across the plaza, marshaling his riders.

Conan parted from Drusandra, who was trying to assemble her company of women. He pressed through the thickening swarm of troops, collaring officers and ordering them to form new ladder-parties. In moments a half-dozen were on their way to fetch ladders from before the walls and haul them through the gate. At this labor the rebels seemed as ready to obey as the mercenaries, or more so.

Moving past the alehouses at one side of the square, Conan found Zeno assembling a dozen men with axes. "I'm ordering them to go into the taverns and smash every ale-cask and wine-jar," he told Conan.

The barbarian nodded, regarding the brightly painted arches of the inns sadly. "A sorry waste of spirits, that."

"But Conan! We don't want these men drunk and reeling in the palace assault!"

"Aye, a wise thought." Conan clapped the red-haired officer on the shoulder and leaned close to confide in him. "Personally I fight better when I'm drunk. But not all of these dogs can stomach it as well. So go ahead!"

Moving on, he found four of Villeza's troopers using a tavern bench to batter in the door of a silk-merchant's. He came up on them unawares, setting his foot against their makeshift ram and kicking it over onto two of them. With a ball-mace he had acquired in the tower, he menaced the other two. "Your orders were no looting the town," he snarled. "There's no time! Any loot of yours is that way, in the cita-del!" The cowed men fell back before his pointing weapon as he herded them out of the plaza and up the lane.

When he looked around, he saw the first of the ladders being trotted forward. "This way!" he shouted, waving Stephany's shield on high and setting out on the familiar road to the palace.

But the way was narrow and steep, and it quickly became jammed with armed men, so that many of those waiting in the rear took diverging streets to speed their progress. The siege-ladders obstructed the lanes, and the troops lost any semblance of formation in trying to get past them. Worse, the horses' hooves tended to slip on the smooth paves of the walkways, posing a hazard to those passing nearby.

Then came a curve so narrow that the foremost ladder would not go through; it had to be lifted almost vertical to clear the ancient walls that over-hung the street on either side.

Conan grew frantic trying to speed the advance. "Briskly now, dogs! Move your mangy hides along there. Curse these wretched streets! Archers, let the pike-squads through! Here, you, Einar! Scout up that lane, and report back to me when you find the citadel!"

After what seemed half a morning of toil, he found Zeno again at his side. Doubts furrowed the lieuten-ant's broad, perspiring face. "As I remember, Conan, the palace walls are higher and steeper than the city ones."

"That's so. But there are buildings close against them. I know because I myself used one to scale the palace wall on the night of our betrayal. These lad-ders will be enough."

"But don't you see how exposed we are?" Zeno stared at his commander and spoke with angry intensity. "The force of our attack is being lost in this city maze!"

"Aye, it will take some sweat to carry the citadel." Conan started back to the corner, waving the next ladder party forward. "Here, take on this task so that I can go forward and keep those rogues out of trouble." He left his lieutenant looking flushed and disconcerted.

On his way up, Conan encountered Aki Wadsai and a handful of horsemen milling in a side-alley. Their steeds looked winded, and some of the riders were binding their saber-cuts. "Conan, beware! There are bands of mounted guards harrying our flank." The desert chief wiped his curved blade and sheathed it at his belt. "They strike at us, then vanish in this tangle of alleys. My band has been split in the confusion."

Conan swore bitterly under his breath. "Aye, these streets are madness!"

"A sly madness. They make a better defense than the city wall." Aki Wadsai frowned darkly. "Guard your flanks, Conan!" He reined away from the crowded avenue and spoke an order to his men.

Pressing further along the flow of troops and horses, Conan happened to glance down a side-road that led into a little square. A noseless, armless statue of Strabonus stood on a pedestal at the center of the plaza. But Conan was surprised to see Villeza's banner flying there; he walked toward the loitering mercenary who held it aloft. Troopers were emerging from the broken door of a stately house, carrying clinking bundles to a barrow at the standard-bearer's feet.

"What are you doing? Is this by your captain's order?" Conan strode up close to the man, who backed away startled, saying nothing.

"Rogues!" The Cimmerian bellowed to the scattered group. "Away from here, and into the fight!" He raised his mace and dealt the wooden bin a mighty blow, knocking out one side of it and spilling silver vessels and trinkets into the street. "No plunder until you take the citadel, I tell you!" He paced forward to berate the looters, who were rapidly ducking out of his sight. "If you waste time cavorting like this you'll never take the town! We'll be cut to pieces!" He turned on his heel. "Knaves! Fools!"

Forcing his way back among the traffic-jammed companies, he hurried up the skein of roads that ran to the citadel. But worse misfortune awaited him, for as he pressed onward he began to encounter smoke—at first only a pungent scent in the air, but soon it was rolling down the lanes in choking clouds, obscuring the narrow expanse of blue sky overhead and the outlines of the palace battlements. The lead troops were being driven back down the street by it.

Conan found Pavlo in a branching street near the foremost ladder, which had been set down when its bearers sought to escape the choking pall. "What treachery is this?" he demanded of his lesser officer. "Our men were told not to set torch to the city! They would have to be lunatics. . . ."

"Conan, the fire is not of our making." The small man's eyes were watering, and his moustache was rumpled from rubbing his face. "As we approached, Ivor's engines on the wall of the citadel threw firepots into the buildings."

"By Mitra! The scoundrel is burning his own city! A costly way to vex us!" He drew breath for more oaths, but coughed instead. "It may save him after all. It will keep us back from his walls for the time—if the palace itself doesn't catch!" He stepped out into the street and squinted up at the gatehouse, which was visible from moment to moment through smoke-billows and waves of shimmering heat. Guards-men with rag-wrapped faces could be seen hurrying along the parapet carrying buckets to douse stray fires. As Conan stood there, a house-wall of burning rubble sagged outward and crashed into the street between him and the looming gate.

"We'll have to fall back," he said to Pavlo, who was already sidling away from him. "These flames might devour the whole town."

They moved down the street, which was crowded more than ever by townspeople fleeing the fires, carrying bundles of their most-prized possessions. The advance had stopped completely, with some men scattering into side-streets while others waited idle. Conan saw a trooper snatch a jingling cloth sack from a distraught housewife; he was immediately set on by three angry town-rebels and knocked down.

"Enough squabbling! Keep to your companies! Pass the word to withdraw in good order."

As Conan railed at the milling crowd a clatter of hoofbeats burst from a smoke-hazed side alley. Suddenly the mob was scattering, crushing back on itself before a flying squad of horse-guards.

They rode down soldiers and refugees alike, leaning left and right to strike from their saddles. Conan blocked a saber-slash with his mace and tried to grasp the ankle of the looming horseman, but he caught only the rowel of a spur, tearing his hand painfully as he was dragged to his knees.

Hoofbeats echoed on all sides, even as a curtain of smoke drifted down, thick enough to smart the eyes. Conan heard hurried steps from behind and turned—to see Zeno's sword over him, raised high. His subordi-nate's lips were clenched in wrath.

Conan threw himself aside, rolling across the cob-bles, but as he did so the lieutenant's sword clanged against another blade overhead. He saw Zeno parry a second stroke and slash the thigh of the horseman who had wheeled back to finish Conan.

Then the Cimmerian saw the face of the rider through the smoke. It was Prince Ivor himself, armored and gray-cloaked, his face contorted with rage at his shallow sword-wound.

The prince spat a curse at both his enemies and jerked his reins away. Moments later he was clattering up the street behind the others. A few arrows and javelins rattled after him, wide of their mark.

"My thanks, Zeno." Conan stood up. "Though I would rather have died jamming this mace down his lying throat."

"Aye." The red-haired man nodded, his voice sounding choked. "May the scratch I dealt him fester and boil." He clapped a hand on Conan's shoulder. "But we had better not loiter here. If Ivor's sally-forths cannot kill us, this smoke might."

"Indeed." Conan glanced darkly up the street once more, then turned back to his troops.

Fortunately, with the lanes so crowded, there had been no room for a full rout. Now the retreat got under way in earnest, with squads of armed men deploying back to cover the approaches. Nevertheless, the going was slow, as swarms of fighters and refugees milled together.

By the time Conan approached the plaza before the city gate, a gray cloud had spread over the town. It made the sun's light seem dark and yellowish. Chaos ruled the surrounding streets, for in spite of the havoc Zeno had wrought in the taverns, some of the men had laid hands on strong drink. Now they lounged noisily in the broken doors of shops and houses.

Conan saw Thranos, his erstwhile fellow-thief, dragging a bulging, rattling sack toward the plaza, while not far behind him a wedge of guardsmen moved forward to harry the mercenaries. At Conan's warning the stout fellow looked back anxiously. But he did not drop his loot and run; he chose only to scuttle forward a little faster with his burden. A moment later, pierced by two arrows, he toppled forward dead onto the paves. The city guards came no nearer, but moved out of sight behind a block of buildings adjoining the plaza.

Conan shrugged away the pathetic scene and walked on. Finally, amid the streaming crowds, he found Stephany. The wounded man was sitting astride a horse, in earnest conference with two rebel leaders.

"The fire could level the city," the elder townsman was soberly telling him. "It may take days to burn out."

"If it does, no structure but the palace will be spared!" The baron gave a solemn shake of his head. "A tragedy for our realm!"

"Devil thrash us all!" Conan interrupted them. "What choice have we then, but to abandon the town?"

"No choice. We must go in hope that Ivor's men will put out the fires." The baron turned toward him, grim-faced. "We are only considering how many of the rebels to leave behind. Captain Villeza has already departed after ordering most of your mercenaries away."

Conan scowled. "And what of the other captains? Surely Aki Wadsai and Drusandra haven't run!"

"Drusandra is yonder, defending our flank." Stephany nodded toward the embattled buildings at the side of the plaza. "Her force was too small, after all, to make much headway. And Aki Wadsai . . . I thought you knew." The baron watched his face closely. "He is dead, Conan, crushed by a stone that was thrown on him from a housetop."

"I see." Conan turned away from them to look at

the crowd. Most of the eyes he saw were watering from smoke, but he knew in his numb heart that those were only the first of many tears that would be shed this day.

24

The Hunters at Bay

"I think we all agree"—Villeza raised his bulky body upright from his padded stump chair and strutted before the burned-out campfire—"the best course is to take what little we gained from the city fight, reform our companies, and go our ways."

"What we gained!" Drusandra shifted impatiently on the sunlit rock where she was resting a bandaged foot. "I and my women now have less than we started with. Perhaps if we had given more effort to looting than to pressing the attack . . ." She turned her glance disdainfully away from the Zingaran. "But not all of us were so . . . provident."

"A shame, truly. You should marry yourself to a provident man." Villeza leered at the captainess, but she ignored him.

"I for one expect an equal division of the spoils from the raid before we leave this mesa." The speaker was Zeno, who sat boldly among the captains. He favored Villeza with a sullen stare. "My fellow-troopers feel the same way."

The Zingaran turned on him. "Feel as you wish, Lieutenant. But if you try to take what is mine, it will come to a fight—and my men will back me." Looking for support to the others standing nearby, he blustered, "After all, why should I have to pay for battles lost by an inept barbarian general and his minions?"

Zeno snarled and arose from his cedar-log bench. But he was restrained from moving against the Zingaran by other lieutenants, who stepped in from the sidelines and expostulated with him amid a general murmur of dispute and ill-temper.

So it had gone among the Free Companions all the morning as they idled about their camp on the Zamanas Mesa. After a grueling night and day riding there, and another day to let their wounds knit, their returning strength was being vented in recrimination. Not pressed by pursuit, they had brought most of their injured with them to the place which, accursed or not, was their only refuge. With them came Baron Stephany, leading those of his rebels who could not hope to stay in hiding among the Kothians.

The rebels had staked out a new area of the camp, which was divided roughly into concentric wedges around the two towering monoliths. The entire place was littered with men groaning with wounds, hunger, and lack of pay. Though the sun was high and bright, shortening the shadows and lighting both sides of the razorback ridge behind the mesa, the day's mood was one of sullen oppression.

The dispute near the ashes of the council-fire was finally silenced by Conan, who walked up to the fireplace in the company of Baron Stephany.

"Calm yourself, Zeno, 'tis no use battling with Villeza. Even if you strip him to the clout, you'll never find the main share of his loot." The Cimmerian looked the stout captain up and down. "Doubtless he buried it somewhere between Tantusium and here, availing himself of his long head start on the rest of us.

"But there is a mote of truth in what he says." Speaking on, Conan had the ears of the assembled officers. "Our failure to take the city wasn't only due to his laggardliness." His words brought murmurs of agreement from the crowd and a furious scowl from

Villeza. "The fault is mine in part, for bad planning, and for underestimating the prince's recklessness. But know this, dog-brothers," he went on. "I'm not finished with Ivor. Now isn't the time to squabble, but to plan our next attack!"

At these words a new argument began, with most of the watchers vehemently disputing Conan. One, a gray-haired, black-skinned senior of the late Aki Wadsai's troop, gave strident voice to the opinion of many. They fell silent to let him speak.

"Conan of Cimmeria! Why should we linger in this unblessed land after our defeat and the loss of our leader? The payment owed us by the Kothian betrayer is gone, if ever it existed. At any moment bloody sorceries may fly at our heads! We would be fools to fight on!"

Conan spoke loudly to be heard over the chorus of assent from the growing crowd. "But know you—it is for Aki Wadsai, the much-mourned, that I fight. And for another brave leader slain by the prince's cunning. Do any here remember Hundolph? Killed by treachery, along with so many of our fellows!" He gazed around the silent span of his listeners. "To avenge them I'll go on fighting. Even if I have to storm Ivor's palace alone!"

After Conan's words the argument gradually resumed, and out of it the old desert trooper stepped forward and spoke gravely. "Success to you in your profitless revenge, Conan. Would that I might join you—but our company has bellies to feed. Today we ride south."

Villeza grinned to mask his red-faced ill-will. "Aye, Conan. I hope that you do meet your enemies face to face, and that a fitting outcome ensues." He smirked. "And by the way, any of your men who decide to quit you are welcome to join my company. We linger here till tomorrow."

"I would not ride with that swine," Zeno said as

Villeza turned away. "Still, Conan, I cannot say how many of the men will follow us. . . ." He stood wordless for a moment. "I can go and poll them for you." After waiting for Conan's nod, he turned and walked briskly toward the tents.

Stephany looked to Conan. "He is going to recruit them for a band of his own."

"Aye." The Cimmerian settled down on the log near the baron with an air of weary unconcern. "Mayhap there'll still be enough left to me for a small raiding force."

Drusandra slid down from her rock divan to sit between Conan and Stephany. "My women will ride with you, Conan, for the time."

"The rebel cause sorely needs all of you, and I pledge to provision as many fighters as you can muster"—Stephany gazed down into the fragile, dead ashes of the fireplace—"though my manor house may be destroyed, and I will have difficulty defending my lands against Ivor and Strabonus."

"The prince has been weakened, too, if his capital is in ashes," Conan said.

"The courier that Eulalia sent to me last night said most of the city was saved—by citizens working under Randalf's lead, with precious little help from Ivor." Stephany looked up and barely smiled. "I am glad of it—whether it strengthens our enemies or not."

"Your courier had no brushes with the Harangi, then?"

"He saw no sign of them."

"No, Conan, they are not in evidence at all lately." Drusandra, who had idly been pulling weed-bits out of Stephany's rumpled silver hair and combing it back with a twig, paused and looked to Conan. "Perhaps they were blasted by sorcery."

"Or perhaps they still ravage the countryside—or even the city!" The baron's look once again grew solemn. "A trial for Ivor, I know, but a greater trial for my people—"

He was interrupted by a sentry's shout from the brow of the mesa a short distance away. "Riders, ho! All eyes to northward! A force approaches!"

Conan sprang silently to his feet. He led the others in dashing forward to the downward-curving rim of stone at the edge of the plateau. There he stopped and scanned the spreading, sage-green knobs of hills a moment. His eye caught a glint of sun on metal; winding down the front rank of hills, on the ancient road that skimmed the crests above the Harangi town, came a column of riders.

"The hillmen must be returning," Stephany said.

"Hillmen? Nay, my friend. Those are Kothian cavalry!" Conan was already turning back toward camp. "Probably the spearhead of the legion that's been hounding us; they're unlikely to bring anything less into these hills. Count them well!" He strode back into the camp, bellowing. "Troopers! Arm yourselves! Make ready to face an assault."

The idleness and discord of the Free Companions was quickly transformed to action. Mercenaries and rebels alike girded themselves and sought out their officers. In a short time work-parties were hauling more rocks to the mesa rim, brushing up the defenses there, and testing a makeshift long-armed catapult powered by the fall of a heavy stone.

Most of the activity was at the southwest corner of the mesa, where the natural causeway led up steeply to the rim. Here, sharpened stakes had been driven into soil and rock crevices to baffle the charge of horsemen. A low fence of timber and rubble was blocked by a single large log that could be rolled back as a sally-port.

Relatively few troopers were assigned to the rest of the perimeter, for not much could be added to the impregnable natural defense of the long, steep drop.

Some of Drusandra's troop were sent back along the flanks of the ridge as pickets, but attack from that quarter seemed less likely than an assault up the causeway.

While final preparations were being made the captains went repeatedly to the outmost point of the mesa to watch the Kothian deployment. It took hours, for the force numbered in the thousands and was widely scattered along the trail. First horsemen, then footsoldiers filed down from the hill, looking like marching columns of purple-scaled insects. They spread out in the flat area near the confluence of streams, resting and waiting. A mounted company galloped up the foot of the causeway, showing a lively interest in that line of attack; the rest of the force would be in a good position to follow up the onslaught once it came.

"So it comes down to a fight after all," Stephany was telling Drusandra. "Instead of scattering to the four edges of the map, our force will face the enemy once again. I am most relieved."

"Aye." Conan moved up and clapped the older man on the shoulder. "And we fight on ground of our own choosing."

"Do you see that caped one on the gray horse?" Drusandra pointed down into the canyon. "There, under the standard with the other mounted officers? 'Tis the prince, I would bet my Bhalkhana mare."

Conan squinted and looked down at the horseman under the cross-barred, double-pennanted purple standard whose forked ends flapped in the breeze. He came to share Drusandra's certainty. "Aye, 'tis Ivor, blight his luck! That legion must have arrived in Tantusium the day after our siege."

"Strabonus backs his nephew to the hilt now that the family squabble is mended." Stephany shaded his eyes and peered down. "But the king himself doesn't seem to be in the column."

"No, more's the shame," Conan said.

"And what is that they're trundling over the hill?" Stephany asked. "Some kind of siege engine?"

Conan glanced up at the horizon, to feel a chill prickling his neck hairs. For the wagon that the gray-liveried soldiers were practically carrying down the rugged slope had large wheels and a faded black canopy. In the brilliant midday sun it looked like a funeral bier, except that an upright figure could be glimpsed riding in it.

"Aye, a siege weapon," Conan said quietly. "The deadliest I know."

Others promptly heard of the approach of Agohoth's chariot and came to watch it manhandled down to the canyon floor.

"The wizard! I thought you killed him, Cimmerian!" Villeza's swarthy features were pale as his eyes followed the progress of the flapping black shape.

Drusandra said grimly, "If so, the news has not reached Agohoth yet."

Conan turned away resignedly from the panorama of the deploying army. "There's no sense standing here glooming about it, in any case. We shall need our defenses all the more now." He strode away from the knot of officers. "Look you, troopers, back to your labor! This is not an excuse for you dogs to sit and scratch your fleas. Hoist those rocks! On with it! We'll be at spear-points soon!" Gradually the frightened men resumed their work.

By early afternoon the floor of the canyon, blanketed with soldiers at its widest part, looked like a meadow of purple clover, with the silver-glinting streams joining in its midst and plunging away down the narrow gorge. The bare hillocks and crests that rose amid the general crowd bristled with pikes and helmet-plumes. The army's baggage train was starting to file down the slope: strings of mules with round baskets suspended from either side of their pack-saddles. The besiegers had set up an observation post on the hill opposite the mesa, whence scouts watching the mercenaries flashed messages to the canyon floor by means of silver mirrors.

"What's the count of the enemy?" Conan strode up, his bronze face beaded with sweat under the baking sun. He bent to grab up a goatskin and squeeze water into his gullet.

"Seven thousand and more at last report," Stephany told him.

"Hmmph." Conan sprayed water over his lank-maned scalp before throwing down the waterskin. "I wonder that they haven't opened festivities yet—mayhap we should start. I'm having trouble finding make-work for these rogues."

He looked behind him to where knots of troopers were carrying up a rude catapult—its square fulcrum of logs borne separately from the T-shaped arm and crossbar, with a heavy stone lashed to the short end. Conan raised his voice to a command. "Here! Set it up over here, on this stone shelf! Briskly now, and don't mash your toes."

Conan had them align the weapon to face the nearest bare area of rock at the mesa's foot—for there sat Agohoth's wagon with empty traces, seemingly untended. A little apart from it the prince and the Kothian general waited on horseback, issuing orders to couriers and junior officers.

Conan supervised the loading. "That's it, draw the arm back lower—lower yet, that it may carry the full distance. Good! And bind it with a double thong. We'll charge it with a round stone first, to test the range." The men followed suit.

Conan's sword-stroke unleashed the engine with a thud and a fierce whizzing, to the cheers of the troopers. But the stone fell far short, smashing somewhere among the tumbled rock debris that formed the lower slope of the mesa without even drawing the attackers' notice. A burning firebrand flew even less far, flaring brightly and dropping out of sight before the brow of the cliff. More tries confirmed the result.

"It's no use!" Conan waved to his troops. "You men, lug this engine back to the causeway, where it may do some good. Away with it!" Then he stood viewing the scene and stroking his chin. "They are outside the fall of any bow we have."

"A shame, truly," Drusandra added. "For there comes our best target."

As she spoke, all saw that a dark figure was indeed detaching itself from the blacker darkness of the wagon. Thin and tall, awkward-looking, casting an angular black shadow on the rock where he stood— there was no question in the watchers' minds that it was Agohoth. Slowly he moved away from the wagon. Servants scurried near him, but not too near, awaiting his bidding. The mounted officers walked their steeds forward to meet him.

Yet Conan, as he watched the scene, thought he saw something changed about the sorcerer—some odd constraint or lopsidedness about his movements. Raising a hand to shade his eyes, he peered carefully, then let slip an oath. "Mannanan!" He faced the others, eyes wide in consternation. "My arrow is still in his craw!"

And indeed, after studying the slightly hunched or twisted figure of the mage, the keenest-eyed among the watchers agreed. They could see sunlight flashing on the end of a painted, brightly fletched shaft that stuck upward and outward from the junction of the weirdling's neck and shoulder.

And yet, in defiance of the seemingly mortal wound, Agohoth did not appear greatly hampered. He stood somewhat crooked, waving an arm jerkily to expostulate with the prince. Then he pivoted to beckon some riders forward with the same spasmodic motion.

"What are they doing?" Drusandra drew their

attention away from the horrific figure of the sorcerer. "Bringing the baggage train up to the fore?"

So it seemed. The strings of double-basketed sumpter mules had finished their descent of the hill and were being led across the stream. It was their pack-riders that the wizard had waved forward; now he gestured to the broad space of rock that was left open before his wagon, and the first of the animals were drawn up in it.

Then, as Agohoth and Ivor looked on, the pack-baskets were unfastened two by two, carried forward, and dumped. Their contents fell onto the stone with a tinkling clatter that was audible even to those on the cliff-top. For they were the Turanian swords that had been sent to Ivor by Emperor Yildiz, to aid his rebellion.

"Crom and Mitra!" Conan muttered to himself. "He plans to unleash the sword-dervish."

"What is it, then?" Villeza asked anxiously. "Will he conjure up flying ghosts to wield the swords?"

"Worse," Stephany assured him. "The sword-dervish is more ghastly than any other—"

Conan interrupted him. "Just be certain that if Agohoth's powers don't fail him, and if we don't find some way to stop him, those blades will be up here and dancing in our guts a few minutes hence." He turned to Zeno, who had joined the others to watch. "Tell the grooms to have every horse saddled in case we order a mass assault."

The lieutenant blinked. "But how could it possibly help us to give up this position?"

"If, as I fear, the wizard can clear this entire plateau, then it may be our only chance. Now go and make ready." As Zeno sprinted away, Conan gazed at those around him. "But for now we should try every expedient. I need a crossbow, a quiver, and a long rope."

As a trooper hurried off to comply with his request, sorcerous preparations continued below. When the last of the baskets were emptied and the pile of swords was man-high, Agohoth took his place before it. A Kothian scribe came forward to hold up a scroll for him.

Then the wizard began his stilted, one-handed passes. His intonations were not audible at the clifftop, but all the folk of both armies seemed to know that something momentous was at hand. Movement in the canyon stopped, and the silence there and on the mesa was intense; the twittering of birds in the sparse bushes seemed suddenly loud and intrusive. Stillness lay across the ancient stones and the hulking, jagged ridge. Silence shimmered like heat waves in the sun.

Meanwhile a pair of troopers arrived bearing a long coil of rope. Conan looped it once about a thin juniper trunk and knotted the end around his middle. "When I start down, let it out nearly to its full length and make it fast," he said to the men. "And guard the rope well," he added with a side glance at Villeza, who was absorbed in watching the spectacle below.

"What do you expect to accomplish?" Drusandra watched him with fear and wildness dancing in her blue eyes. "Is there really a hope?"

"The cliff falls away so gradually here that our shots can't reach." He shrugged to her. "I'll go down to the lowest rim to shorten the range and see how many more arrows Agohoth can catch. Or Ivor, or perhaps the scroll-bearer. I may at least distract them."

Black-clad Ariel came light-footing it across the cliff, bringing a heavy crossbow and a quiver to Conan. As he took it from her he felt her small, firm hand pressing his against the stock with a gesture of reassurance. He looked up into her earnest dark-brown eyes, surprised. He could not recall her ever having met his gaze before.

She turned away wordlessly, and Conan slung the

quiver over his head. He started down the rock, trying not to think about the fate of the last man who had climbed here. He walked backward, leaning on the rope as the troopers let it feed around the tree and down.

As he went a faint clattering carried to his ears. He was looking over his shoulder, but he had to get past a depression in the cliff-face before he could see anything. Finally the rock curved away beneath him, and there once again was Agohoth standing by the scroll-bearer, gesticulating stiffly, moving his whole body from the knees with an appearance of intense effort.

The scene looked ridiculous at first: the gawky, injured sorcerer trying desperately to mold huge and monstrous shapes from empty air. Conan would have laughed if he had not witnessed the result once before.

Then, with a queasiness in his belly that the dizzy height could never give him, he saw the great pile of metal that was the target of Agohoth's exertions begin sluggishly to shift and stir. Like a corpse reawakening it lurched and heaved upright, giving off a rasping and scraping of steel that echoed up and down the canyon.

25

The Greater Evil

From that moment Conan could not ignore the growing noise and turbulence of the spell taking shape beneath him. Yet he could not give much heed to it, either, because of the danger of his position. With the rope being paid out unremittingly and the cliff-face growing ever steeper and less regular, he had to watch his footing closely.

At one point he was lowered past an overhanging brow of rock to dangle and twist helplessly in space. After an anxious time his feet again found the sheer slope. He approached the next dropoff, hoping that the rope would run out and that his invisible cohorts at the top would make it fast. But it did not, and when he reached the rim, he had to take up the extra length of line hand over hand and wait for it to stop coming. When it finally did, he knotted it through the loop at his waist to anchor himself, leaving a dozen paces of slack rope doubled beneath him.

Now the line was firm, as was his footing, although there was not enough of a ledge to support his weight. He braced his feet wide against the cliff and unstrapped the crossbow from his shoulder. He began to wind the bow-winch back while leaning out to view the canyon floor.

His enemies were much nearer now, he saw at a glance; what he had lost in altitude would be more than compensated in range. He had gone far out and down the side of the mesa's outermost promontory. Now he viewed the heart of the attacking force at an angle, from the causeway side. That his descent had been seen by many, he could not doubt. Yet he was still out of their bowshot, unless they sent archers climbing high up the talus. And that danger was dwarfed by the spectacle below, which was as terrifying as the din that filled his ears.

For the sword-dervish had grown unspeakably. It was a lithe, glinting funnel ten paces broad and thrice that in height, narrowing sinuously toward its top, where it tapered out in a halo of glittering blades. Agohoth was dancing stiffly, driving the horror forward up the cliff by the arching, spasmodic movements of his body. His capering was dreadfully mimicked by the halting progress of the dervish, which had now gone far up the slope of broken rock. As it advanced, its base canted upward to remain perpendicular to the slope, while its top end curved skyward like a towering waterspout.

Whether because of the rugged terrain or the difficulty the wounded sorcerer had in controlling such a huge dervish, it was not as silent as before. Instead of gliding with a low brushing and snicking of steel against steel, it shrieked now into the cliff like an angry millstone, striking showers of sparks and shattering the age-old silence of the canyon. The very rock where it passed looked strangely scoured and bare, and the wind of its whirling raised a yellow veil of dust and debris, sending smaller dust-dervishes skittering away among the rock crannies. Conan sweated to think of the havoc it would wreak among his fellows on the mesa. Twirling like a heavy-skirted dancer, the thing had nearly reached the top of the talus. It was more than halfway to Conan's perch on the face of the cliff.

He finished winding the winch, his motions quickened by the fear that Agohoth might notice him and turn the dervish aside to consume him. But the sorcerer's eye, like every other, seemed fixed on the lurching, veering progress of the steel hurricane, as every ear was full of its unholy din. Conan steadied himself and flicked the trigger of the crossbow forward, backing off the winch to let the trigger-catch take up the urgent stress of the bowstring.

He reached across his shoulder for a shaft, eyeing the clear spot below where Agohoth cavorted—with Ivor standing rapt, forming an equally tempting target just beyond.

But then a new sound intruded: a deep rumbling and scraping. Conan's ears had scarcely acknowledged it, when he realized that it was also sensible as a vibration in the stone beneath his feet.

Swiftly the tremor grew, turning into a violent quaking that set Conan's buskins pattering sideways in a desperate dance along the cliff. The taut rope oscillated and jerked above him, its loop digging into his back, and the deep rumblings grew ever more intense—until finally they were drowned out by the crash of falling rocks.

Great stones were being dislodged from the clifftop. Some bounded near Conan with smashing impacts, along with the writhing and spinning bodies of falling defenders. The air became acrid with the smell of pulverized rock-dust. Then a wave of small debris struck the dangling man, battering his helmet and his upraised arms while blinding him with flying grit.

He rubbed his eyes clear, his still-reverberating ears becoming attuned to the continuing rumble of the earthquake and the ringing of screams from below. The quaking had become intermittent, though it was going on longer than any earth-tremor Conan had ever felt. His crossbow was gone, he realized, lost in the avalanche.

Dangling from his loop of rope and bracing against

the unquiet cliff, he looked down through shifting dust-curtains to see that the great rocks had bounded far out among the besiegers and struck down many of them.

Although the worst of the avalanche seemed past, the tide of screams from below still swelled and mounted in a way that could hardly be caused by the residual rockslides, or even by the continued trembling and shifting of the bedrock. And the focus of the Kothians' fear, as he glimpsed them staggering away through the dust-clouds or looking up with widened eyes, seemed to be at the front of the mesa.

Conan looked to the cliff-base. He saw no sign of the sword-dervish, unless—yes, was that a gleam of burnished steel blades, scattered unmoving on the dusty talus? Agohoth was standing in a stilted posture near the crushed wreckage of his wagon; Ivor was frozen just beyond him. The object of their fixed stares was invisible to Conan because of the curve of the cliff and the sifting haze of sun-rayed dust.

Then the barbarian felt a new, ponderous shifting of the bedrock and saw something huge and gray go forward from the front of the cliff. It was long and snakelike, with a rough, gleaming texture; its target was the sorcerer, and with a quickness and dexterity that was astonishing for something so large, it smote him, seeming to double around his writhing form, and bore him back toward the cliff. Only his shrill scream lingered in the air as he was snatched out of sight.

The stones lurched under Conan's feet as the thing struck again, this time sweeping up three struggling Kothians and a mule; then it licked back to the cliff. Ivor dove out from under the plunging tentacle and scampered frantically away.

What was it? Staggering and rolling along the cliff because of the violent agitation of the rope, Conan craned his neck for a view around the curving rock.

He heard a sharp, scraping clash of stone from overhead. He looked up and stared without quite believing what he saw.

Set into the recess of the cliff above him was a titanic, living eye, bright and glistening though filmed with a pale membrane of immemorial age. Its gaze darted and refocused across the stricken field, seeking out living morsels. Meanwhile from the invisible mouth below, the darting thing that he now knew to be a tremendous tongue lashed forth again and again. As Conan watched in primal awe, the massive, rock-rimmed eyelid clashed shut and open in another vast, reptilian blink.

The sawing and bowing rope that supported Conan hung straight down in front of the monstrous eye. Now, due to some unknowable stress at its anchorpoint, it slipped and let him fall several man-lengths farther down the cliff, well past the brick of the next sheer drop. Under the jarring impact of his weight, the knot at his waist pulled loose, and the slack length of rope beneath him began to play out, burning the skin of his belly as it slid around his entangled sword-hilt. Unable to grasp the running line, Conan felt himself dropping even faster.

Jerking to a halt farther down, he could no longer see the monstrous eye, but amid the crazy oscillations of the rope, which slammed him against the cliff one moment and swung him far out into space the next, he caught a single, telling glimpse. It was a view back along the edge of the mesa to the ridge. The jagged crest of stone was rumbling along with the entire plateau in a strangely smooth, coordinated motion, like the flank and head of a great beast, while the sloping causeway that was really a titanic leg and claw lumbered forward to rest atop a scattering host of Kothian cavalry.

As the tormented rope finally slipped free of its mooring above, plunging Conan straight downward, a feverish vision came to him of the true shape and immensity of the monster, from its stony face and broad, armored head, with two pale horn-spikes rising like great monoliths at its center, up the rock-scaled neck to the jagged, ridgelike plates of its backbone and down along rough flanks, half-buried in ancient rubble, to the tail and haunches that vanished from sight somewhere in the stone of the time-lost Kothian hills.

Then Conan struck bottom, and all thought was driven from his brain.

His unconsciousness could not have lasted long. Feeling his life vaguely threatened, he struggled back to awareness; he imagined himself caught in the toils of a great serpent. But it was only the rope, which had coiled atop him as it fell.

Bruised and sore, he heaved it aside and set about extracting himself from the tangle of brush and gravel that had accumulated at the top of the talus. As he was sawing the rope-knot loose from his middle with his dagger, a sudden fear dawned on him—the mesa at his back might lumber forward and crush him. Then he sensed that the perturbations of the earth had stopped, except for the occasional rattles of rocks finding their new levels. Looking up at the cliff now, he sought the shape of the monster-lizard in vain. It was difficult to see the mesa as a living thing, or even to glimpse the lineaments of a face.

The rock-beast was slumbering again, Conan realized. Vexed in its aeons-long rest by the petty scratching of a human sorcerer, it had half-awakened and stirred, like a cow flicking its tail at a gnat, just long enough to silence the nuisance. Then it had subsided again. Its contours were now so masked by the accumulated debris of centuries that it was hard to be sure it had ever really existed. Conan knew the beginning of a numbing and strangely comforting doubt. Yet what he had seen was undeniable—wasn't it?

He turned his attention back to the canyon floor, which was a shambles, with hundreds of Kothian corpses in view. There was no telling how many more had been hidden from sight, but red rivulets spread from under many of the great stones which had not formerly lain there.

Dazed men and riderless horses wandered aimlessly across the scene, while the more purposeful remnants of the routed army crowded together on foot and horseback beyond the stream, battling for a place on the upward road. Others had doubtless found the trail down the canyon to the Harangi town—but for the moment at least, it seemed that all order in the Kothian ranks had been blasted.

Conan spied friendly horsemen trotting down from the mesa along the causeway—the position of which had been massively altered. It was nearer the stream now; soon the descending mercenaries would meet the milling remnants of the Kothian force.

With a last, wary glance at the stone cliff towering behind him, Conan started down the slope. He strode and jumped from rock to rock, his pace becoming faster and surer as the lingering pangs of his fall were shaken out of his limbs. Some of the new-fallen stones shifted under his weight, but most were so large that his passing mattered little. After a long downward jog he began to see gravel in the rock interstices, and then soil, edged with grass and small wildflowers. Finally he found himself back on the rock-strewn canyon bottom, where dead men and horses lay in a litter of purple and red.

The first riders from the mesa were already down off the causeway, for they had spurred their horses beyond the limits of safety on the steep, broken ground. Conan recognized the lead horseman as

Villeza, squat in the saddle, with leather pouches of booty riding heavily behind him.

It seemed that the captain was panic-stricken. He drove his mount onward without waiting for his companions to catch up, riding heedless of the dozens of footborne Kothians lingering on the near stream-bank.

Though demoralized, the Kothians were still dangerous. With a chorus of yells they converged on Villeza and halted the progress of his horse, grabbing at his reins and saddle-gear. Doubtless each one was eager to use the animal for his own escape. Though there was little logic in it, they dragged the rider down. He struck wildly about him with a chain-mace, but soon vanished in their midst.

Conan drew his sword and started toward the broil, but the redness of the Kothians' rising and falling weapons quickly told him that he was too late. The two following riders reined in likewise, to watch helplessly as their chief was murdered.

Conan turned and ran to intercept the growing numbers of his comrades who were picking their way down the causeway by various paths.

"Free Companions! Do not flee!" he called, whirling his sword high. "The day is ours! Come and rout these Kothians!"

The mercenaries were not as badly battered nor as frightened as their enemies. They rallied to Conan first with waves of the hand, then with cheers, as the momentum of their flight was gradually converted to battle-zeal. They swept forward and fell on the Kothians in growing numbers. Of the latter, many threw down their weapons and begged for mercy, while others set on their own fellows in frenzied efforts to escape.

Then distant, raucous war-cries echoed from the top of the hill. Drusandra, who was just moving past Conan in a crowd of mercenary women, shoved her way to his side and pointed up. "Look there! The Harangi!"

And indeed, high on the road a number of the small, fierce horsemen were attacking Kothian fugitives. As Conan watched, another party of hillmen swept out of the lower canyon in a flying charge, riding down purple-clad soldiers all the way to the stream-bank. There, with eyes carefully averted from the mesa, they wheeled their mounts and galloped away.

"They are back from their raiding," Drusandra said. "I pity any Kothians who try to escape through the hills."

"Aye, but I think we are safe from them—at least on this accursed ground." Conan turned back to Drusandra, but she had already left his side and was running toward a swordfight clanging on the bare rock of the canyon.

One of the fighters was Ariel, as Conan could see by her black costume and deft, dancing thrusts. The undersized maid seemed hard-pressed, yet her skill and spirit would scarcely let her give ground. Her adversary, a bareheaded, robust man in gray garb, demonstrated a wild ferocity that caught Conan's attention.

Then, with a thrill of antipathy, he recognized him—it was Ivor, fighting as Conan had not known he could, driving recklessly forward and swinging his saber as lightly as a riding-crop.

Ariel made a nimble leaping stroke and whittled the prince's arm. But he seemed not even to notice; at the same instant he stepped forward and struck her a clanking blow on the brow of her helm. Then, drawing back his saber as she staggered, he ran her straight through the middle.

Immediately, automatically, he raised his boot and kicked her collapsing body off his sword. The slight girl fell straight back against Drusandra, who was running to her aid, and both of them tumbled to the ground.

Conan was upon the nobleman, roaring. "Traitor! Wizard-monger! Have at me, devil's knave! Hyaa!" His voice pummeled at his enemy like hammer blows. "By the grim Lord of the Mounds, I'll butcher you as I killed your demon sire! Slayer of innocents! . . ."

But then Conan's maledictions ceased, for he could see that they all went unheard and wasted. The pale eyes under the tossing shock of brown hair were soulless. Ivor fought fixedly, efficiently enough to force the raging Cimmerian back, and back, but without any real awareness. His mind was utterly blasted by what he had seen. With an eerie insight Conan guessed that the prince's every step and stroke had the sole purpose of bearing him straight away from the mesa.

By way of a test he moved to one side, out of the prince's path. When Ivor lowered his saber and started forward, Conan brought his own blade down from aside and behind in a whistling sweep. The silent man's head leaped from his shoulders and thudded down bleeding on the rock, while his body toppled to rest nearby.

"He was mad," the barbarian said. He stepped around the corpse with a slight shudder.

"Aye, many of them are maddened with fear, but of what?"

The speaker was old Horus, who had moved near to watch the fight. "One Kothian slew himself rather than be brought back here! Others rave of monster lizards and frogs . . . but I saw no such. Did you?" The grizzled man's eyes searched Conan's face, but found no answer in it. "True, the groundshaking was bad. But I can't puzzle out why they gape and gibber so. . . ." His voice trailed away in bafflement.

"We've taken a good many of them, then?" Conan scanned the valley floor, seeing Kothian troops milling in confusion at the stream between his own force and the Harangi.

"Captured many, yes, and killed most of the rest." Horus nodded with evident satisfaction. "We have horses, supplies—the loot of a Kothian legion, less what the hillmen have taken"—he shrugged—"and some valuable hostages, I would guess."

"Our enemies destroyed . . . our own losses not heavy . . . 'tis a notable victory." Conan looked down to Drusandra, who knelt beside dead Ariel. Two female warriors were kneeling at either hand, lamenting quietly.

The captainess rose to her feet, her eyes meeting Conan's briefly. "It is still too much, Conan." She frowned darkly and shook her head. "Too, too great a price!"

The following day dawned golden-bright, with birds trilling among the rocks. It was a stiff and weary morn for the captives, who had huddled under guard all night in the sheltering arm of the mesa. But for those rebels and troopers who had not feared to return to the camp it was a busy dawn, devoted to rolling tents, saddling horses, and loading mules.

Conan was ebullient, going among the different parties of mercenaries, striking terms, and securing pledges. While climbing astride his war-horse he told Stephany, "All of the men have agreed to ride with me. Their old leaders are dead, they lack prospects, and I have great plans." He swept an arm toward the horizon of hills that were deeply shadowed by the sun's low light. "We ride southward and eastward to carve a kingdom out of the hinterlands of Koth, Shem, and Turan. We can unite the roving *kozaki* of the plain and lead them against the local warlords. Soon I will meet the Harangi chiefs and seek their alliance too."

The baron, who had somehow retrieved his tame

forest-cat, waited in the saddle with the sullen-looking creature in his lap. "I hope that you will escort my rebels home when we carry Ivor's head to Tantusium. The citizens will welcome us, of course. 'Tis the hillmen I trust not."

"Oh, aye." The Cimmerian nodded soberly. "Else how would we collect the payment your city owes us?"

The baron smiled in wry resignation. "Indeed, I had almost forgotten. There should be something left in the prince's well-hoarded treasury."

"I know that the captain's demands will not exceed what is fair." Drusandra walked close beside the baron, reaching up to rest a hand on his knee. "Incidentally, Conan, you need not collect anything on my troop's behalf." She turned her sun-blazing face up to his, squinting against the light. "We will be staying on with Stephany in Tantusium to begin our employment as his palace guard."

Conan looked in surprise from Drusandra to the mercenary women, who were saddling up their horses nearby. "Why not follow me south? You can help us forge a strong neighbor-kingdom for Stephany's dominion."

Drusandra shook her head. "Of all of us, Conan, Ariel might have gone with you. But she is no more." She sighed. "Perhaps it is a woman's way. I and my girls would rather nurse an ailing kingdom back to health than snatch two or three new ones on the wing."

Conan shrugged, hoping that he showed no evidence of the strange, numb pang in his chest. "I will miss the sleeping arrangements, Drusandra. Your tent was so much more—hospitable than my own."

She glanced to Stephany, who reached down and rumpled her blond hair. Then the warrior-woman smiled frankly up at Conan. "I will miss those times, too, but I expect to find the baron's palace more hospitable than any tent.''

Zeno had ridden up close to the group, and now he broke the silence between the leaders. ''Conan, the troops are ready. I have given them the marching order.''

Conan scanned the groups of horsemen on the mesa and saw Bilhoat, Pavlo, and the other lieutenants hailing him to signal their readiness. With fresh exuberance he wrenched his sword from its scabbard and waved it on high. ''Onward, then, Free Companions! Follow me to wealth and glory!'' To those nearest him he winked and added, ''Why should we remain petty thieves and spoilers forever, when the great thieves and spoilers are kings!''

Amid a rising chorus of cheers, Conan spurred his horse onward.

Conan
the
Indestructible

by L. Sprague de Camp

The greatest hero of the magic-rife Hyborian Age was a northern barbarian, Conan the Cimmerian, about whose deeds a cycle of legend revolves. While these legends are largely based on the attested facts of Conan's life, some tales are inconsistent with others. So we must reconcile the contradictions in the saga as best we can.

In Conan's veins flowed the blood of the people of Atlantis, the brilliant city-state swallowed by the sea 8,000 years before his time. He was born into a clan that claimed a homeland in the northwest corner of Cimmeria, along the shadowy borders of Vanaheim and the Pictish wilderness. His grandfather had fled his own people because of a blood feud and sought refuge with the people of the North. Conan himself first saw daylight on a battlefield during a raid by the Vanir.

Before he had weathered fifteen snows, the young Cimmerian's fighting skills were acclaimed around the council fires. In that year the Cimmerians, usually at one another's throats, joined forces to repel the warlike Gundermen who, intent on colonizing southern Cimmeria, had pushed across the Aquilonian border and established the frontier post of Venarium. Conan joined the howling, blood-mad horde that swept out of the northern hills, stormed over the stockade walls, and drove the Aquilonians back across their frontier.

At the sack of Venarium, Conan, still short of his full growth, stood six feet tall and weighed 180 pounds. He had the vigilance and stealth of the born woodsman, the iron-hardness of the mountain man, and the Herculean physique of his blacksmith father. After the plunder of the Aquilonian outpost, Conan returned for a time to his tribe.

Restless under the conflicting passions of his adolescence, Conan spent several months with a band of Æsir as they raided the Vanir and the Hyperboreans. He soon learned that some Hyperborean citadels were ruled by a caste of widely-feared magicians, called Witchmen. Undaunted, he took part in a foray against Haloga Castle, when he found that Hyperborean slavers had captured Rann, the daughter of Njal, chief of the Æsir band.

Conan gained entrance to the castle and spirited out Rann Njalsdatter; but on the flight out of Hyperborea, Njal's band was overtaken by an army of living dead. Conan and the other Æsir survivors were led away to slavery (''Legions of the Dead'').

Conan did not long remain a captive. Working at night, he ground away at one link of his chain until it was weak enough to break. Then one stormy night, whirling a four-foot length of heavy chain, he fought his way out of the slave pen and vanished into the downpour.

Another account of Conan's early years tells a different tale. This narrative, on a badly broken clay prism from Nippur, states that Conan was enslaved as a boy of ten or twelve by Vanir raiders and set to work turning a grist mill. When he reached his full growth, he was bought by a Hyrkanian pitmaster who traveled with a band of professional fighters staging contests for the amusement of the Vanir and Æsir. At this time Conan received his training with weapons.

Later he escaped and made his way south to Zamora (*Conan the Barbarian*).

Of the two versions, the records of Conan's enslavement by the Hyrkanians at sixteen, found in a papyrus in the British Museum, appear much more legible and self-consistent. But this question may never be settled.

Although free, the youth found himself half a hostile kingdom away from home. Instinctively he fled into the mountains at the southern extremity of Hyperborea. Pursued by a pack of wolves, he took refuge in a cave. Here he discovered the seated mummy of a gigantic chieftain of ancient times, with a heavy bronze sword across its knees. When Conan seized the sword, the corpse arose and attacked him ("The Thing in the Crypt").

Continuing southward into Zamora, Conan came to Arenjun, the notorious "City of Thieves." Green to civilization and, save for some rudimentary barbaric ideas of honor and chivalry, wholly lawless by nature, he carved a niche for himself as a professional thief.

Being young and more daring than adroit, Conan's progress in his new profession was slow until he joined forces with Taurus of Nemedia in a quest for the fabulous jewel called the "Heart of the Elephant." The gem lay in the almost impregnable tower of the infamous mage Yara, captor of the extraterrestrial being Yag-Kosha ("The Tower of the Elephant").

Seeking greater opportunities to ply his trade, Conan wandered westward to the capital of Zamora, Shadizar the Wicked. For a time his thievery prospered, although the whores of Shadizar soon relieved him of his gains. During one larceny, he was captured by the men of Queen Taramis of Shadizar, who sent him on a mission to recover a magical horn wherewith to resurrect an ancient, evil god. Taramis's plot led to her own destruction (*Conan the Destroyer*).

The barbarian's next exploit involved a fellow thief, a girl named Tamira. The Lady Jondra, an arrogant aristocrat of Shadizar, owned a pair of priceless rubies. Baskaran Imalla, a religious fanatic raising a cult among the Kezankian hillmen, coveted the jewels to gain control over a fire-breathing dragon he had raised from an egg. Conan and Tamira both yearned for the rubies; Tamira took a post as lady's maid to Jondra for a chance to steal them.

An ardent huntress, Jondra set forth with her maid and her men-at-arms to slay Baskaran's dragon. Baskaran captured the two women and was about to offer them to his pet as a snack when Conan intervened (*Conan the Magnificent*).

Soon Conan was embroiled in another adventure. A stranger hired the youth to steal a casket of gems sent by the King of Zamora to the King of Turan. The stranger, a priest of the serpent-god Set, wanted the jewels for magic against his enemy, the renegade priest Amanar.

Amanar's emissaries, who were hominoid reptiles, had stolen the gems. Although wary of magic, Conan set out to recover the loot. He became involved with a bandette, Karela, called the Red Hawk, who proved the ultimate bitch; when Conan saved her from rape, she tried to kill him. Amanar's party had also carried off to the renegade's stronghold a dancing girl whom Conan had promised to help (*Conan the Invincible*).

Soon rumors of treasure sent Conan to the nearby ruins of ancient Larsha, just ahead of the soldiers dispatched to arrest him. After all but their leader, Captain Nestor, had perished in an accident arranged by Conan, Nestor and Conan joined forces to plunder the treasure; but ill luck deprived them of their gains ("The Hall of the Dead").

Conan's recent adventures had left him with an aversion to warlocks and Eastern sorceries. He fled northwestward through Corinthia into Nemedia, the second most powerful Hyborian kingdom. In Nemedia he resumed his profession successfully enough to bring his larcenies to the notice of Aztrias Pentanius, ne'er-do-well nephew of the governor. Oppressed by gambling debts, this young gentleman hired the outlander to purloin a Zamorian goblet, carved from a single diamond, that stood in the temple-museum of a wealthy collector.

Conan's appearance in the temple-museum coincided with its master's sudden demise and brought the young thief to the unwelcome attention of Demetrio, of the city's Inquisitorial Council. This caper also gave Conan his second experience with the dark magic of the serpent-brood of Set, conjured up by the Stygian sorcerer Thoth-Amon ("The God in the Bowl").

Having made Nemedia too hot to hold him, Conan drifted south into Corinthia, where he continued to occupy himself with the acquisition of other persons' property. By diligent application, the Cimmerian earned the repute of one of the boldest thieves in Corinthia. Poor judgment of women, however, cast him into chains until a turn in local politics brought freedom and a new career. An ambitious nobleman, Murilo, turned him loose to slit the throat of the Red Priest, Nabonidus, the scheming power behind the local throne. This venture gathered a prize collection of rogues in Nabonidus's mansion and ended in a mire of blood and treachery ("Rogues in the House").

Conan wandered back to Arenjun and began to earn a semi-honest living by stealing back for their owners valuable objects that others had filched from them. He undertook to recover a magical gem, the Eye of Erlik, from the wizard Hissar Zul and return it to its owner, the Kahn of Zamboula.

There is some question about the chronology of Conan's life at this point. A recently-translated tablet from Asshurbanipal's library states that Conan was about seventeen at the time. This would place the episode right after that of "The Tower of the Elephant," which indeed is mentioned in the cuneiform. But from internal evidence, this event seems to have taken place several years later. For one thing, Conan appears too clever, mature and sophisticated; for another, the fragmentary medieval Arabic manuscript *Kitab al-Qunn* implies that Conan was well into his twenties by then.

The first translator of the Asshurbanipal tablet, Prof. Dr. Andreas von Fuss of the Münchner Staatsmuseum, read Conan's age as "17." In Babylonian cuneiform, "17" is expressed by two circles followed by three vertical wedges, with a horizontal wedge above the three for "minus"—hence "twenty minus three." But Academician Leonid Skram of the Moscow Archaeological Institute asserts that the depression over the vertical wedges is merely a dent made by the pick of a careless escavator, and the numeral properly reads "23."

Anyhow, Conan learned of the Eye of Erlik when he heard a discussion between an adventuress, Isparana, and her confederate. He invaded the wizard's mansion, but the wizard caught Conan and deprived him of his soul. Conan's soul was imprisoned in a mirror, there to remain until a crowned ruler broke the glass. Hissar Zul thus compelled Conan to follow Isparana and recover the talisman; but when the Cimmerian returned the Eye to Hissar Zul, the ungrateful mage tried to slay him (*Conan and the Sorcerer*).

Conan, his soul still englassed, accepted legitimate employment as bodyguard to a Khaurani noblewoman, Khashtris. This lady set out for Khauran with Conan, another guard, Shubal, and several retainers. When the other servants plotted to rob and murder their employer, Conan and Shubal saved her and escorted her to Khauran. There Conan found the widowed

Queen Ialamis being courted by a young nobleman who was not at all what he seemed (*Conan the Mercenary*).

With his soul restored, Conan learned from an Iranistani, Khassek, that the Khan of Zamboula still wanted the Eye of Erlik. In Zamboula, the Turanian governor, Akter Khan, had hired the wizard Zafra, who ensorcelled swords, so that they would slay on command. En route, Conan encountered Isparana, with whom he developed a lust-hate relationship. Unaware of the magical swords, Conan continued to Zamboula and delivered the amulet. But the nefarious Zafra convinced the Khan that Conan was dangerous and should be killed on general principles (*Conan: the Sword of Skelos*).

Conan had enjoyed his taste of Hyborian-Age intrigue. It became clear that there was no basic difference between the opportunities in the palace and those in the Rats' Den, whereas the pickings were far better in high places. Besides, he wearied of the furtive, squalid life of a thief.

He was not, however, yet committed to a strictly law-abiding life. When unemployed, he took time out for a venture in smuggling. An attempt to poison him sent him to Vendhya, a land of wealth and squalor, philosophy and fanatacism, idealism and treachery (*Conan the Victorious*).

Soon after, Conan turned up in the Turanian seaport of Aghrapur. A new cult had established headquarters there under the warlock Jhandar, who needed victims to be drained of blood and reanimated as servants. Conan refused the offer of a former fellow thief, Emilio, to take part in a raid on Jhandar's stronghold to steal a fabulous ruby necklace. A Turanian sergeant, Akeba, did however persuade Conan to go with him to rescue Akeba's daughter, who had vanished into the cult (*Conan the Unconquered*).

After Jhandar's fall, Akeba urged Conan to take service in the Turanian army. The Cimmerian did not at first find military life congenial, being too self-willed and hot-tempered to easily submit to discipline. Moreover, as he was at this time an indifferent horseman and archer, Conan was relegated to a low-paid irregular unit.

Still, a chance soon arose to show his mettle. King Yildiz launched an expedition against a rebellious satrap. By sorcery, the satrap wiped out the force sent against him. Young Conan alone survived to enter the magic-maddened satrap's city of Yaralet ("The Hand of Nergal").

Returning in triumph to the glittering capital of Aghrapur, Conan gained a place in King Yildiz's guard of honor. At first he endured the gibes of fellow troopers at his clumsy horsemanship and inaccurate archery. But the gibes died away as the other guardsmen discovered Conan's sledgehammer fists and as his skills improved.

Conan was chosen, along with a Kushite mercenary named Juma, to escort King Yildiz's daughter Zosara to her wedding with Khan Kujula, chief of the Kuigar nomads. In the foothills of the Talakma Mountains, the party was attacked by a strange force of squat, brown, lacquer-armored horsemen. Only Conan, Juma, and the princess survived. They were taken to the subtropical valley of Meru and to the capital, Shamballah, where Conan and Juma were chained to an oar of the Meruvian state galley, about to set forth on a cruise.

On the galley's return to Shamballah, Conan and Juma escaped and made their way into the city. They reached the temple of Yama as the deformed little god-king of Meru was celebrating his marriage to Zosara ("The City of Skulls").

* * *

Back at Aghrapur, Conan was promoted to captain. His growing repute as a good man in a tight spot, however, led King Yildiz's generals to pick the barbarian for especially hazardous missions. Once they sent Conan to escort an emissary to the predatory tribesmen of the Khozgari Hills, hoping to dissuade them by bribes and threats from plundering the Turanians of the lowlands. The Khozgarians, respecting only immediate, overwhelming force, attacked the detachment, killing the emissary and all but two of the soldiers, Conan and Jamal.

To assure their safe passage back to civilization, Conan and Jamal captured Shanya, the daughter of the Khozgari chief. Their route led them to a misty highland. Jamal and the horses were slain, and Conan had to battle a horde of hairless apes and invade the stronghold of an ancient, dying race ("The People of the Summit").

Another time, Conan was dispatched thousands of miles eastward, to fabled Khitai, to convey to King Shu of Kusan a letter from King Yildiz proposing a treaty of friendship and trade. The wise old Khitan king sent his visitors back with a letter of acceptance. As a guide, however, the king appointed a foppish little nobleman, Duke Feng, who had entirely different objectives ("The Curse of the Monolith," first published as "Conan and the Cenotaph").

Conan continued in his service in Turan for about two years, traveling widely and learning the elements of organized, civilized warfare. As usual, trouble was his bedfellow. After one of his more unruly adventures, involving the mistress of his superior officer, Conan deserted and headed for Zamora. In Shadizar he heard that the Temple of Zath, the spider god, in the Zamorian city of Yezud, was recruiting soldiers. Hastening to Yezud, Conan found that a Brythunian free company had taken all the available mercenary posts. He became the town's blacksmith because as a boy he had been apprenticed in this trade.

Conan learned from an emissary of King Yildiz, Lord Parvez, that High Priest Feridun was holding Yildiz's favorite wife, Jamilah, in captivity. Parvez hired Conan to abduct Jamilah. Meanwhile Conan had set his heart on the eight huge gems that formed the eyes of an enormous statue of the spider god. As he was loosening the jewels, the approach of priests forced him to flee to a crypt below the naos. The temple dancing girl Rudabeh, with whom Conan was truly in love for the first time in his life, descended into the crypt to warn him of the doom awaiting him there (*Conan and the Spider God*).

Conan next rode off to Shadizar to track down a rumor of treasure. He obtained a map showing the location of a ruby-studded golden idol in the Kezankian Mountains; but thieves stole his map. Conan, pursuing them, had a brush with Kezankian hillmen and had to join forces with the very rogues he was tracking. He found the treasure, only to lose it under strange circumstances ("The Bloodstained God").

Fed up with magic, Conan headed for the Cimmerian hills. After a time in the simple, routine life of his native village, however, he grew restless enough to join his old friends, the Æsir, in a raid into Vanaheim. In a bitter struggle on the snow-covered plain, both forces were wiped out—all but Conan, who wandered off to a strange encounter with the legendary Atali, daughter of the frost giant Ymir ("The Frost Giant's Daughter").

Haunted by Atali's icy beauty, Conan headed back toward the South, where, despite his often-voiced scorn of civilization, the golden spires of teeming cities beckoned. In the Eiglophian Mountains, Conan rescued a young woman from cannibals, but through overconfidence lost her to the dreaded monster that haunted glaciers ("The Lair of the Ice Worm").

Conan then returned to the Hyborian lands, which include Aquilonia, Argos, Brythunia, Corinthia, Koth, Nemedia, Ophir, and Zingara. These countries were named for the Hyborian peoples who, as barbarians, had 3,000 years earlier conquered the empire of Acheron and built civilized realms on its ruins.

In Belverus, the capital of Nemedia, the ambitious Lord Albanus dabbled in sorcery to usurp the throne of King Garian. To Belverus came Conan, seeking a patron with money to enable him to hire his own free company. Albanus gave a magical sword to a confederate, Lord Melius, who went mad and attacked people in the street until killed. As he picked up the ensorcelled sword. Conan was accosted by Hordo, a one-eyed thief and smuggler whom he had known as Karela's lieutenant.

Conan sold the magical sword, hired his own free company, and taught his men mounted archery. Then he persuaded King Garian to hire him. But Albanus had made a man of clay and by his sorcery given it the exact appearance of the king. Then he imprisoned the king, substituted his golem, and framed Conan for murder (*Conan the Defender*).

Conan next brought his free company to Ianthe, capital of Ophir. There the Lady Synelle, a platinum-blond sorceress, wished to bring to life the demon-god Al'Kirr. Conan bought a statuette of this demon-god and soon found that various parties were trying to steal it from him. He and his company took service under Synelle, not knowing her plans.

Then the bandette Karela reappeared and, as usual, tried to murder Conan. Synelle hired her to steal the statuette, which the witch needed for her sorcery. She also planned to sacrifice Karela (*Conan the Triumphant*).

Conan went on to Argos; but since that kingdom

was at peace, there were no jobs for mercenaries. A misunderstanding with the law compelled Conan to leap to the deck of a ship as it left the pier. This was the merchant galley *Argus*, bound for the coasts of Kush.

A major epoch in Conan's life was about to begin. The *Argus* was taken by Bêlit, the Shemite captain of the pirate ship *Tigress*, whose ruthless black corsairs had made her mistress of the Kushite littoral. Conan won both Bêlit and a partnership in her bloody trade ("Queen of the Black Coast," Chapter 1).

Years before, Bêlit, daughter of a Shemite trader, had been abducted with her brother Jehanan by Stygian slavers. Now she asked her lover Conan to try to rescue the youth. The barbarian slipped into Khemi, the Stygian seaport, was captured, but escaped to the eastern end of Stygia, the province of Taia, where a revolt against Stygian oppression was brewing (*Conan the Rebel*).

Conan and Bêlit resumed their piratical careers, preying mainly on Stygian vessels. Then an ill fate took them up the black Zarkheba River to the lost city of an ancient winged race ("Queen of the Black Coast," Chapters 2–5).

As Bêlit's burning funeral ship wafted out to sea, a downhearted Conan turned his back on the sea, which he would not follow again for years. He plunged inland and joined the warlike Bamulas, a black tribe whose power swiftly grew under his leadership.

The chief of a neighboring tribe, the Bakalahs, planned a treacherous attack on another neighbor and invited Conan and his Bamulas to take part in the sack and massacre. Conan accepted but, learning that an Ophirean girl, Livia, was held captive in Bakalah, he out-betrayed the Bakalahs. Livia ran off during the slaughter and wandered into a mysterious valley, where only Conan's timely arrival saved her from being sacrificed to an extraterrestrial being ("The Vale of Lost Women").

Before Conan could build his own black empire, he was thwarted by a succession of natural catastrophes as well as by the intrigues of hostile Bamulas. Forced to flee, he headed north. After a narrow escape from pursuing lions on the veldt, Conan took shelter in a mysterious ruined castle of prehuman origin. He had a brush with Stygian slavers and a malign supernatural entity ("The Castle of Terror").

Continuing on, Conan reached the semicivilized kingdom of Kush. This was the land to which the name "Kush" properly applied; although Conan, like other northerners, tended to use the term loosely to mean any of the black countries south of Stygia. In Meroê, the capital, Conan rescued from a hostile mob the young Queen of Kush, the arrogant, impulsive, fierce, cruel, and voluptuous Tananda.

Conan became embroiled in a labyrinthine intrigue between Tananda and an ambitious nobleman who commanded a piglike demon. The problem was aggravated by the presence of Diana, a Nemedian slave girl to whom Conan, despite the jealous fury of Tananda, took a fancy. Events culminated in a night of insurrection and slaughter ("The Snout in the Dark").

Dissatisfied with his achievements in the black countries, Conan wandered to the meadowlands of Shem and became a soldier of Akkharia, a Shemite city-state. He joined a band of volunteers to liberate a neighboring city-state; but through the treachery of Othbaal, cousin of the mad King Akhîrom of Pelishtia, the volunteers were destroyed—all but Conan, who survived to track the plotter to Asgalun, the Pelishti capital. There Conan became involved in a polygonal power war among the mad Akhîrom, the treacherous Othbaal, a Stygian witch, and a company of black mercenaries. In the final hurly-burly of sorcery, steel, and blood, Conan grabbed Othbaal's red-haired mistress, Rufia, and galloped north ("Hawks Over Shem").

Conan's movements at this time are uncertain. One tale, sometimes assigned to this period, tells of Conan's service as a mercenary in Zingara. A Ptolemaic papyrus in the British Museum alleges that in Kordava, the capital, a captain in the regular army forced a quarrel on Conan. When Conan killed his assailant, he was condemned to hang. A fellow condemnee, Santiddio, belonged to an underground conspiracy, the White Rose, that hoped to topple King Rimanendo. As other conspirators created a disturbance in the crowd that gathered for the hanging, Conan and Santiddio escaped.

Mordermi, head of an outlaw band allied with the White Rose, enlisted Conan in his movement. The conspiracy was carried on in the Pit, a warren of tunnels beneath the city. When the King sent an army to clean out the Pit, the insurrectionists were saved by Callidos, a Stygian sorcerer. King Rimanendo was slain and Mordermi became king. When he proved as tyrannical as his predecessor, Conan raised another revolt; then, refusing the crown for himself, he departed (*Conan: The Road of Kings*).

This tale involves many questions. If authentic, it may belong in Conan's earlier mercenary period, around the time of *Conan the Defender*. But there is no corroboration in other narratives of the idea that Conan ever visited Zingara before his late thirties, the time of *Conan the Buccaneer*. Moreover, none of the rulers of Zingara mentioned in the papyrus appear on the list of kings of Zingara in the Byzantine manuscript *Hoi Anaktes tês Tzingêras*. Hence some students deem the papyrus either spurious or a case of confusion between Conan and some other hero. Everything else known about Conan indicates that, if he had indeed been offered the Zingaran crown, he would have grabbed it with both hands.

We next hear of Conan after he took service under Amalric of Nemedia, the general of Queen-Regent Yasmela of the little border kingdom of Khoraja. While Yasmela's brother, King Khossus, was a prisoner in Ophir, Yasmela's borders were assailed by the forces of the veiled sorcerer Natohk—actually the 3,000-years-dead Thugra Khotan of the ruined city of Kuthchemes.

Obeying an oracle of Mitra, the supreme Hyborian god, Yasmela made Conan captain-general of Khoraja's army. In this rôle he gave battle to Natohk's hosts and rescued the Queen-Regent from the malignant magic of the undead warlock. Conan won the day— and the Queen ("Black Colossus").

Conan, now in his late twenties, settled down as Khorajan commander-in-chief. But the queen, whose lover he had expected to be, was too preoccupied with affairs of state to have time for frolics. He even proposed marriage, but she explained that such a union would not be sanctioned by Khorajan law and custom. Yet, if Conan could somehow rescue her brother from imprisonment, she might persuade Khossus to change the law.

Conan set forth with Rhazes, an astrologer, and Fronto, a thief who knew a secret passage into the dungeon where Khossus languished. They rescued the King but found themselves trapped by Kothian troops, since Strabonus of Koth had his own reasons for wanting Khossus.

Having surmounted these perils, Conan found that Khossus, a pompous young ass, would not hear of a foreign barbarian's marrying his sister. Instead, he would marry Yasmela off to a nobleman and find a middle-class bride for Conan. Conan said nothing; but in Argos, as their ship cast off, Conan sprang ashore with most of the gold that Khossus had raised and waved the King an ironic farewell ("Shadows in the Dark").

Now nearly thirty, Conan slipped away to revisit his Cimmerian homeland and avenge himself on the Hyperboreans. His blood brothers among the Cimmerians and the Æsir had won wives and sired sons, some as old and almost as big as Conan had been at the sack of Venarium. But his years of blood and battle had stirred his predatory spirit too strongly for him to follow their example. When traders brought word of new wars, Conan galloped off to the Hyborian lands.

A rebel prince of Koth was fighting to overthrow Strabonus, the penurious ruler of that far-stretched nation; and Conan found himself among old companions in the princeling's array, until the rebel made peace with his king. Unemployed again, Conan formed an outlaw band, the Free Companions (*Conan the Renegade*). This troop gravitated to the steppes west of the Sea of Vilayet, where they joined the ruffianly horde known as the *kozaki*.

Conan soon became the leader of this lawless crew and ravaged the western borders of the Turanian Empire until his old employer, King Yildiz, sent a force under Shah Amurath, who lured the *kozaki* deep into Turan and cut them down.

Slaying Amurath and acquiring the Turanian's captive, Princess Olivia of Ophir, Conan rowed out into the Vilayet Sea in a small boat. He and Olivia took refuge on an island, where they found a ruined greenstone city, in which stood strange iron statues. The shadows cast by the moonlight proved as dangerous as the giant carnivorous ape that ranged the isle, or the pirate crew that landed for rest and recreation ("Shadows in the Moonlight").

Conan seized command of the pirates that ravaged the Sea of Vilayet. As chieftain of this mongrel Red Brotherhood, Conan was more than ever a thorn in

King Yildiz's flesh. That mild monarch, instead of strangling his brother Teyaspa in the normal Turanian manner, had cooped him up in a castle in the Colchian Mountains. Yildiz now sent his General Artaban to destroy the pirate stronghold at the mouth of the Zaporoska River; but the general became the harried instead of the harrier. Retreating inland, Artaban stumbled upon Teyaspa's whereabouts; and the final conflict involved Conan's outlaws, Artaban's Turanians, and a brood of vampires ("The Road of the Eagles").

Deserted by his sea rovers, Conan appropriated a stallion and headed back to the steppes. Yezdigerd, now on the throne of Turan, proved a far more astute and energetic ruler than his sire. He embarked on a program of imperial conquest.

Conan went to the small border kingdom of Khauran, where he won command of the royal guard of Queen Taramis. This queen had a twin sister, Salome, born a witch and reared by the yellow sorcerers of Khitai. She allied herself with the adventurer Constantius of Koth and planned by imprisoning the Queen to rule in her stead. Conan, who perceived the deception, was trapped and crucified. Cut down by the chieftain Olgerd Vladislav, the Cimmerian was carried off to a Zuagir camp in the desert. Conan waited for his wounds to heal, then applied his daring and ruthlessness to win his place as Olgerd's lieutenant.

When Salome and Constantius began a reign of terror in Khauran, Conan led his Zuagirs against the Khauranian capital. Soon Constantius hung from the cross to which he had nailed Conan, and Conan rode off smiling, to lead his Zuagirs on raids against the Turanians ("A Witch Shall Be Born").

Conan, about thirty and at the height of his physical powers, spent nearly two years with the desert Shemites, first as Olgerd's lieutenant and then, having ousted Olgerd, as sole chief. The circumstances of his leaving the Zuagirs were recently disclosed by a silken scroll in Old Tibetan, spirited out of Tibet by a refugee. This document is now with the Oriental Institute in Chicago.

The energetic King Yezdigerd sent soldiers to trap Conan and his troop. Because of a Zamorian traitor in Conan's ranks, the ambush nearly succeeded. To avenge the betrayal, Conan led his band in pursuit of the Zamorian. When his men deserted, Conan pressed on alone until, near death, he was rescued by Enosh, a chieftain of the isolated desert town of Akhlat.

Akhlat suffered under the rule of a demon in the form of a woman, who fed on the life force of living things. Conan, Enosh informed him, was their prophesied liberator. After it was over, Conan was invited to settle in Akhlat; but, knowing himself ill-suited to a life of humdrum respectability, he instead headed southwest to Zamboula with the horse and money of Vardanes the Zamorian ("Black Tears").

In one colossal debauch, Conan dissipated the fortune he had brought to Zamboula, a Turanian outpost. There lurked the sinister priest of Hanuman, Totrasmek, who sought a famous jewel, the Star of Khorala, for which the Queen of Ophir was said to have offered a roomful of gold. In the ensuing imbroglio, Conan acquired the Star of Khorala and rode westward ("Shadows of Zamboula").

The medieval monkish manuscript *De sidere choralae*, rescued from the bombed ruins of Monte Cassino, continues the tale. Conan reached the capital of Ophir to find that the effeminate Moranthes II, himself under the thumb of the sinister Count Rigello, kept his queen, Marala, under lock and key. Conan scaled the wall of Moranthes's castle and fetched Marala out. Rigello pursued the fugitives nearly to the Aquilonian border, where the Star of Khorala showed its power in an unexpected way ("The Star of Khorala").

Hearing that the *kozaki* had regained their vigor,

Conan returned with horse and sword to the harrying of Turan. Although the now-famous northlander arrived all but empty-handed, contingents of the *kozaki* and the Vilayet pirates soon began operating under his command.

Yezdigerd sent Jehungir Agha to entrap the barbarian on the island of Xapur. Coming early to the ambush, Conan found the island's ancient fortress-palace of Dagon restored by magic, and in it the city's malevolent god, in the form of a giant of living iron ("The Devil in Iron").

After escaping from Xapur, Conan built his *kozaki* and pirate raiders into such a formidable threat that King Yezdigerd devoted all his forces to their destruction. After a devastating defeat, the *kozaki* scattered, and Conan retreated southward to take service in the light cavalry of Kobad Shah, King of Iranistan.

Conan got himself into Kobad Shah's bad graces and had to ride for the hills. He found a conspiracy brewing in Yanaidar, the fortress-city of the Hidden Ones. The Sons of Yezm were trying to revive an ancient cult and unite the surviving devotees of the old gods in order to rule the world. The adventure ended with the rout of the contending forces by the gray ghouls of Yanaidar, and Conan rode eastward ("The Flame Knife").

Conan reappeared in the Himelian Mountains, on the northwest frontier of Vendhya, as a war chief of the savage Afghuli tribesmen. Now in his early thirties, the warlike barbarian was known and feared throughout the world of the Hyborian Age.

No man to be bothered with niceties, Yezdigerd employed the magic of the wizard Khemsa, an adept of the dreaded Black Circle, to remove the Vendhyan king from his path. The dead king's sister, the Devi Yasmina, set out to avenge him but was captured by Conan. Conan and his captive pursued the sorcerous Khemsa, only to see him slain by the magic of the

Seers of Yimsha, who also abducted Yasmina ("The People of the Black Circle").

When Conan's plans for welding the hill tribes into a single power failed, Conan, hearing of wars in the West, rode thither. Almuric, a prince of Koth, had rebelled against the hated Strabonus. While Conan joined Almuric's bristling host, Strabonus's fellow kings came to that monarch's aid. Almuric's motley horde was driven south, to be annihilated at last by combined Stygian and Kushite forces.

Escaping into the desert, Conan and the camp follower Natala came to age-old Xuthal, a phantom city of living dead men and their creeping shadow-god, Thog. The Stygian woman Thalis, the effective ruler of Xuthal, double-crossed Conan once too often ("The Slithering Shadow").

Conan beat his way back to the Hyborian lands. Seeking further employment, he joined the mercenary army that a Zingaran, Prince Zapayo da Kova, was raising for Argos. It was planned that Koth should invade Stygia from the north, while the Argosseans approached the realm from the south by sea. Koth, however, made a separate peace with Stygia, leaving Conan's army of mercenaries trapped in the Stygian deserts.

Conan fled with Amalric, a young Aquilonian soldier. Soon Conan was captured by nomads, while Amalric escaped. When Amalric caught up again with Conan, Amalric had with him the girl Lissa, whom he had saved from the cannibal god of her native city. Conan had meanwhile become commander of the cavalry of the city of Tombalku. Two kings ruled Tombalku: the Negro Sakumbe and the mixed-blood Zehbeh. When Zehbeh and his faction were driven out, Sakumbe made Conan his co-king. But then the wizard Askia slew Sakumbe by magic. Conan, having avenged his black friend, escaped with Amalric and Lissa ("Drums of Tombalku").

Conan beat his way to the coast, where he joined the Barachan pirates. He was now about thirty-five. As second mate of the *Hawk*, he landed on the island of the Stygian sorcerer Siptah, said to have a magical jewel of fabulous properties.

Siptah dwelt in a cylindrical tower without doors or windows, attended by a winged demon. Conan smoked the unearthly being out but was carried off in its talons to the top of the tower. Inside the tower Conan found the wizard long dead; but the magical gem proved of unexpected help in coping with the demon ("The Gem in the Tower").

Conan remained about two years with the Barachans, according to a set of clay tablets in pre-Sumerian cuneiform. Used to the tightly organized armies of the Hyborian kingdoms, Conan found the organization of the Barachan bands too loose and anarchic to afford an opportunity to rise to leadership. Slipping out of a tight spot at the pirate rendezvous at Tortage, he found that the only alternative to a cut throat was braving the Western Ocean in a leaky skiff. When the *Wastrel*, the ship of the buccaneer Zaporavo, came in sight, Conan climbed aboard.

The Cimmerian soon won the respect of the crew and the enmity of its captain, whose Kordavan mistress, the sleek Sancha, cast too friendly an eye on the black-maned giant. Zaporavo drove his ship westward to an uncharted island, where Conan forced a duel on the captain and killed him, while Sancha was carried off by strange black beings to a living pool worshipped by these entities ("The Pool of the Black Ones").

Conan persuaded the officials at Kordava to transfer Zaporavo's privateering license to him, whereupon he spent about two years in this authorized piracy. As usual, plots were brewing against the Zingaran monarchy. King Ferdrugo was old and apparently failing, with no successor but his nubile daughter Chabela. Duke Villagro enlisted the Stygian super-sorcerer Thoth-Amon, the High Priest of Set, in a plot to obtain Chabela as his bride. Suspicious, the princess took the royal yacht down the coast to consult her uncle. A privateer in league with Villagro captured the yacht and abducted the girl. Chabela escaped and met Conan, who obtained the magical Cobra Crown, also sought by Thoth-Amon.

A storm drove Conan's ship to the coast of Kush, where Conan was confronted by black warriors headed by his old comrade-in-arms, Juma. While the chief welcomed the privateers, a tribesman stole the Cobra Crown. Conan set off in pursuit, with Princess Chabela following him. Both were captured by slavers and sold to the black Queen of the Amazons. The Queen made Chabela her slave and Conan her fancy man. Then, jealous of Chabela, she flogged the girl, imprisoned Conan, and condemned both to be devoured by a man-eating tree (*Conan the Buccaneer*).

Having rescued the Zingaran princess, Conan shrugged off hints of marriage and returned to privateering. But other Zingarans, jealous, brought him down off the coast of Shem. Escaping inland, Conan joined the Free Companions, a mercenary company. Instead of rich plunder, however, he found himself in dull guard duty on the black frontier of Stygia, where the wine was sour and the pickings poor.

Conan's boredom ended with the appearance of the pirette, Valeria of the Red Brotherhood. When she left the camp, he followed her south. The pair took refuge in a city occupied by the feuding clans of Xotalanc and Tecuhltli. Siding with the latter, the two northerners soon found themselves in trouble with that clan's leader, the ageless witch Tascela ("Red Nails").

Conan's amour with Valeria, however hot at the start, did not last long. Valeria returned to the sea;

Conan tried his luck once more in the black kingdoms. Hearing of the "Teeth of Gwahlur," a cache of priceless jewels hidden in Keshan, he sold his services to its irascible king to train the Keshani army.

Thutmekri, the Stygian emissary of the twin kings of Zembabwei, also had designs on the jewels. The Cimmerian, outmatched in intrigue, made tracks for the valley where the ruins of Alkmeenon and its treasure lay hidden. In a wild adventure with the undead goddess Yelaya, the Corinthian girl Muriela, the black priests headed by Gorulga, and the grim gray servants of the long-dead Bît-Yakin, Conan kept his head but lost his loot ("Jewels of Gwahlur").

Heading for Punt with Muriela, Conan embarked on a scheme to relieve the worshipers of an ivory goddess of their abundant gold. Learning that Thutmekri had preceded him and had already poisoned King Lalibeha's mind against him, Conan and his companion took refuge in the temple of the goddess Nebethet.

When the king, Thutmekri, and High Priest Zaramba arrived at the temple, Conan staged a charade wherein Muriela spoke with the voice of the goddess. The results surprised all, including Conan ("The Ivory Goddess").

In Zembabwei, the city of the twin kings, Conan joined a trading caravan which he squired northward along the desert borders, bringing it safely into Shem. Now in his late thirties, the restless adventurer heard that the Aquilonians were spreading westward into the Pictish wilderness. So thither, seeking work for his sword, went Conan. He enrolled as a scout at Fort Tuscelan, where a fierce war raged with the Picts.

In the forests across the river, the wizard Zogar Sag was gathering his swamp demons to aid the Picts. While Conan failed to prevent the destruction of Fort Tuscelan, he managed to warn settlers around Velitrium and to cause the death of Zogar Sag ("Beyond the Black River").

Conan rose rapidly in the Aquilonian service. As captain, his company was once defeated by the machinations of a traitorous superior. Learning that this officer, Viscount Lucian, was about to betray the province to the Picts, Conan exposed the traitor and routed the Picts ("Moon of Blood").

Promoted to general, Conan defeated the Picts in a great battle at Velitrium and was called back to the capital, Tarantia, to receive the nation's accolades. Then, having roused the suspicions of the depraved and foolish King Numedides, he was drugged and chained in the Iron Tower under sentence of death.

The barbarian, however, had friends as well as foes. Soon he was spirited out of prison and turned loose with horse and sword. He struck out across the dank forests of Pictland toward the distant sea. In the forest, the Cimmerian came upon a cavern in which lay the corpse and the demon-guarded treasure of the pirate Tranicos. From the west, others—a Zingaran count and two bands of pirates—were hunting the same fortune, while the Stygian sorcerer Thoth-Amon took a hand in the game ("The Treasure of Tranicos").

Rescued by an Aquilonian galley, Conan was chosen to lead a revolt against Numedides. While the revolution stormed along, civil war raged on the Pictish frontier. Lord Valerian, a partisan of Numedides, schemed to bring the Picts down on the town of Schohira. A scout, Gault Hagar's son, undertook to upset this scheme by killing the Pictish wizard ("Wolves Beyond the Border").

Storming the capital city and slaying Numedides on the steps of his throne—which he promptly took for his own—Conan, now in his early forties, found himself ruler of the greatest Hyborian nation (*Conan the Liberator*).

A king's life, however, proved no bed of houris. Within a year, an exiled count had gathered a group of plotters to oust the barbarian from the throne. Conan might have lost crown and head but for the timely intervention of the long-dead sage Epimitreus ("The Phoenix of the Sword").

No sooner had the mutterings of revolt died down than Conan was treacherously captured by the kings of Ophir and Koth. He was imprisoned in the tower of the wizard Tsotha-lanti in the Kothian capital. Conan escaped with the help of a fellow prisoner, who was Tsotha-lanti's wizardly rival Pelias. By Pelias's magic, Conan was whisked to Tarantia in time to slay a pretender and to lead an army against his treacherous fellow kings ("The Scarlet Citadel").

For nearly two years, Aquilonia thrived under Conan's firm but tolerant rule. The lawless, hard-bitten adventurer of former years had, through force of circumstance, matured into an able and responsible statesman. But a plot was brewing in neighboring Nemedia to destroy the King of Aquilonia by sorcery from an elder day.

Conan, about forty-five, showed few signs of age save a network of scars on his mighty frame and a more cautious approach to wine, women and bloodshed. Although he kept a harem of luscious concubines, he had never taken an official queen; hence he had no legitimate son to inherit the throne, a fact whereof his enemies sought to take advantage.

The plotters resurrected Xaltotun, the greatest sorcerer of the ancient empire of Acheron, which fell before the Hyborian savages 3,000 years earlier. By Xaltotun's magic, the King of Nemedia was slain and replaced by his brother Tarascus. Black sorcery defeated Conan's army; Conan was imprisoned, and the exile Valerius took his throne.

Escaping from a dungeon with the aid of the harem girl Zenobia, Conan returned to Aquilonia to rally his loyal forces against Valerius. From the priests of Asura, he learned that Xaltotun's power could be broken only by means of a strange jewel, the "Heart of Ahriman." The trail of the jewel led to a pyramid in the Stygian desert outside black-walled Khemi. Winning the Heart of Ahriman, Conan returned to face his foes (*Conan the Conqueror*, originally published as *The Hour of the Dragon*).

After regaining his kingdom, Conan made Zenobia his queen. But, at the ball celebrating her elevation, the queen was borne off by a demon sent by the Khitan sorcerer Yah Chieng. Conan's quest for his bride carried him across the known world, meeting old friends and foes. In purple-towered Paikang, with the help of a magical ring, he freed Zenobia and slew the wizard (*Conan the Avenger*, originally published as *The Return of Conan*).

Home again, the way grew smoother. Zenobia gave him heirs: a son named Conan but commonly called Conn, another son called Taurus, and a daughter. When Conn was twelve, his father took him on a hunting trip to Gunderland. Conan was now in his late fifties. His sword arm was a little slower than in his youth, and his black mane and the fierce mustache of his later years were traced with gray; but his strength still surpassed that of two ordinary men.

When Conn was lured away by the Witchmen of Hyperborea, who demanded that Conan come to their stronghold alone, Conan went. He found Louhi, the High Priestess of the Witchmen, in conference with three others of the world's leading sorcerers: Thoth-Amon of Stygia; the god-king of Kambuja; and the black lord of Zembabwei. In the ensuing holocaust, Louhi and the Kambujan perished, while Thoth-Amon and the other sorcerer vanished by magic ("The Witch of the Mists").

Old King Ferdrugo of Zingara had died, and his throne remained vacant as the nobles intrigued over the succession. Duke Pantho of Guarralid invaded Poitain, in southern Aquilonia. Conan, suspecting sorcery, crushed the invaders. Learning that Thoth-Amon was behind Pantho's madness, Conan set out with his army to settle matters with the Stygian. He pursued his foe to Thoth-Amon's stronghold in Stygia ("Black Sphinx of Nebthu"), to Zembabwei ("Red Moon of Zembabwei"), and to the last realm of the serpent folk in the far south ("Shadows in the Skull").

For several years, Conan's rule was peaceful. But time did that which no combination of foes had been able to do. The Cimmerian's skin became wrinkled and his hair gray; old wounds ached in damp weather. Conan's beloved consort Zenobia died giving birth to their second daughter.

Then catastrophe shattered King Conan's mood of half-resigned discontent. Supernatural entities, the Red Shadows, began seizing and carrying off his subjects. Conan was baffled until in a dream he again visited the sage Epimitreus. He was told to abdicate in favor of Prince Conn and set out across the Western Ocean.

Conan discovered that the Red Shadows had been sent by the priest-wizards of Antillia, a chain of islands in the western part of the ocean, whither the survivors of Atlantis had fled 8,000 years before. These priests offered human sacrifices to their devil-god Xotli on such a scale that their own population faced extermination.

In Antillia, Conan's ship was taken, but he escaped into the city Ptahuacan. After conflicts with giant rats and dragons, he emerged atop the sacrificial pyramid just as his crewmen were about to be sacrificed. Supernatural conflict, revolution, and seismic catastrophe ensued. In the end, Conan sailed off to explore the continents to the west (*Conan of the Isles*).

Whether he died there, or whether there is truth in

the tale that he strode out of the West to stand at his son's side in a final battle against Aquilonia's foes, will be revealed only to him who looks, as Kull of Valusia once did, into the mystic mirrors of Tuzun Thune.

L. Sprague de Camp
Villanova, Pennsylvania
May 1984

CONAN

☐ 54238-X   CONAN THE DESTROYER $2.95
   54239-8   Canada $3.50

☐ 54228-2   CONAN THE DEFENDER $2.95
   54229-0   Canada $3.50

☐ 54225-8   CONAN THE INVINCIBLE $2.95
   54226-6   Canada $3.50

☐ 54236-3   CONAN THE MAGNIFICENT $2.95
   54237-1   Canada $3.50

☐ 54231-2   CONAN THE UNCONQUERED $2.95
   54232-0   Canada $3.50

☐ 54246-0   CONAN THE VICTORIOUS $2.95
   54247-9   Canada $3.50

☐ 54248-7   CONAN THE FEARLESS (trade) $6.95
   54249-5   Canada $7.95

☐ 54242-8   CONAN THE TRIUMPHANT $2.95
   54243-6   Canada $3.50

☐ 54244-4   CONAN THE VALOROUS (trade) $6.95
   54245-2   Canada $7.95

Buy them at your local bookstore or use this handy coupon:
Clip and mail this page with your order

TOR BOOKS—Reader Service Dept.
49 W. 24 Street, 9th Floor, New York, NY 10010

Please send me the book(s) I have checked above. I am enclosing
$_____ (please add $1.00 to cover postage and handling).
Send check or money order only—no cash or C.O.D.'s.

Mr./Mrs./Miss _____

Address _____

City _____ State/Zip _____

Please allow six weeks for delivery. Prices subject to change without
notice.

For the millions of people who have read the books, enjoyed the comics and the magazines, and thrilled to the movies, there is now —

THE CONAN

FAN CLUB

S.Q. Productions Inc., a long time publisher of science fiction and fantasy related items and books is announcing the formation of an official Conan Fan Club. When you join, you'll receive the following: 6 full color photos from the Conan films, a finely detailed sew-on embroidered patch featuring the Conan logo, a full color membership card and bookmark, and a set of official Conan Fan Club stationary.

Also included in the fan kit will be the first of 4 quarterly newsletters. **"The Hyborian Report"** will focus on many subjects of interest to the Conan fans, including interviews with Conan writers and film stars. And there'll be behind-the-scenes information about the latest Conan movies and related projects, as well as reports on other R.E. Howard characters like Red Sonja and King Kull. Fans will also be able to show off their talents on our annual costume and art contests. **"The Hyborian Report"** will be the one-stop information source for the very latest about Conan.

Another aspect of the club that fans will find invaluable is the **Conan Merchandise Guide,** which will detail the hundreds of items that have been produced, both in America **and** Europe. And as a member of the club, you'll receive notices of **new** Conan products, many created just for the club! Portfolios, posters, art books, weapon replicas (cast from the **same** molds as those used for the movie weapons) and much, much more! And with your kit, you'll get coupons worth $9.00 towards the purchase of items offered for sale.

Above all, The Conan Fan Club is going to be listening to the fans, the people who have made this barbarian the most famous in the world. Their suggestions, ideas, and feedback is what will make the club really work. The annual membership is only **$10.00.** Make all checks and money orders payable to: **CONAN FAN CLUB**
PO Box 4569
Toms River, NJ 08754

Response to this offer will be tremendous, so please allow 10-12 weeks for delivery.